REVIE'

'Raina's skill is evident the mom
impressive is the script he has fashioned by creating characters
that share a deeply moving experience of cross cultural and
cross national sympathy'
Rajni Srikanth, M.I.T Boston, 23rd November 2003

'Raina spins a fine web of human contacts in which the
ambivalence of the globalised business world is revealed.'
Wiener Zeitung 24.05.2007

'A beautiful evening, one that addresses the major issues
with simple means of storytelling.
Felicity Amman, Zurich, 21 August 2008

'The Indian tells a wonderful story about India and Linz. A
magical, touching and very funny story developed over India
and Linz.'
Nachrichten, Linz, 18.02.2009

Staging a 70-minute drama where you can only see the actors
from chest-up and no physical interaction sounds limiting.
But, this production, with its live music, sound effects,
appropriate exits and entries, immersive acting and a friendly
narrator to take you through it all, does it effectively.
Bageshri Savyasachi 15.10.2020 Indiaink.com.au

In 'Hawking the Bard...' Arjun Raina presents a wry
contemporary commentary on just how Australians' attitudes
to immigrants of colour may - or may not - have changed
since the first Punjabi hawkers toured Victoria in the late
1800s. Arjun's character sketches intermixed with video and

audio segments make for an entertaining evening of theatre; sometimes funny, sometimes sad, but always very much to the point.

Dr Alison Richards
Adjunct Senior Lecturer,
Centre for Theatre and Performance
Faculty of Arts, Monash University

NINE CONTEMPORARY PLAYS

ARJUN RAINA

ZORBA BOOKS

ZORBA BOOKS

Published by Zorba Books, March 2023
Website: www.zorbabooks.com
Email: info@zorbabooks.com

Title: **Nine Contemporary Plays**
Author Name: Arjun Raina
Copyright © Arjun Raina
Printbook ISBN :- 978-93-95217-54-5
Ebook ISBN :- 978-93-95217-53-8

Zorba Books Pvt. Ltd. (opc)
Sushant Arcade,
Next to Courtyard Marriot,
Sushant Lok 1, Gurgaon – 122009, India

Printed in India

CONTENT

AN INTRODUCTION

There are nine plays in this collection written over a period of two decades (2004-2022). The first four plays were written while the Author was living and working out of India. The rest of the plays were written after the Author migrated to Australia. A brief introduction to each text follows.

The first play, **_A Terrible Beauty is Born_** was a commissioned work for the Vienna Festwochen and was written after the author had worked as a Voice Coach in the International Call Center Industry in India, witnessing the difficult conditions of the calling work done primarily through the night, with the additional stress of putting on fake accents and identities. A suicide by a worker was the seed to write the play. Then 9/11 happened, giving a kind of larger connection, linking the world of the Call Centers of Gurgaon- India, with life as experienced in New York-U.S.A post the 9/11 attacks.

The Weight Loss Hour is the story of three bodies, one a saint lying in his tomb, second a politician on a fast unto death, and third, a young woman lying on a bed in a weight loss centre. While lying on the weight loss 'bed' clients spend their time watching T.V, showing contemporary news events and stories. The interweaving of the stories of these three bodies, and the news events, leads to a kind of a slice of life play, with many dramatic characters and themes playing off, and intercutting each other.

Ecdysis: The snake sheds its skin was a commissioned work for the European Culture Capital organisation Linz 09. The author spent a large part of a year in Linz, Austria (the birth town of Adolf Hitler) first researching, then writing, and finally performing the show. The play was first written in English and was then translated into German to facilitate subtitling. Some of the text was also translated into Punjabi. This is the English version of the text. There are three characters in this show. One, the Austrian Uncle of Indian/Punjabi origin, who speaks fluent German. Second, his niece who he has brought to Austria and who is keen enough to learn German and speaks it with some level of fluency. The third character is Kuldip, a maverick, who has married Priya on the gamble of a good life in Austria. However, he refuses to speak German, resists integrating, and ends up fighting with most people. At the end of the play, the Uncle has him transported back to India.

I am no feeble rice eater was a play written after the year spent by the author in Linz, Austria. The play works with the seed idea of the still raw wound of the Jewish people and their complex relationship with Austro-German history. It sets up a sort of inter- cultural, and international situation, with the theme of a German theatre company out to perform a play about India titled *The New Taj Mahal*. Various dis jointed scenes work to create an unsettled narrative furthered by the strange imagery of a naked woman covered in ashes hanging from a rope looped into the ceiling. Was this some kind of ancient Indian religious/spiritual practice? While the play refuses to answer this and other questions, a strange tension runs through its narrative, a tension that finally explodes at the end, when the 'monkey men' come in, and violently interrupt the play within the play. Written in 2010 the play is tense with a concern for a rising tide of religious intolerance in India.

The Colonial the Convict and the Cockatoo was written as a response to the author's own migration to Australia in 2010. It works as an Indian migrants view of Colonial Australian history. On the first day there, he stood under a very large tree with a great number of Cockatoos angrily trying to chase him out of their territory. From this visceral and angry welcome came the character of the Cockatoo and an impulse to tell a story of its world. The play emerged from research into the arrival of the First Fleet in 1788 and the effect it had on the Aboriginal populations. This devastating effect is seminal to this play but only reveals itself right at the end. Till then it is in most parts a view of Australian Convict/ Colonial history. The play was first performed at the Adelaide Fringe Festival and then toured India for the Bharat Rang Mahotsav and the International Theater Festival of Kerala.

Straight from a horse's heart was a play written in response to the impressions received over the first two years of the author's migration to Australia. One of the first experiences that surprised the author was the number of friends and acquaintances who had Cancer. These recurring stories of Cancer patients led to the play being set in a Cancer healing centre. In writing the play the author was also influenced by the story of the mining magnate and

Australia's richest woman Gina Rhineheart and her troubles with her children over their inheritance and control of the business. The characterization of Victoria, the owner of the healing centre, is influenced by Ms. Rhineheart's story. A central character in the play is Paro, a robotic nurse created by an Indian inventor to take care of the patients in the healing centre. However, while the patients think she is a robot, the audience knows it's a South Asian migrant woman pretending to be one. The play is a social satire and works with humour to throw light on the end-of-life-existence of ageing Australians. While this play was written in 2012, it finally got performed as a 'Zoom drama' in 2020-the first year of the pandemic. Nine actors, from nine separate rooms in Melbourne and the surrounding areas, never having met each other, rehearsed, and performed the play for a week in October 2020, and then again for four shows in April 2021. The play is set in a two storied cottage, with patient's rooms on the ground floor, and Victoria, the owner's office, on the first. The text in this collection is the script used for the online zoom performance.

Hawking the Bard in the Heart of Whiteness begins with Dr. Hari/Harry Singh the historian narrating, in verse, the story of 19th century Indian/Punjabi migration to Australia. Hawking their wares, these Punjabi men and their presence in rural country Victoria, were perceived as a threat to the female sections of the 'White' settler populations. Moving on from the narrative of these prejudiced perceptions we get introduced to the real lives and experiences of these hawkers through a courtroom scene in which Sir Barnaby Higgenbottom argues a case for Hardayal Singh the 'Hindoo hawker,' who has been robbed of his hard earned money.

While looking back at the 19th century experience of Indian Hawkers, the play simultaneously works to turn the gaze forward, to interrogate 21st century Indian migration to Australia. The set up for this contemporary investigation is the scene of a widow Barbara and the party thrown by her to celebrate her husband's life. To this party and into Barbara's home comes Nitin Sethi, an Indian I.T worker, who, uninvited, joins in the party celebrations, and on his real identity being discovered, is taken to court for criminal trespass, consequently losing his job. The discursive narrative works to explore issues of race and prejudice in rural Victoria where the author now lives.

Camp Darwin Written during the ongoing Coronavirus Pandemic is a slice of life play emerging out of the author's experience of quarantine on returning from India to Australia. While the first five days of quarantine were spent in a hotel in India, the next fourteen were spent at the Howard Springs Center for National Resilience, Darwin. The play details the living out of time in quarantine by six characters, two Indian Australians, three Anglo Saxon Australians, and one Australian of Chinese origin, who while being bound within the limits of their porches, interact, communicate, tell stories, sing, laugh, do yoga, fight, are terrorised by, and survive the situation they find themselves in. The play documents their experiences, and places on record, through the life of these characters, the unique experience of the pandemic.

The house of a great Victorian playwright Mr. Brandon Smith, local Stardale playwright lives with his married partner Mr. Arthur Hall. To his home, on a writer's residency, he invites Mr. Hari Gunesekhara, a South Asian playwright, to collaborate on a new play he is writing on the

Mahabharata. Contrary to Mr. Smith's expectations, instead of creating text around this ancient epic, Mr. Gunesekhara is more interested in what he observes happening in Mr. Smith and Mr. Hall's home. The marriage of Mr. Smith and Mr. Hall, the eccentric behaviour of Mr. Smith's mother, all are intriguing subjects for a contemporary play. Suspicious of Mr. Gunesekhara's intentions, Mr. Smith pries into his writing and what he discovers sends him into a rage. He humiliates and throws Mr. Gunesekhara out of his house. It is in Mr. Hall that Mr. Gunasekhara not only finds a friend, but a co-conspirator in plotting revenge. This revenge, when executed, leads to a very unexpected consequence. The story, the plot, the characters and their interactions, all set inside a Victorian Cottage, offer an opportunity for satire, for humour, and for drama. A contemporary play about race relations and more, set in regional Victoria, Australia.

I hope you will enjoy reading these nine plays.

ARJUN RAINA

A TERRIBLE BEAUTY IS BORN

Characters

Elizabeth, a 65 year old American woman

Ashok Mathur/ John Small a 25 year old Indian man

Lisa Washington a forty year old African American woman (on video)

Stage setting

Upstage right is a video screen

Downstage left is a roadside bench

On the left of the stage hangs a painting of Brooklyn Bridge, New York.

On the right of the stage is a large poster/ banner of 'Chuck E Cheese Ice Cream Parlour.'

Elizabeth, a 65 year old woman, sits on the bench.

Elizabeth: Welcome to Brooklyn Bridge. Right there across the bridge to the left is where the twin towers were. And then on that terrible morning of September 11th, those mother-fucking terrorists flew those planes into them. You know, there are a few events that are so big that you know exactly what you were doing at that point in time, I mean even years later. Like the killing of President Kennedy. That was like a long time ago but I can still remember exactly what I was doing. I was sitting in my room on my bed drinking coffee and my mother comes in, she's standing there at the door, crying. I can see those tears coming down her cheeks, and all she's saying is: 'He's dead, they killed him, they shot him in the head.' And I kept asking her, 'Who? Who died? Who got killed? Who got shot in the head?' just like that screaming back at her, and she just standing there crying. It took her a long time to say it, she just couldn't, and then she said 'the President, they killed the President, they killed Kennedy.'

I remember it even today, like it was yesterday.

There are other moments too of course but only a few that match that.

Like when Neil Armstrong took those first steps on the moon, that was a thrilling unforgettable moment. And now these planes, flying into these buildings.

I am going to walk across this bridge to Brooklyn. I think it will take me an hour to cross it. The jogger who ran past me must do it in less than ten but I walk slow now, real slow.

I am here to search for my daughter. She was here that day. I mean she lives in New York but I haven't seen her. You see she left home some time ago and I have no address. No telephone number, no way to get to her. I had to come to New York myself to look for her but it isn't easy, it's such a big city.

It's so odd, you know the guy that just ran past me, he had a tee shirt that said at the back, 'I survived the wall street crush of 1999.' It said crush not crash. That was such a ridiculous statement. I mean who cares, we've had two buildings crashing, thousands of people dying, don't people see what they're wearing anymore. I don't know. I just found that very odd.

And then, just as he runs past me this Rasta guy comes along, he's sitting in one of these automated chairs for the physically challenged, they move pretty quick and he zips past me. He has this big wild beard and his dreadlocks are all held in a sky blue cap, and he's laughing just like that to himself. He was laughing pretty loud because I could hear him even when he's well past me. It was strange seeing him and hearing that laugh. I mean I am not trying to say there was some great meaning in this but it was kinda sad, terribly sad seeing him laugh.

And then just as his laugh fades I see this guy way down there to the left on the bank, he's doing a kind of strange slow moving dance. I mean I liked that. I read about this dance somewhere, all those slow hand movements, they were about warding off evil, changing the air around you, getting rid of bad feelings you know, I liked that. The air needed healing. There are all these helicopters crackling their way through the sky breaking it up into pieces.

It's hard remembering those days immediately after the tragedy.

I live outside of New York, it's four hours by a Greyhound bus, in Little Town, it's a little village really.

See, I bought this map here, it has all five boroughs, Brooklyn, New York, Manhattan, Queens, Bronx.

It's a big city but I have an idea you know where she might be. A geographic location. I am going to begin there and hope. I mean it's been quite a journey how I got this far.

The first few days were terrible, there seemed no way to find out. Then my husband came to New York, he checked out all the hospitals, the police records, did everything everyone was doing to find the missing.

But she was nowhere. We really were lost, did not know what to do next.

Then this credit card guy called. I mean called and gave us hope.

It's really quite a story from having no hope to being here but it's not been easy, oh no, I have terrible pain in my knees.

But I have to keep trying.

I am trying.

I am trying to do the best I can.

She gets up and starts walking slowly off stage.
Lights fade.
On the video we see a night scene of Gurgaon, the Millenium city. The city is full of skyscrapers, all well lit from within, suggesting work happening at night, in the numerous International Call Centers.
Hindu religious music plays in the background.
Lights come on centre stage.
Ashok Mathur, a young man of 25 years old enters. Ashok is a calling agent at an International Call Center in India. His 'fake' calling identity is John Small. We meet him as John Small.

John: Hi, welcome to this International Call Center in Gurgaon, India. My name is John and I was Magdalena's supervisor. We were both a part of the Montmerry Ward Credit Card Collections team. It's true though what you have just heard. Magda, as we liked to call her, killed herself on that precise September 11th morning, only of course it was evening here, the sun had just set, we had only just begun calling.

It was all very sad.

This is Magda. I keep this photograph in the drawer now or I just get sad looking at her. She was a strange one, she was beautiful with a kind of beauty that withdrew from you the moment she saw you noticing it.

She once told me she loved giving blood, donating blood, she said her heart felt cleansed each time she gave blood.

She was an excellent caller. She collected a lot of money every day. She was the best. She'd mastered the art.

That's 'Bull' over there. He's Vice President-Operations. He was doing a security briefing when he was told about Magda. They call him Bull for two reasons. Because he takes no crap from no one and because he can gore your ass bloody with his horns.

He is known to have the reflexes of a Cowboy, he is always the first to draw and the first to shoot. That's why they made him VP operations. He is a powerful man in the company and Magda's biggest boss.

Collections is the most successful operation in the call center. Collecting money for credit card companies across America. This was tough calling. You had to learn to let the customer feel the knife-edge but no you could never, never, draw blood. Unless of course they forced you to!

Then you had to be hard, real hard.

And through all this you had to keep the game going, you had to keep the accent going, the mask was never off, they never knew who they were speaking to, they never knew we were not Americans, that we were Indians calling from India.

When Bull read Magda's suicide note he knew this was a bomb that could blow the whole operation up. The press would just love it. Desperate action had to be taken. Before the world spread, before the Police got there.

Magda had beautiful handwriting with every line and curve crafted. Time taken to write something from the heart. I wrote down what she'd written. It was very moving.

> For all you creatures of the night
>
> That sings false songs to a heartless moon
>
> Wearing masks and fangs and twisted tongues
>
> A farewell, my nightmares over.

She had signed it as Magdalena Falco. This was her calling name. Her real name was Uttara Bhatnagar.

The Police were bribed and taken care of. We were told to keep things quiet. And we did. The press got to know nothing about it.

I was calling when I was told about her. I was so disturbed I kept calling that night without a break.

The following text is performed with an artificially learnt American accent, the kind he would use while calling American customers.

> 'Hi this is John calling. Can I speak with Freddy please?
>
> Hi Freddy I am calling on behalf of the Montgomery Ward Credit Cards collections office. My records here show me you owe us fifty dollars. Now when are you gonna pay up Freddy because I see here you are four weeks overdue. You don't want me getting

tough on you, do you now Freddy. So you better buckle up and get that check across to us, right?

Okaey ...what I suggest you do is

Okaey...let me rephrase that for you

Okaey...Okaey... Okaey

Then on to the next call

Good morning this is John calling on behalf of Montgomery Ward Card services. Can I speak with Mrs. Julian Smith please?

Hi Julian

Hi...this is John calling

Hi...this is John calling

Hi... this is John calling'

Through the night without a break.

They gave me a prize for that night. It was an employee boost up plan. The highest money collector each week was to get a snazzy Phillips three-in-one player. An audiotape, CD and VCD player. A shining silver grey in colour.

It was a tough job calling to collect money. Especially at the beginning for young girls like Magda, handling abusive calls was tough, they'd never heard language like that from the small towns they'd come from.

'You sharks, all you want is my money huh, here I tell you my mama died and all you want is your hundred dollars, go fuck yourself man, shove that money up your ass.'

On her first day of calling I remember Magda lost her innocence violently.

> 'Suck my cock sweetheart I'd love to fill that sweet mouth of yours with my honey that's a fair exchange huh honey for money'

She was so shocked she didn't know what to do. She gave me the phone to handle. I did. No problem.

Later I taught her to be polite but firm and take no abuse.

Speaks with an American accent.

> 'Sir, If you carry on like this we'll have to get very serious about this and that'll be trouble for you sir, real trouble. You don't want us making things more tough for you than they already are huh?'

That was Magdalena Falco.

I miss her a lot now. Keep imagining I see her sitting there. Still taking calls.

Lights fade.

On the video screen we see projected a very old photograph of Brooklyn bridge. The photograph has been animated and brought alive. Through this old photograph there is conveyed a feeling of nostalgia, of something lost forever.

Nora Jones plays in the background, her song, "I don't know why I didn't come" plays hauntingly, sentimental.

Lights come on Elizabeth, standing, resting. She has been walking along the bridge.

Elizabeth: So there I was, sitting in front of my television. It was terrible seeing that second plane hit that tower. One knew then it was a terrorist attack. I just wanted to get up and go that minute, drive hard across to that terrified city, to that city terrified by terror where my daughter was, and her little baby, my granddaughter, who I had seen only once.

I couldn't move of course, my ankles, my knees, arthritis you know. My mother, my grandmother, they all suffered terrible pain.

'Leda,' I cried out just sitting there in front of the TV, 'My beautiful Swan. Oh My God. Where are you?'

My husband woke up then. He works nights you see keeping watch at a night shelter for juvenile delinquents. He had just fallen asleep. I said to him

'Honey. America has been attacked. They flew planes into the WTC buildings. Let's go honey we need to go now'

I mean, like I was shouting, hysterical.

Seeing me shout Bacchus, our little Chihuahua began yodelling. My daughter had taught him that. I speak loud you see and my daughter couldn't stand that so she'd taught Bacchus to put his snout up like that and yodel a sweet little tune every time I spoke out loud something like this…

Does a little dog yodel

It used to be very funny when he did that but that day with all that horror happening it just broke me up. It looked so sad, this little yodelling dog, it reminded me so much of the happy times we'd had, when Leda was home, that I began to cry. I don't do that too often you know but that morning I began to cry.

Anyway, I've now lived in Little Town for quite a while. It's a small village surrounded by forests about a four hour drive by car from New York city. I used to take Leda often to see her grandpa. He used to stay upstate New York. We'd hire a car for the day, eighty dollars, fill in the gas and then drive upstate and sometimes drive back late into that same night. All in one day. I couldn't do that now, not with my knees and ankles. My hands too are not too steady, keep shaking, shivering. It's funny.

You know I never liked travelling by Amex or a Greyhound bus by public transport I mean. Never liked that. In trains and buses you gotta suffer all kinds of other people with all kinds of strange attitudes, and when I smell an attitude, oh man, I am ready, ready for a fight.

I grew up in the Bronx in the sixties. It was no pretty neighbourhood then, you can bet your sweet ass it wasn't. I lived on the main street and all around me you get these buildings coming up and the noise, it just stays in your ears forever. You had to shout to be heard in your own kitchen. All those years I shouted, and now I can't talk softly, and here it's so quiet. you can hear a mouse breathe.

My husband and I just love it here. His name is Leo. His father named him after the great Russian revolutionary Leon Tolstoy. People here often like to call him Lee. That drives me mad. I mean they do that to my name too. I tell them I am not Liz or Lizzy. Please call me Elizabeth as in the Queen of England. Is that so very difficult? Must everything be reduced, shortened, made simple. No! Not my name nor my husband's. His name is Leo, that is Lee with an O and if you can't say the O, then you can shove it up your own great O, and get the hell outta here. I mean it drives me crazy.

I work for the government as a community aid worker. I help all the little people of my village deal with government bureaucracy. Well, for example, there are cooks in the restaurant down the main street, they're Korean, they speak nor read nor write English but they're making a lot of money. So who helps them fill up their income tax forms? Well yours truly here does. WellCare provides ten dollars a month for Medicare but the local forms are so complicated, well, they need me then. The other day there's this family here from the Dominican Republic. They speak English, they're getting their green card but they still want me there. They call me 'Little Angel,' I suppose I am that for all the little people of the village.

It's a pretty village. I am really proud of my house, a living room, a kitchen, two small rooms, a study and a basement. Outside on the porch it's beautiful. Soon, in the fall, the leaves will turn a magic red. 'The color of God's blush' I say. When I saw my house for the first time I thought, Yes! I could live here and die here too. OK, we never had much money but with God's beauty around I thought we'd be happy here.

Then one day Leda walked out.

She left for New York. I've seen her for only one day after that.

It was tough for her. I mean that ballet woman was so nasty and then maybe I wasn't there for her when her world was crashing. Maybe I added to her pain. I don't know.

She was such a beautiful ballet dancer. She'd worked so

hard for all those years from the age of four to seventeen till she was the star of the Norfield Ballet Company. That's the big town close to Little Town. They were touring the Edinburgh festival all these young ballerinas wild with their first taste of freedom. This was how that bitch Michelle Bernard, the director of the ballet company chose to see it. Leda was at the bar drinking and dancing with a Lithuanian dancer or was he Yugoslavian,whatever, she's having all this innocent fun and then this old bitch walks up to her and calls her a slut right there in the open in front of everyone. It was terrible for Leda. And then next morning she sacks her for corrupting the morals of the company.

It was terrible pain losing that chance to live a life of beauty and some ease. Maybe when she came home that day I was too disappointed in myself, too angry with her for having lost out. For the poor like us the chances, choices aren't too many. I too had worked hard all those years living that dream taking her to every one of those damn classes for all those damn years. I know I should have been more gentle, been there for her. But I wasn't and she walked out, left home never to come back.

I didn't hear from her for a year then she called one day.

'I am in Nu York' she says

'Doing what' I asked her, almost screaming.

There was silence for a while. I waited, then I asked her again.

'Doing what?'

'I am working at the World Trade Center' she says

I was sure she was making that one up to impress me or something. I mean she hadn't finished school, what would she do there?

Maybe I should have let her be but I was so worried for her, I don't know

I asked her again.

'Doing what?'

She hung up on me. Without saying another word.

She didn't call for a long time after that. Then suddenly she called one day. She said she'd had a baby. A girl.

'Is the baby's father with you?' I asked.

Her silence gave me the answer I did not want.

I knew why she had called. I knew she was my daughter and too proud to ask. But I knew she needed help.

I told her I would give her a credit card and that she could use it for two hundred and fifty dollars a month. That's all I could afford to give her and that it was only for my granddaughter. I told her if she spent a dollar more I would ask the credit card company to cancel the card.

It was the only time Leda came back home with my little granddaughter. I went and saw her at the local restaurant, The Piranhas, where she had worked often.

I saw the little one. It was terrible, she looked just like me. I mean I could see myself there. All little and bundled up. I was so happy.

It wasn't easy seeing them go that day (*cries*).

And now look at what they did to those buildings. They've flown planes into them and my daughter, oh my god.

And here I was crying and wailing not knowing what to do and there is Leo sitting in front of the TV saying repeatedly, 'this is evil, this is evil.'

For a while we were too shocked to do anything.

Then we started to do all those things that everyone was doing in America. I mean everyone in America has someone or the other they know in New York and everyone was worried not knowing what was going to happen next.

Leo and I, we started calling friends, the police, people we knew in New York. You couldn't get through because the lines were jammed, we heard the airports closed down, I mean there was chaos and panic all around.

And then suddenly in all this I get a call. I mean the phone rings. We're both right there. Leo picks up the phone and says it's for me from that credit card company that I take credit from Montgomery Ward.

Now I know I've not paid these guys. I am way overdue again this time. But normally on a day like this I would have just slammed that phone down and told the guy to f... off but something clicked at that moment. I mean way back in my unconscious maybe a little voice spoke up telling me to talk, not to hang up, but to talk to this guy.

And thank god I did. Thank god I talked to that Credit Card guy.

Lights fade.

On the video screen we see an image of an old stone gate of Mughal architecture. It's a gate that leads into the old city of Delhi. Through the arch of the gate you can see the crowded streets of the old city.

Lights come on centre stage
Ashok Mathur enters

Ashok Mathur: I live in this old, forgotten city. This is Ajmeri gate. I wait here, on the street, every evening for the company transport to pick me up

This old city has seven gates like the classical city of Thebes. In the old days when you would ride on a horse or in a chariot, each road led you to a different city in a distant land. As the name suggests this road would take you to Ajmer that's where the shrine of the famous Sufi saint is.

This way, right at the end of this road, is the Jama Masjid. Some nights you can see the moon rise over it, it looks magical. And the *muezzin* calling the faithful to the last prayer of the day.

I am a Hindu my name is Ashok Mathur. It's when I go past this gate in the morning that I leave John behind and become Ashok Mathur again. It's the other way round in the evening. I leave Ashok behind and become John, John Small calling for Montgomery Ward Credit Card Services.

Imagine if I actually were John Small I would live in a very different world than this that is around me. Of course I'd be paid a lot more than the 250 dollars a month I am paid now.

I know in America I would be paid at least ten times that amount.

We have a fairly clear picture of American life and culture. The first month and half of training is all about the way Americans live, eat, sleep, how they buy groceries, how they earn and spend money, the fact that they often don't carry any cash with them which is why their plastic money is so important to them.

All these details help us understand and sympathise, empathise with their situation. Empathy is a very important part of our work, then the customer trusts us helping us do our job better.

In the initial training we were shown films, all kinds, we spent hours discussing them. Initially I used to try and imagine what John Small looked like. How he walked, talked, how he woke up in the morning, what was the first thing he did, did he go out of his apartment to get milk, a newspaper etc.

I imagined his home, his family, and his children.

I mean it was all very mixed up in my imagination not having ever been to America of course but I started getting a picture of this man and I started believing it, this idea of who John Small might be.

This really helped me succeed with my work. It helped my calling persona stay stable. I mean even if the customer was shouting at me, cursing me I would just imagine what John Small would do and then that would immediately help me find a way out. Soon I found John Small being able to handle all situations, it was a good feeling.

But then I found I was carrying my work back to this old, forgotten city.

I mean all night I would be imagining the life of each of the calls I was making. When you called someone in America you couldn't escape that. Often you'd hear the TV in the background, people talking, parents scolding their children, couples fighting, you could imagine the life in those apartments, the pets, the cats, the dogs barking

All night my imagination would be alive with the sights and smells of America and I would carry them back through the gates of this forgotten city to my home, to my room.

At moments little details in my room would change, transform, start looking different, American in a way. I mean I would lie in my room and imagine my three bladed fan was actually a four bladed one as they are in America.

You can imagine on a blazing hot summer day with the temperature at 115 degrees Fahrenheit you come home and try to sleep in the day time, and the electricity goes off, so you're hot and sweating and staring at the fan which is not working and slowly the three blades change to four and then the fan seems to move from three to four and back again to three and then again to four. In the initial months of my job the fourth blade in the fan became a symbol for me, a sign that this was not just a difficult job but also, mentally a challenging and perhaps a dangerous one, that I had to be careful.

I had to consciously remind myself that fans have three blades here that switches turn up down not down up. That I needed to be aware while making the transition from one virtual world to another more real one.

I mean it was tough, this dual reality, and when finally the electricity came all the T.V channels were showing America bombing Afghanistan and the news readers saying Kaboool not Kabul. I mean why couldn't someone tell them it was Kabul they were bombing and not Ka booool. It almost drove me crazy.

But what perhaps tilted the scales was a strange coincidence that my mind was obsessed with for a while, it sort of possessed me, this idea.

We were being shown films of American Cowboys and Indians. This was part of the history lesson, the story of the origin settlers.

There was this wonderful one about a battle of the wounded leg or foot or knee or something in which the Indians are about to surrender and then suddenly the rifle goes off and the cowboys start shooting and all the Indians get killed. The image of all those Indians lying wounded or dead in the snow stayed with me for a long time.

In this film you had this character who kept warning you that the American Indians would rise from the dead and take revenge for what the White Man had done to their civilization and the sign would be the sighting of this strange creature half beast half man, a kind of live shadowy furry spirit, 'The *Ojibwa.*'

It was a wonderful film. I loved watching it. But then around the time I saw it a strange coincidence seemed to occur where I lived, right there in my street and in a number of slums and shanty towns in and around Delhi.

People reported first occasionally and then in large numbers the sighting of a 'Wolf Man,' half beast half human, a kind of live furry shadowy spirit. It was there everywhere on T.V on the radio. People were reporting seeing it at night, what it looked like, what it smelt like, what it did, they were showing their wounds, their scars from its claws.

Everywhere, even in the street where I lived people said they had seen him. Now I am not someone who believes in all this. I was convinced it was someone playing a trick to terrify and that rumours spread fast in slums where there are no walls to hold them in.

Like the one about Ganesha, the elephant headed god drinking milk, I mean the whole nation went crazy believing that one.

But somewhere, I don't know, I began to lose control.

Maybe I was just too tired, I mean we were working all night and trying to sleep in the day was difficult in the heat with all those power cuts.

I was losing my sanity a little and for a while I got obsessed with the link between the prediction made in that cowboy film and the 'Wolf Man' seen even in my street, in my city, in my world. It was an unreal, bizarre connection and I caught myself almost wanting to tell someone, like share this incredible discovery I seemed to have made that the American Indian prediction had come true in the streets of this old forgotten city in the shape of a terrifying wolf man.

Thank god I didn't. I mean even the 'Wolf Man' sort of disappeared and. things were calm for me too. I made sure I was sleeping better.

But then to make sure it didn't happen again I decided to consciously use the Ajmeri Gate as a separating line between John Small and Ashok Mathur.

I don't speak in English the moment I go past these gates. It's a golden rule I never break. It keeps me sane, helping me do my job well as well as live my life …my real life.

And when my transport picks me up John Small comes alive and blabbers away speaking only in English and with an American accent on call.

Well that's the story of my life.

Ah here comes the transport for work, a Tata Sumo.

Lights fade
On the video screen seen we see excerpts from a documentary of the 'Wolf Man.' Set in Old Delhi, at night, with crowds bustling about, the night streets are filled with people anxiously reporting various sightings of the 'Wolf Man,' what it looks like, half ape half wolf, what it

does, how it attacks people at night, how it appears from nowhere and disappears into the night. The documentary footage leaves one with a sense of dread and an anxious desperation.

Lights fade
Lights come on Elizabeth in spot on stage right

Elizabeth: The phone rang for quite a while before Leo actually heard it and picked it up. We were so caught up in our worries we didn't hear it and it's there right under our noses loud as a bomb.

'It's for you,' Leo said, 'It's that credit card company guy, I mean what's with these guys man don't they ever let up, don't these guys know what's happening in the world, should I ask him to call you later?'

Leo looked mad. Angry. It was crazy getting this call right then, when the world was blowing up, when we were sitting there crying, terrified, but something told me, you know that little voice in my head that I've learnt to listen to, that little voice told me not to hang up. I mean I know I hadn't paid my dues, this guy had called a few days back and I had told him I would go down to the store and mail him the check but give me a break this was the last thing I wanted to worry about that morning. But something told me, no not told, forced me to talk.

Even Leo said to me just slam it down honey, but I …I listened to that voice and thank god I did.

'Hi Elizabeth Frenner here, who is that?'

The voice on the other end was a little unclear

'Can you speak up please, I can't hear you?' I said raising mine

It immediately got better. I think the caller wasn't talking directly into the mouthpiece. I mean when I told him he immediately seemed to focus his voice. I could hear him clear.

We hear John Small over the PA system

'Hi Elizabeth. My names John and I am calling on behalf of Montgomery Ward Credit Card services. Do you have a few minutes to talk to us. I mean we do need to talk right?'

You know I liked his voice when I heard it. He was being aggressive in a way, but it was still a rich, deep and kinda warm voice. It also seemed calm, detached, and distant. In the chaos around it seemed reassuring in a strange kind of way. I don't know. It made me want to talk to him.

'Yes John, we can talk. I think I know what you're calling about'

'Thanks Elizabeth, that's a help. How are you doing today, isn't it terrible what's happening in New York?'

'Yes John.' I told him, 'It's terrible out there and for me personally I have a daughter in New York and we have no news of her we're really very worried. So what's this about John?'

'Yes Elizabeth this must be very tough on you I apologise for bringing up your account matters at this moment but I've got a job to do and I am trying to do the best I can to try and serve you well ma'am'

'Yes, son,' I told him, 'you must always do your job well. In any circumstance. That's America for you. That's why we are such a great country.'

You know, normally, I am not a patriot but at that moment with all those planes flying and the talk of war I too waved the flag.

'Yes Ma'am and god bless America.'

He waved the flag too. It was a little moment of communion. Of a strange feeling of togetherness. Then I could hear him change his tone.

'Yes Elizabeth. I see your account in front of me and I see you owe us $480 which should have been paid up by the 1st of September. I called you up on the 2nd and you said you would pay up by the 7th right? It's the eleventh today. Now you don't want me getting tough on you, do you now Elizabeth? So when can I expect a payment?'

You know this was getting very tough. I asked Leo to shut the TV down but he only lowered the volume. I mean I understand that. You couldn't break away from it, not at that moment you couldn't.

Of course I was on the verge of slamming down the phone myself when I heard that voice you know get threatening in that controlled kind of way. I thought to myself why am I doing this, why am I suffering this? I don't need this. Not now. Not when I am sick to death with worry about my daughter's life and my granddaughter. This was the loud voice then. Bellowing inside me. But then there was a little voice. Quiet, but there.

'Talk to him' it said, 'Keep going, don't hang up.'

And so I didn't.

'You've been our valued customer Elizabeth.' He was carrying on.' What's happened to you lately.Last time it took you three reminders before you paid up. You know my supervisor, he didn't like that, that didn't go down well on our record. You understand that Elizabeth. You're not paying up shows up bad on my team's record. We let that happen last time but not this time Elizabeth, right? So I am not paying the price for your delays. Ok?Ok? Did you get that? So why don't you just go down to the store and mail us a check and I mean that right away. You know Elizabeth, you know I mean that now. And let me tell you what I will be forced to do if you don't pay up this time Elizabeth. I have your credit bill here with every detail right? Here is the last bill with everything you bought and paid for in the last two months. Aha, what do I see here Elizabeth. I see you got yourself a nice new cooking stove eh!Wow, that's 1500 hundred dollars. That's a smart piece of fire you bought Elizabeth. You must be cooking up a lot of great meals for your friends down there, right? Well then Elizabeth you don't pay up today, you get me into trouble with my supervisors and I am going to see to it that the money runs out on your payment schedule. They're going to come to get it soon, they'll tear it out, rip it out of your kitchen wall. They'll leave a hole there Elizabeth right there for everyone to see. You don't want that to happen right? So you're going to go down to that store and you're going to send us our money right?

It was violent, terrible. I mean I felt destroyed but it was precisely at that instant I realised why I had come this far.

'Just a moment John' I said, forcing my voice to stay calm. 'Please believe me I am not trying to avoid the issue of paying the present dues. There is something else and it is very important. I just need you to look at my bill more carefully. Can you please do that for me?'

He wasn't listening to me. He was mechanical, aggressive.

'There is no problem with that bill Elizabeth. If there was, it would have come up on my screen. Your bill is here and I am looking at it and I can continue to look at it but nothings going to change that. It's you who's got to decide and go to that store, and now. Now if you say you will I'll go through your bill in all the detail you want me to. That's my job, we've no problem with that. I am here to help you, you know that Elizabeth right? But you know we've done enough for you and you've got to pay up and pay up quick right?'

I stayed calm through this.

'Honey' I said 'just hang in there. I am not questioning the billing. That's all fine...'

And then I decided at that moment to accept it and make a deal for the future, to fill that hole not in my kitchen but in my heart.

'It's something else,'I said, 'I'll write out that check right now and go down to the store and mail it to you but there's something else, just hold it while I get myself a copy of the bill. I need your help please, can you do that? Can you help me please?

After a brief silence he answered

'Yes Ma'am, of course I can ma'am.'

I put down the receiver and opened the drawer where I kept all the bills.

Leo had in the meantime made coffee and placed a mug

right there on the telephone table. Ah! That smell of coffee. It always wakes you up even from desperate grief sometimes.

The bill was where I thought it was. I gave myself full marks for being organised. I looked to check whether it was the latest then picked up the receiver.

There were in that bill, besides all the others, eight entries, which were clearly for a child and they all totaled up to 250 dollars.

1. There were diapers
2. Baby food
3. A pram
4. A baby's alarm clock
5. Baby's clothes
6. Medicines
7. Toys
8. A visit to a Chuck E cheese

I went through that entire list with that Credit Card guy, they have like all these credit records on their computers and he saw all these entries there. I convinced him, I said...

> 'Hey honey, just look carefully at all these items, no's 3,17,25,46,48,56,60 and 65. There's diapers here in no 3. Now what is an old lady like me going to do with diapers, there's baby food here, what's me and my husband going to do with baby food. Look at each of these items. They are all a baby's items, just check them up. You can see from our earlier records I never bought any baby items earlier. These are all my daughter's expenses for my granddaughter. And

like I told you she's in New York. You can see only these items are the ones bought from a store in New York. Now what happened was this. I gave her my card. She'd had this little baby you see and the father he'd just walked out. Now what was a grandmother supposed to do, so I gave her my card and you can see for the past few months every month she's bought two hundred and fifty dollars worth of stuff and now here's the tough part honey here's what I am dealing with right now. My daughter lives in New York but I don't know where she lives or what she does. Now I tell you and you got to believe me and seeing what has happened today it is driving me sick. The only time she spoke to me about what she does she told me she was working at the world trade centre. Now this may be hard to believe but it is God's truth. I hope and pray to god that she was making it up. Kind of putting on the airs saying she was like working in this fancy place. The only time I saw her some months back she'd come with her baby. I wanted to see my granddaughter, she said she'd come if I asked her no questions, so I didn't and now I don't know where she is and if she's alive or not.

I know, this is none of your concern but here is where I think you can help me. See, sooner or later she's going to use that credit card of mine right? That's the only link I have to her and then I can breathe again. I 'll know that my daughter is alive and that my little granddaughter is not just abandoned in some terrible apartment somewhere in that terrible city. So honey you got to help me. I'll keep my side of the deal. I'll pay up right away and go down to the store and drop that check so that you get it soon and your boss gets nothing to complain about. I understand that, I respect that. But you son you gotta make me a promise. You will not forget about me after this call. You will keep an eye on my account, keep checking on my credit entries as they happen. You can do that, I know you can do that, that's how you always know everything, everything about me right? As soon as you see a credit entry for a baby's item from a store in New York you'll let me know, you'll call me, please I beg you, don't, don't pass me over. I know this is asking a lot of you, you must be making hundreds of calls each day, I have no right to but please son, please, please do this for me.

It was tough. I was crying, shaking by the end of it all. Leo was holding me, consoling me. I was waiting, desperate for an answer.

Lights fade
Lights on centre stage.
John Small enters

John: So there I was taking hundreds of calls that night. Without a break. This beautiful girl had just died, just killed herself. Planes were being flown into buildings, people were dying, the world was coming apart. It took the systems a while to react before they blocked out all calls, first New York, and then the rest of America. However, for a while even after the second plane hit that tower we were taking calls.

I was aggressive, real aggressive that night. I'd never been that aggressive ever and never that successful too.

And then there is this call. There is this call to an old lady Elizabeth. My team had been handling her business for a while and I saw she had delayed payment a couple of times before and this time she was late again. I mean it was bad news for her, she was up for the saw. You see our team had to show results or else the axe would fall on us. Low scores meant tough times, lesser breaks, more calls per hour, no benefits, no promotions. It all just added up. In fact low results forced us to send some of our team members back for re-training and that was an issue with Magda too. She'd drop her accent sometimes. I think she'd just get tired and also she wasn't aggressive enough, the real aggression that cracks the hardest nut there is to crack. You have to come down on them real hard and then they pay up, I mean everyone pays up. I once had this guy who was refusing to pay and finally I told him I was coming to get his truck the next morning and sure enough the check was on my table.

But Magda, she had too sweet a heart.

Miss Pamela Price thought she needed retraining. Pamela Price, Voice, Accent and Business Communication trainer. Her training sessions were hilarious. She trained you on speaking 'International English' with an American accent.

How to roll your are r's and soften the t into a d...wader not water.

How to roll the l and how to speak with an American intonation.

Pretending to be on call.

Good morning, customer service. This is Maggie speaking. How can I help you?

All in a kind of singsong way.

We all found it very funny. I mean she was British. She was the local British School Principal's daughter. She was still in college. And here she was heading the communication program in a multinational corporation. She had the power to decide the future of thousands of call takers. I mean after the anxiety and stress she caused with her harsh decisions, they had to remove her, especially after what happened to Magda. They were forced to bring in someone with greater skill.

They got this wonderful African American voice trainer Lisa Washington who was flown in from America, to work with us for six weeks. Those of us who were talented with doing accents were coached by her to become accent trainers.

We had a great time with her. She was a master with accents. She spoke in all kinds of accents. She also brought in some very interesting ideas. She said we were all trying to speak 'White' American English. That America was also Black America, Spanish speaking America, all kinds of Americas and that perhaps we could also speak as Indian Americans. An Indian who has been in America for a few years and speaks with, and understands the style and rhythm of the different kinds of English spoken in America.

That helped the stress ease out. We had to pretend to be only a version of ourselves. As Indian Americans, that really helped.

She played all these wonderful recordings for us of American writings, monologues from plays, essays, and famous speeches, and then there were her favourites. She made us read all these wonderful poems of black writers in America. I mean we all loved that. My favourite one was by a guy who had written it like a hundred years ago, he had died young at 32. Here's how it went

Lights fade
We see on the video an accent training session with an African American lady coaching John Small. She recites a couple of lines of the poem with an American Accent and John repeats. She corrects him on certain words like mask to demonstrate the American accent.

Paul Laurence Dunbar (1872 –1906)
We wear the mask

We wear the mask that grins and lies
It hides our cheeks and shades our eyes
This debt we pay to human guile
With torn and bleeding hearts we smile
And mouth with myriad subtleties

Why should the world be over-wise?
In counting all our tears and sighs?
Nay let them only see us, while
We wear the mask.

The trainer ends the session
Lights up on stage

John: This was great stuff for us reading all these wonderful words that seemed to connect with us, we had a feeling we were being cared for, a rare feeling in our corporate world. There was one poem however that I specially connected to. It reminded me of Magda, and our situation as Callers calling with a fake accent and name.

Lights fade.
We see on the video screen the African American lady reading another poem. After a line or two she makes John read it.

To a dark girl

I love you for your brownness
And the rounded darkness of your breast
I love you for the breaking sadness in your voice
And shadows where your wayward eyelids rest

Something of old forgotten queens
Lurks in the little abandon of your walk
And something of the shackled slave
Sobs in the rhythm of your talk

Oh little brown girl born of sorrows mate
Keep all you have of queenliness
Forgetting that you once were slave
And let your full lips laugh at fate

The video ends. The stage stays dark for a brief while.
Lights on stage.
Elizabeth is on the bridge near it's Brooklyn end

Elizabeth: You know I have walked for about forty minutes without a break. It's the longest I've walked for a while now. It's really like a penance. Offering my tired flesh at the altar of my grief (*laughs*).

So here I am at the end of my walk across the bridge. Down there is the Brooklyn promenade and that's my destination. There is an ice-cream shop there and that's where I hope to meet my daughter.

You know I have to thank John for this.

He brought us news of the first credit entry that was about four days after the eleventh of September.

Those four days were hell.

But then she bought some baby food from a store and we knew she was alive. My husband and I hugged each other, we celebrated, we were really happy, we thanked John, really blessed him.

But that was not enough.

I mean even John knew we had to see her. I mean there was this chance that she had let someone else use the card or something complicated like that. We couldn't just rest assured on the basis of that one buy.

So we waited and John began to track all the credit entries as they came in. I mean it's amazing the kind of love and effort he put in to help us, we would have been lost without him. We can't stop asking God to bless him.

For a while the credit entry showed no pattern, gave us no lead to where she may be, no pattern to follow.

And then over the next two weeks John noticed a credit entry to the Blue Bunny ice-cream parlour, Brooklyn Promenade, at 5 p.m. on Wednesday and Friday, and it repeated itself the next week 5 p.m. Wednesday and Friday.

So here I am next Wednesday.

I hope to hell she'll come.

I mean I'll be devastated if she doesn't but if she doesn't I'll be back on Friday and I am sure she will come on Friday.

Of course if she doesn't I'll be shattered. I'll really not know what to do next. I mean how long can we keep asking John to help us. He's done enough, by god in heaven, he's done more for me than anyone has in a long long time. He's been a true brother and I can only bless and thank him for bringing me this far and giving me hope. It's been really hard but I am here and I am sure I will see my daughter today, oh yes, I will, and my granddaughter.

Oh gawd, I'm sure she is looking more and more like me.

I am sure she is.

Sure she is. Sure she is (cries).

Lights fade. On the video screen we see Elizabeth breaking down, crying. This happens slowly, taking its time. In the distance we hear the aazaan, the muslim call to prayer..

THE END

THE WEIGHT LOSS HOUR

Characters

Chorus: Middle aged man or woman

T.V anchor/presenter: A young woman

Kalpana Katkar: A young Indian Hindu woman

Zahira: A young Indian Muslim woman

Citizen 1,2,3: Any age and gender

Aurangzeb: Aged Mughal Monarch

Mahavir Acharya: Middle aged Bengali man

Maulvi 1: Middle aged Muslim man

Sarmad Sufi: Middle Aged man of Armenian heritage. Nude on stage.

Commissioner: Young Indian Hindu male

Translator: Any gender/age

Right in the middle of the stage is the weightloss room. A curtain/ screen is drawn across its front, to make it private. The Chorus stands downstage right. The Chorus projects from his laptop onto the curtain. Whenever appropriate he pauses the projection.

The Chorus addresses the audience

Chorus: Hello and welcome. I am an only lonely chorus. I apologise. As you can see, I am alone. There is no one else with me. I tried to get others but in today's times it is difficult to get people together. I am a chorus member of 'One.' However, armed with this laptop and this curtain for a screen, I am a chorus of millions. I represent this great nation called India and its people. Now, in the year 2007, I reveal to you its people and their lives.

Projects an image of the facade of Sunita Sharma's Weight Loss Clinic.

Here in Delhi I take you to Sunita Sharma's Weight Loss Clinic. Sunita Sharma is recorded in the Limca book of world records for the maximum weight loss in the shortest length of time. Her formula for personal success is now an entire business strategy known as the SS way to SS that is Sunita Sharma's way to Stay Slim. She uses the latest techniques of electronic controlled weight reduction as well as personalised massage service and body care.

Here in Sunita Sharma's weight loss clinic we will meet Kalapana Katkar. Now a slim woman of 52 kgs she has lost 20 kgs over the past year but still wants to lose more weight. She wants to lose more weight not because she wants to make her body look even more beautiful than it already is, but because she wants to be fighting fit. That is right. Kalpana's life is going to change very radically very soon and for once she is fighting to stay in control.

From Sunita Sharma's weight loss clinic we will move to the wonderful state of Bengal where Samta Ganguli the firebrand politician is on a fast protesting the forced acquisition of a thousand acres of fine agricultural land for a car manufacturing project.

We see images of a protest site where Samata Ganguly is on a fast

She has been on a fast for twenty days and her condition is fast deteriorating making life extremely difficult for the Marxist Chief Minister Mahavir Acharya who is wracking his brains to try and come up with an innovative solution to the political problem.

We see an image of Sarmad Sufi's Dargah in Jama Masjid, New Delhi

We are then back to the capital city of Delhi where a Supreme Court controlled demolition drive is breaking down all illegally constructed structures and buildings. Shops are being sealed and lakhs of traders are losing their business. Simultaneously old structures and buildings that are impeding the path to progress are also to be demolished and their inhabitants relocated. One such building is the Dargah of a 17th century Sufi saint Sarmad right next to the Jama Masjid. For those unfamiliar a Dargah is a shrine where the grave of a Muslim saint is located. In a Dargah the saint is considered to be asleep, and not dead, by the faithful. Hence the scared character of the structure.

So dear Janta, dear great people of this great country, let us waste no further time and get the show moving.

The chorus projects from his laptop onto the curtain. Behind the curtain is the weight loss room.

Zahira, the slim and beautiful weight loss assistant enters and sits on a stool kept in front of the curtain watching a TV program the chorus is projecting.

Signature tune of CNN IBN

An attractive TV anchor is smiling over cheesily and presenting the days story

T.V anchor: Welcome to the day's top story. Organ trade twist to Noida horror. You thought the Nithari killings could not get more morbid. Well they have. Morbid details are emerging from the house of horrors in the Nithari village in Noida's Sector 31.

Four days after U.P. Police unearthed grisly details of young children being kidnapped, sexually assaulted and butchered to death in businessman Moninder Singh Pandher's D-5 bungalow, police are now exploring a possible organ trade angle.

Officials, who have recovered skeletal remains of at least seventeen of the nearly thirty one children so far, say that the torsos of most of the bodies are missing, lending credence to the organ trade theory, which was earlier, ruled out.

Moving on to the next headline of the day it is confirmed that Abhishek and Aishwarya are getting married. They were both seen with the Bachchan family at the Sankat Lochan temple in Benares.

Kalpana presses the bell and a loud ring is heard.
Zahira draws the curtain and enters the room.
The chorus stops the projection.
In the weight loss room:
There is a bed
A massage table
An electronic tapping machine
TV
Cupboard, table etc.

Kalpana Katkar lies on the bed all wired up for the session. .
She has been watching TV, which shows the same program the
chorus projects onto the curtain. She lowers the sound.

Kalpana: Zahira this one, here, it's not working at all, no
buzz no feeling. Can you please do something? Kuch karo.

Zahira moves to the machine and goes about readjusting the vibrating
pads attached to Kalpana's body, adjusting the control of the flow of the
electric vibration. She checks very carefully with Kalpana that each pad
is reactivated. Kalpana helps her fix the right level.

Kalpana: Han, now it's there, just a little more without
giving me a shock. *Ab ismey bhi aa raha hai* how old is this
machine? Half the time is taken up adjusting levels. That is
why I am losing weight so slowly now. The first fifteen kilos
took just four months, then the next ten another four, and
now these last five have already taken me five months. When
I told Sunita Sharma about it she spun some weight loss *gyan*
at me, that first the fat is loose so weight loss is easier but
then the muscle has to lose water or some rubbish like that,
so it takes longer. But the truth is the machine has been here
since I started over a year ago, a year is a long time these
days. *Aajkal toh saal main pati basi ho jata hai machine toh kya.*
Tell Sunita Sharma she is making all this money she needs to
reinvest it in her business. She herself is putting on so much
weight. The Limca book of records *ki* champion weight loser
is now looking like a 'Before' and 'After' ki ' Before' model.
I don't want that to happen to me.

Zahira (laughing) That won't happen, you've slimmed down a lot, you look so attractive now. It's just that you've decided to lose more weight, for me your figure is perfect now. Acha, if you need anything else just ring the bell *abhi* ten minutes are left.

Kalpana: Today, what's after this?

Zahira: Today Sunita madam has for you twenty minutes of electronic tapping, then massage, then twenty minutes of tummy tuck.

Saying this she tries to change the channel pointing it towards the curtain. The remote is not working.

Areey the remote isn't working, *yeh kaam nahi kar raha hai…nayee* battery *lagani padegi.* I'll just change the batteries, put in new ones.

She leaves the room exiting downstage left and leaving the curtain drawn.

Kalpana's phone starts ringing. She looks at the number calling says a loud 'fuck' under her breath. She takes the call.

Kalpana: What the fuck do you want? I've told you not to call me in my sessions you can't hold your fucking tongue like you can't hold your fucking semen. Who the hell are you to tell me to mind my tongue and who the fuck are you to tell me to stop losing weight, it is my body and my fat, and I will get rid of it and do whatever I want with it. When I was fat you liked it because then I would just sit at home and cook meals for you. Well you screwed it all up for yourself. That fat slob who you could walk all over is now past tense. This is me now and if the new me is too threatening then I am through with you. I should have walked out the day I found out but I stayed on because of your mother. She has only me to care for her in the house, but the more I have found out about what you've been up to, the more it makes me sick that I have spent so much time with such a bloody asshole.

She switches off the phone. She begins to cry, suddenly overwhelmed by her anger. Just then Zahira comes in.

Zahira: What happened, your husband on the phone again? I am sorry I heard you, you did just right. Men think they still own us, our bodies, give them half a chance and they even want to control our weight. My husband too tried that, encouraged me to grow fat so I'd just stay at home and cook for him. Like his mother has done for him his whole life. But I stayed slim even after two children. He doesn't even know the number of men who want me, who desire me, but I am tired of them all. I like to be with women now, *marey sarey mardlog meri bala sey.* The next time your husband calls, just give the phone to me *aisi galiyan doongi uska raang udh jayeega.* At this time in the clinic there is no one else, I'll just let him have it.

Kalpana starts laughing.

Kalpana: *Bilkul sahi kaha* the time has come to let them really have it *marey saaley sab ke sab. Achcha* give me the remote. I have to watch these TV anchors *kal mera* audition *hai* CNN IBN mai and I am feeling very under confident but I have decided. I am going to get this job and start a new life. I need to now live for myself and when I decide something *tab vo hokar hi reh jata hai.* I make sure it's done.

Zahira gives her the remote then leaves the room drawing the curtain behind her.

The chorus projects onto the screen. It's TV news time. The lead header goes 'Samta Ganguli goes on a fast unto death against the TATA car factory.' Then a TV anchor presents at her sexy stylish best. It's an image at odds with the fasting Samta Ganguli.

T.V anchor: On the twenty third day of her fast, drinking only water every day Samta Ganguli the Chartaka Congress Chief's condition has very seriously deteriorated causing grave concern to her supporters. The Chief Minister Mahavir Acharya in a surprise political move has requested Samta Ganguli to give up her fast and has invited her to a feast of excellent Bengali cuisine, which he promises to personally supervise. As the chief minister in his address to the Bengali TV channels insisted, its an offer Samta cannot and must not refuse. Samta Ganguli who has been in and out of consciousness for the past two days is yet to respond to the Chief Minister's offer. With her fast deteriorating health the Chief Minister has a serious crisis on his hands. This channel has done a survey on people's reactions to the fast and the political battle ahead and here is what ordinary people had to say

The Chorus projects onto the curtain responses of common citizens to Samta Ganguli's fast. Some are in support while a few are critical.

Citizen 1: Samta Ganguli is a great Bengali leader, she is an inspiration for all Bengali women, Ma Kali speaks through her. If she led the nation the whole nation would prosper. I totally support her hunger strike.

Citizen 2: All this *dharna sharna* fasting business only creates public disturbance. At the time of our freedom struggle this kind of politics was fine. If work stopped then the British suffered. Now we are all suffering because of her *dramabaazi*. They should feed her intravenously, or somehow, I don't care.

Citizen 3: I totally support this peaceful way of resisting. She is a great lady. Totally incorruptible. I will myself go tomorrow and sit in dharna with her. I will not eat for 24 hours in support. *Jai Ma Kali.* Jai Mamta Ganguli.

Zahira draws the curtain open and comes into the room to check the time left.

Zahira: This Samta Ganguli is quite amazing. Twenty three days on just water, nothing else. Here in the clinic there are customers who cannot stay without food for twenty three minutes. There was one who just came in a short while back, in nine months she hasn't lost 500 gms. I've done them all on her, electronic tapping, tummy tucks, massages, hot towels. Everything. But she is still where she was, twenty five kgs overweight. I have to call her everyday to keep a check on what she is eating. She will tell me with a straight face 'today I have been very good, just had water all day'. Then when she comes here her weight is up two kgs. She's really shameless. She'll say sorry I forgot I had a lot at tea time, three *samosas*, *gulab jamuns* and three *emertis*. I told Sunita madam that this one is a gone case and we should let her go. But Sunita Madam says if she doesn't have a problem wasting her money why should we? Well, she has a point. She has to run her business but for me, I feel sick and tired sometimes of massaging her fat body. Like with you it's different, you've put your heart in losing weight, that makes me feel so good. I mean even if this is a strange thing to do, if we do it with our hearts one feels one has achieved something. But with her one feels humiliated. *Acha* has six minutes left. If you need anything just buzz.

She steps out drawing the curtain behind her.

The chorus projects onto the curtain, another TV anchor presents the news

T.V anchor: The demolition drive in the city of Delhi ordered by the Supreme Court has now found a new and controversial victim. The Supreme Court has instructed its Commissioner to inform the authorities that run the shrine of Sufi Sarmad fakir, right next to the Jama Masjid, that the court has directed the shrine to be relocated to another site, under the supervision of the Archaeological Survey of India. This move will be seen as very controversial for Sarmad, a well revered Sufi Saint, by the people not only of old Delhi but even worldwide. Sarmad's body is buried in the shrine. In fact the local people believe that the Saint is in fact alive and only sleeping, resting in his shrine.

The Chorus*:* For those unfamiliar with Sarmad's story he was a Sufi fakir in the times of Aurangzeb who the emperor beheaded accusing him of being a sympathiser and well wisher of Dara Shiko, Aurangzeb's elder brother and rival, whom Aurangzeb defeated and killed in battle. Sarmad was charged, for being nude, which is against the teachings of the *sharia*. He was further charged with not speaking the full *kalmah* and only reciting part of the first line saying "There is no god but god" while continuing no further. By this charge he was accused of attempting to question or deny the existence of god by cunningly stopping at the negation of god's existence in the *kalma*

> There is no God but Allah
>
> And Mohammad is the messenger of Allah

His replies were found unacceptable and he was ordered to be beheaded. The next day he was taken to the execution spot. When the executioner came near him with a gleaming sword in his hand, he smiled on seeing him and while lifting his eyes to the heavens spoke these historic words:

We see Sarmad upstage right for the first time. He is standing nude. Sarmad speaks in an ancient dialect of Persian. A translator steps up and translates.

> **Translator:** There was a commotion and I opened my eyes from the dream of non-existence. I saw that the night of sedition still remained, and so went back to sleep! "May I be sacrificed for you? Come, come, for whichever guise you come in, I will recognize you!"

Chorus: After his martyrdom the words, "There is no god but Allah, and Mohammad is the messenger of Allah" were heard from his mouth thrice. Not only did his severed head recite the *kalmah* but it continued to praise Allah almighty for some time afterward. The people in Delhi greatly venerate the grave of Sarmad and daily burn candles and incense and sprinkle fresh rose water and flowers on it.

Zahira draws open the curtain and comes in to the room
Zahira looks at the weightloss machine clock

Zahira: Just two minutes left. *Arrey,* did you see the story on my dear saint Sarmad Sufi's Dargah. I love him a lot. I live very close to his shrine. Often returning from work, before going home, I spend time there. They say he fulfils any secret desire expressed to him. No one knows this, but my first child I wanted was a girl, and a girl is what he gave me. It was his blessings that made it happen. If you have any desire or dream I will take you there, you can ask him and it will get fulfilled.

The time for the vibrating pads is up and Zahira starts taking all the pads off even as she keeps talking.

But you'll have to hurry. They say the government is planning to build a hotel there. A lot of people come to the Masjid from all over the world but there is no decent hotel nearby. Especially for millionaire Arab Sheikhs, a five star hotel is being planned there. All over India old buildings are being removed. In Baroda there was a four hundred year old Dargah that was demolished. They ask what's the problem in relocating a gravesite? But I say a Dargah is not just any graveyard, it is no ordinary grave there, in a Dargah we believe the saint is resting. He's sleeping there. Dargahs don't hold corpses within them, there a saint lives, it's his home. It's a way to keep goodness alive, not letting it die and disappear from the world. Amongst thousands do you find one good human being and our Sarmad Sufi was a good man among millions. He came from Armenia as a merchant, then fell in love with a Hindu boy and got distracted and so lost in love that he wore no clothes. People see him as a saint of love and goodness. They say when the emperor Aurangzeb had him beheaded, his disembodied head kept reciting the holy *kalma*, kept repeating Allah's name and his headless body holding his bleeding head in one hand walked right up the steps of the sacred Jama Masjid.

Zahira has just finished the removal of the weight loss machine pads. Kalpana has stood up for Zahira to make the bed for an oil massage.

Just then the phone rings. It's Kalpana's husband again, she paces around the room talking to him. Zahira prepares the bed, then the oil for the massage

Kalpana: Why are you calling again? Don't you get the message? I don't want to talk to you. Not now, not tonight and maybe not ever if I can help it. What are you sorry about? It's not just enough to say you are sorry you have to spell it out. What are you sorry about? Have you any idea what it feels like to live with someone for two years who has been lying to you?

Yes you have been lying to me. I know what a travel agency is about and now I know what kind of travel business you are in? Does your mother know? Do any of your relatives know? What you really do for a living? For two years you fooled me and now I know why you carried that laptop of yours so close to you. It was because it contained all the secrets of your dirty business you bastard. What you didn't know is that despite your disapproval I had learnt to use the computer. I learnt to use the email, have my own account and then one day you leave your laptop behind and I get to find out the truth.

Don't tell me that it's legal business, you bastard, you lied to me, for all these months and I will never forgive you for that. Go find yourself some other body to do your dirty business with.

Once again Kalpana is overwhelmed by her anger, she breaks down crying. Zahira doesn't say anything; she is ready for the massage. Kalpana lies down on the bed on her stomach with her head buried in the pillow. Zahira begins to massage her while telling her a story of Zebunissa, daughter of Aurangzeb the Mughal emperor.

Zahira: I love poetry, ghazal anything in verse, have you heard this poem by Zebunissa

> "Though I am Laila of Persian romance,
> my heart loves like ferocious Majnu.
> I want to go to the desert
> but modesty has chains on my feet.
> A nightingale came to the flower garden
> because she was my pupil.
> I am an expert in things of love.
> Even the moth is my disciple!"

Zeb-un-Nissa was the daughter of Aurangzeb the Mughal Emperor. A poet and a wild one it is rumoured she was a lover of women writing her poems under the name of *makhfi* or the hidden one. She was 21 years old, when her father seized the throne from his father, Shah Jahan. One day he invited Nasser Ali, a handsome Persian noble, to a contest with his daughter. The challenge was that Ali would recite the first *misra*/line of a couplet. and Zeb would have to complete it within three days. If she failed she would have to renounce her poetry forever. Ali composed the following

Durre ablaq kase kam deeda maujud

Rare it is to find a pearl both black and white

For three days Zebunissa failed to find an apt response. She preferred to die than give up her poetry, so she prepared for her last moments by calling a Hindu girl she was in love with to her quarters. As Zebunissa prepared to eat her own diamond ring, her beautiful friend wept tears of distress. As she wept, Zeb began to smile and then spoke out joyously

Weep no more, dear one for I have found the second line of the couplet.

She summoned Aurangzeb immediately to her palace and recited

Durre ablaq kase kam deeda maujud

Rare it is to find a pearl that is both black and white
and

Bajus ashqe butane surma aabud

Except a teardrop in the darkened eye of a lover

Delighted, the Chorus sings Sarmad Sufi's song

Along the road you were my companion

Seeking the path you were my guide
No matter to whom I spoke it was you who answered
When Sun called Moon to sky it was you who shone
In the night of aloneness you were my comforter
When I laughed you were the smile on my lips
When I cried you were the tears on my face
When I wrote you were the verse
When I sang you were the song
Rarely did my heart desire another lover
Then when it did you came to me in the other.

Lights fade
Light on a centre spot.
A thin wiry old man walks on stage. Dressed as an emperor in silks and pearls

Aurangzeb: Aadab arz hai my countrymen my greetings to you. Perhaps you don't know who I am, in the 17th century I ruled over India for half a decade that is nearly fifty years. I am Aurangzeb the Mughal emperor.

During my reign I gathered peace in my hand and held it tight and fought only to maintain it, to keep my empire as one, so that ordinary people could work and earn their living, their families safe and secure. The country that has a new ruler every six months, a new vision of growth and progress every twelve, is a country that lives in perpetual chaos driving itself in many directions and going nowhere. With enemies on its border and enemies within constant strife and change burns the energy of its people wasting a nation's time, life and existence. One emperor and one empire for fifty years, that was my rule. When the heart beats strong the body is healthy, grows, flowers. It is no easy task to rule a country for half a century. It was Allah's will of course but it was also the love and trust of my courtiers, my kinsmen and my people… or else…some enemy, some thug, courtier, friend, or even my own security guard would have plunged a knife into my back. Whatever happened was the final truth. For fifty years I put my heart, breath and every muscle into making this a country of peace and prosperity where ordinary people could work, live, and prosper.

Despite all this I am accused of many terrible crimes.

The Chorus: That is correct Emperor Aurangzeb. You in fact are one of the most reviled and controversial men in Indian history. It is for this that I have decided to give you a chance, here in the people's court, to defend yourself. Here are the charges made by the ordinary people of India.

Chorus projects on curtain

Citizen 1(*on screen***):** The first charge you are accused of is the murder of your own elder brother, the crown prince to the Mughal throne, Dara Shikoh, a man loved both by your Hindu and Muslim subjects, a Sufi by nature, a man of inquiry and wonder, a poet. You fought battles with him and eventually ordered his beheading. Besides Dara Shikoh you also drove your brother Prince Murad into exile, where he died a terrible death, as well as you had your youngest brother, Murad murdered. How can you argue against this terrible crime?

Aurangzeb: Dear Countrymen, citizens of free India, I have an answer for each of these accusations, however terrible they may seem from your point of view in history, and I am thankful for this opportunity given to me to personally clarify each charge made against me.

First my brothers and my terrible treatment of them, their defeat, the death of Dara was in War. I fought them in battle, used the fairest means to battle and they in turn fought back, warred with me. If they at the first instance had laid down their arms at my first battle cry then their death, exile could have been avoided. As you don't clap with one hand you also don't battle alone. War only takes place when two decide to fight. It is never ever a singular choice.

Yes I defeated and killed my elder brother Dara to become emperor of India. What is the truth? Is Dara's right to the throne the truth? Why? Where is it written and whose hand is it that has written it? Did I too not have a right to the throne? And my brothers and sisters too, in fact it was my belief that it was everyone's right, each countrymen's right to become emperor. He who had the strength and power to rule and control this kingdom had the right to be king. And how was this strength to be judged, by a singing competition, by playing dice, or horse racing, playing *gulli danda*, Or, by warring on the battlefield, putting your life at stake, either you or I, and the survivor becomes the emperor.

Yes I became the emperor by defeating and killing Dara Shikoh.

Yes I became emperor by defeating and exiling Shah Shuja.

Yes I murdered Prince Murad.

All this because they fought me in battle. And I defeated each of them in battle.

I am not proud of the fact that I killed my brothers but

then we were not flying kites together, this was a fight for the throne of Hindustan. A King after all is a King and consequently a crown, a crown that is something worth fighting and dying for. It is not easy to speak truths simply, clearly but years later to say what I have known all along brings peace to my own heart.

Chorus: Well spoken Aurangzeb. I am not here to pass judgement on you, but to give you a chance to speak your truth. The final decision will however be by the people, whose court you are standing in. I, as the only lonely chorus, am only their representative. Here comes the next charge.

Citizen 2: Emperor Aurangzeb, in Hindustan there is nothing as sacred as a parent and nothing as reviled as the ill treatment of one. You imprisoned your father, the great Shah Jahan, the creator of the most exquisite Taj Mahal for seven long years, in the Red Fort, at Agra. Was this just, fair, necessary? Was this an act of an emperor? Or was it a reflection of your petty paranoid personality that lived out of fear, and controlled the world around you, through fear and terror, even imprisoning a dear wonderful man like Shah Jahan who besides all other wonderful things was your father. How can you not be regretful of this act?

Aurangzeb: It is true that I imprisoned my father for seven long years in the Red fort at Agra. Agra was where my father had built the Taj Mahal as a tomb for my mother Mumtaz Mahal. However I request you to see the reason in my following words. If I killed my dear elder brother was it then so difficult to kill an ageing father? But I didn't kill him.

Hindus believe that old age is a time to be spent in the forest. I too was hoping that for my father, that he would choose to live away from the chaos of city life but he chose not to, he wanted to be near the tomb of my dear mother, his dear Mumtaz. I found a room for him in the red fort from where he could see his beloved Taj Mahal. Was this a crime? I had seen my parent's love and I had also seen my father's broken heart at my mother's death. Only I know how happy he was those seven years near his beloved Mumtaz, near her tomb the Taj Mahal. Only I know how happy he was there in the red fort. I knew how precious the Taj Mahal was to Shah Jahan. I also know how precious it is to the world to each one of you. But the truth is that right from its beginning I was against it being built. For me a tomb is six yards of land, some dust sprinkled with respect, and at the most extravagant a tombstone. Perhaps you have not read my will and testament. In it I have left the two rupees and fifty paisa that I earned darning socks, to my courtiers, to my gardener. That's the kind of simplicity I believe kingship should be made of. When your countrymen don't have enough to eat, when they sleep unprotected from nature's fury, when disease wracks and death stalks your people, a marble monument for an emperor's wife is nonsensical, in fact is ugly, vulgar.

An emperor does not need to wear silk

An emperor can do well without pearls and diamonds

An emperor's tomb should be of ordinary stone and earth

An emperor should build only those buildings where people can gather and shade themselves from the sun and pray, like a mosque.

Was all this a crime? And if it was then the accusation

holds true but if not, then I have wrongly been accused and slandered by history.

Chorus: Well argued Aurangzeb. You have made your point. This is the truth of perspective, that given time everything can be made to look different, for better or worse. Who am I, an only lonely chorus to pass judgement? My job is to set things up and observe. The charges against you are endless but we will restrict ourselves to this final charge, which above all others concerns us today. If your answer to this too is as sharp as the other two then perhaps historians will look at your case differently. Judge you differently, for better or worse. Now for the third and final charge.

Citizen 3: You are charged Alamgir Aurangzeb with the cruel beheading of the saint of love and goodness Sarmad Sufi. What was his crime? That he wore no cloak to hide a dagger in? That he tread terribly dangerous ground by his denial of god's existence in the first part of the *kalma* stopping at 'there is no god but god.' Was this so very threatening to your existence that you needed him dead? Why? Why did you kill this naked poet?

Aurangzeb: Dear friend, a king must know both how to make a horse gallop as well as to reign it in, and that sometimes he does this with a terrible crack of the whip, as I did with Sarmad the naked Sufi fakir.

The truth is always simple. On the one hand was the great fakir, with his wisdom and his poetry, his songs and his followers and the other was his naked body. It is an ugly sight in the public space to see a naked man.

Sarmad was never mad, only madly in love with a Hindu boy. These two were so busy taking their clothes off that they were never able to put them back on again!

For the majority to prosper, an emperor's supreme task is to maintain law and order. And that is why when I saw crowds gather around this nudity I decided to do away with him. To maintain the sacred dignity of my reign I was willing to do anything.

Dance, music, art, ecstasy, joy, happiness were on one side and the hunger of my people was on the other.

For me two simple meals a day

A set of clean clothes covering my body

And prayer, five times a day

This was my strength

This is what helped me rule for 48 years, helped me keep secure an empire.

In all of history's many lies, these are a few of my own simple truths now spoken. They bring a quietude and peace to my heart. The rest is for you to judge fairly or with the worst prejudice as has been the case so far.

Lights fade as Aurangzeb exits

Lights on weightloss room

Zahira continues to massage Kalpana and sing Sarmad's verses. We can see them in the weight loss room through the curtain. For a while nothing happens. Then a middle-aged man walks on stage. He speaks in a rhetorical and elaborate style as if addressing a vast crowd. He speaks English with a heavy Bengali accent.

Lights on Mahavir Acharya

Mahavir Acharya: My fellow Bengali comrades and friends.

I address to you the good people of Bengal but I also know that the rest of the nation is listening and that is why I am not speaking in our sweet mother tongue Bengali. English is a very deceptive language, however, be rest assured I am not here to deceive you. I am here to say what I do know as our good friend Brutus once said. I am here today as an ordinary man caught in extraordinary circumstances. Of course I am chief minister of Bengal, of course I am member of the Communist Party's Politburo, but above everything else I speak to you as an ordinary man, as just one more Bengali amongst you many wonderful Bengalis.

What is the extraordinary circumstance this ordinary man is facing? Is it about the industrialization of Bengal? Is it about the conflict between the agrarian and city world? Is it about the dialects of materialism that speak with different tongues in different languages? Or is it more specifically about the car project? Have the Tata's not done business honourably in India for the past seventy five years? And now they want to start a car project. Is it a luxury car project? No. They want to make the cheapest car in the world. And why do they want to build it because they want to make lakhs of families that ride dangerously on scooters safe. Is this a sin I ask you? There are so many questions my friends that if you want you can keep raising them and I can keep answering them. But the issue I want to place before you is not the Tata's and the car project. It is not about the acquisition of a thousand acres of land. It is not about compensation and rehabilitation. It is not even about Samta Ganguli and her reactionary politics. But it is about her fast. Today I speak to you dear Bengali people not as a Chief Minister but as another fellow Bengali. Samta Ganguli's fast is twenty-three days old. Her condition is critical. I have to grant that when she first started I thought she was throwing a tantrum, it will soon be over. But she is serious. I have to grant her that.

Samta says she will die fasting. As a chief minister I am faced with a grave political situation. If Samta dies fasting it will mean political disaster for me. I know that. I have offered to discuss all issues with her but she refuses sipping water only for the past twenty-three days. In the morning water, afternoon water, evening water. No food. Please note no *Bengali* food.

He is almost hysterical now.

Let me repeat that for you, dear Bengali people, this critical detail. For twenty three days and seventy two meals Samta Ganguli has refused to eat Bengali food. In my opinion this is a shameful degradation and disrespect of Bengali culture. It is unpardonable. Let me clarify my position further. This whole business of fasting was made successful by the father of the nation Mahatma Gandhi. God bless him. Firstly, he was a thin man. Unlike Samta who is definitely not. My point is that she likes food. And secondly and more importantly he was not a Bengali but a Gujarati which implies quite naturally that he ate Gujarati food. Now I do not want to offend any of my many Gujrati friends but I ask you to think of a *dhokla* on one side and a well cooked *chingari macher malai curry* on the other. Is there any comparison? Friends this is my understanding of historical processes, that the political weapon of fasting became successful in the hands, or belly of the Mahatma, not because it was a non violent act against the British but because in the first instance it was so easily done. It was possible because it was so easy to avoid eating Gujarati food.

I speak to you as a Bengali and a true Bengali speaks. Can any one of us stay without Bengali food even for a day? Wherever I go in the world, if I meet a fellow Bengali the first and last thing we discuss is food, *ilish mach, luchi, tangra mach, chorchori*. Ladies and gentlemen it is my contention that Bengali food is at the heart of Bengali culture and civilization and a rejection of Bengali food is consequently a rejection of the Bengali people. This is unacceptable, intolerable and must end.

Samta Ganguli must end her fast. So as Lenin said, what is to be done? Very good question. I Chief Minister of Bengal tell myself that I am not an Emperor of India in the seventeenth century like Aurangzeb. I cannot ask a political rival like Sarmad to be beheaded. Nor am I like Indira Gandhi to impose emergency and throw all opposition to jail. As a true democrat and a true Marxist I can only offer a dialogue, a true and honest discussion on every issue. And that is what I propose to do. Fellow Bengali friends, I have decided to cook a feast for Samta Ganguli and invite her to it. This is an offer she can't refuse. We as a people must not allow her to refuse. Samta Ganguli must end her fast. See what we plan to cook for her, the finest *macher matha*, yes the finest fish head.

The chorus of one sings the song of the macher matha —the fish head, in Bengali

O what joy to be a Bengali
and eat macher matha
On a rainy day
O hilsa ma
You great giver of joy and anando
Whose Matha forehead is split into two
And body smeared with salt and turmeric
Who twists and turns and squirms in a frenzy
And is fried in bubbling burning boiling oil
And lying there all bathed and slippery
Is showered and blessed with
A curry of Coconut and Coriander
And in this cooks the fish's head
O what joy it is to be a Bengali
What joy to eat a *macher matha*
On a rainy monsoon day
O great fish who swam in the great sea
All day happily with your family
Till one day a fisherman's net
Brought you out to the sandy shore
I watched as with the others of your family
You were sold to a fat woman of sixty
Who chopped your head into two
And sang to you as the oil boiled
O what joy to be a Bengali?
What joy to eat a *macher matha*
On a rainy monsoon day

*As the Chorus sings the song of the macher matha, in the weightloss
room the massage is over.*

Kalpana gets up and rubs herself all over with a towel

Zahira is preparing material for a tummy tuck. It's like a gluey paste that concretizes once pasted over a newspaper spread over the belly
Kalpana slips out of the room briefly saying

Kalpana: Just be back. I need to do some piss loss, a piss loss during the session helps reduce the final weight by at least three hundred grams…be back soon.

They laugh.
Things are quiet as Zahira prepares a tummy tuck
She is singing a Sufi song. She switches the channel and on the TV there is Kaun banega crorepati (Who will be a Millionaire)
Kalpana returns and settles down to a tummy tuck. Watching KBC.
Kalpana's phone rings
Zahira looks at her to say shall I take it?
Kalpana indicates she can handle it.

Kalpana: What is it you want you bastard? Can't you leave a woman alone? Don't you get it? I am through with you. I am not coming home tonight. It's over *(pause)*.

That is none of your business. I have friends who you don't know. If you think you are the only one with a secret life, well I have a secret life too. That's exactly what happens. When a marriage is based on a lie, then you get two people with two secret lives *(pause)*.

Well that is why I have suffered you for so long you bastard and you've taken full advantage of that. Well that too is over. Tonight you give her the medicine. Call Dr. Nath now. His number is stuck on the refrigerator. Tell him my wife has left me. And I now need to take responsibility for my mother's medicines. Do that not just for your mother but also for yourself. Not that I really care. And don't push me to tell you what I really want to say. This is not a game of cards with your buddies that you can choose to play another round and try your luck again. For me at least this is as real as it gets and I am out finally. Please don't call me again. If you call me again even the smallest care or respect I have for you, for any of the brief moments of happiness that we may have shared together will be gone. So please just leave me alone.

Zahira who has been there watching TV lowers the volume.

Zahira: *Agar aap bura na maney* may I ask what your husband does?

Kalpana: It's really quite shameful. He runs a travel business. Where people from rich countries come to India, but not for tourism, they come for an organ transplant. Usually a kidney, or a lung, or sometimes even a heart. He sets up everything, from the donor, to the doctor and the hospital, to their hotel and stay and all the travel arrangements. So in a way it is the travel arrangement that he had told me about, but of course it's not. All the donors are poor people, labourers, beggars. It's terrible.

Let me show you something. Saying this Kalpana closes the curtain

The Chorus projects form his laptop onto the curtain a powerpoint presentation

The power point shows the hospitals, the hotels and the donors.

The donors are the poor with their gaunt, sad faces. We see X-rays of their bodies and details of their organs as seen through ultrasound examination.

Slide after slide after slide. Like a horror show.
Suddenly there is a black out, and we hear Zahira shout.

Zahira: Oh ho power cut, Zahid generator 'on' karo.

Zahid takes his time to switch it on.
Kalpana grumbles in the dark.

Zahira: *Sunita madam ko kitni bar mainey kaha inverter laga do lekin vohi purana broken generator chala rahi hai.*
Shahid *(she shouts again)* Start the generator.

In the darkness we see Aurangzeb pacing, agitated. With him is his chief courtier a Maulvi-muslim priest carrying a lamp.

Aurangzeb: Has anyone even the slightest sympathy with an emperor? Of what he has to bear, to suffer all in a good day's work. There to the North the Khalsa Sikh army is roaring like lions wanting to tear our bowels out. Next, in the East there is famine and thousands are dying everyday and food has to somehow be gotten across to them. Now while you think of a solution for that you must also solve the problem of robbers and bandits that are looting the highways. In all this come the horses from Arabia and I must be sure to choose the best hundred for my personal army. Finally if all this was not enough comes this disgusting spectacle, of a naked fakir coming to this great court of my ancestors the great Moghuls.

What are all of you here for, you good for nothings? All of you courtiers and Maulvis and wise men of Dilli? Could you not put your silly heads together and solve the problem, then come to me and say Emperor, here is the solution, here is the way for you to avoid being attacked by this horrid man's horrid nudity. But no, even this problem I must solve.

Maulvi 1: Forgive my saying so my lord but we did try, it's only that it is such a delicate matter that we…

Aurangzeb: Delicate, nonsense, rubbish. I will tell you what to do since there is no help from any of you. I hate to be faced with this man's naked thing. Perhaps for the first time in this great court of the Moguls, where for centuries people have come from near and far, dressed in the finest of silks, adorned with gold and diamonds and pearl ornaments, bedecked, bejewelled and always covered from head to toe, and now for the first time, this naked thing faces us, dares to confront us. Well here is how we will deal with this.

Let there be a curtain hung here in the middle of this stage that I might see him smokey, cloudily, his thing hidden from me as I stand on one side of the curtain and he on the other.

I shall only briefly hold court while you question him, then I shall have his skin stripped off his back, and if anyone questions I will say I was only taking off his shirt *(laughs cruelly)*.

Hang a curtain here in the middle of the stage and hide this ugliness.

Maulvi 1: Your highness forgive me but we had thought of this option and we came to this conclusion that by hanging a curtain/a *purdah* in a way, the emperor, that is you my lord will be on one side and since it will clearly be seen that the naked *fakir* is male, only because it will be so obvious, that as a consequence this side, that is the side of the emperor will be perceived as feminine, which I am sure your lordship will not consider the appropriate position you would like to be. Please forgive me if in my haste to advise you I have said anything that would be inappropriate.

Aurangzeb: All right all right enough of this fawning. For once, and I am amazed you are right. This curtain thing will put me in the *zenana* which is the wrong place for me to be in. So if you have thought so much, what is the solution? Facing his manhood straight on is also degrading for me, it is obscene, it's vulgar.

Maulvi 1: Yes your highness it is. You are very right, it is for this that we Maulvis have after great deliberation come to the conclusion that perhaps there is only one solution out of this. If you allow me to show you, when I turn around like this with my back to you I am in a way making my back into a curtain through which I cannot see you. In this way I have placed myself as if within a curtain, and while you can see both me and my back clearly I, the fakir, cannot see you. Now it is obvious that in this position his naked backside will offend your imperial eyes but in a way it is better than seeing the naked frontside. I mean, if we see the Fakir's front as masculine, we can say that the back is feminine, and your highness will therefore be looking at the feminine, and be clearly masculine. Of course this will only be for a short time, the length of four questions and four answers and then his fate is sealed. This was our logic. The decision of course can only be yours.

Aurangzeb: What a bloody headache. Does anyone have any idea what an emperor has to go through in a day? What I have to suffer?

Call that naked fakir and let him turn around there and cover himself with his own curtain. It is after all just a little play we are putting on, the real has already been decided. I shall have him beheaded. I will colour his back, his curtain a bloody red.

Call him, let him come.

Brief interval

After the interval the chorus projects on the curtain the shrine of Sarmad right next to the Jama Masjid

On stage the Commissioner walks in. He addresses the shrine projected onto the curtain. He is a very honest, earnest looking bureaucrat/ government officer.

Commissioner: My dear Saint. My apologies that I come here to disturb you. I have been appointed by the Supreme Court of India to serve you notice of your eviction and relocation. I am here as the court's representative. I am here to do a job. I hope you will forgive me. Perhaps I need to explain the court's decision. India is changing, moving fast, racing forwards. It is developing. But certain communities in India are being left behind. The Muslim minority is one. As the courts observed, due to Islamic ideals of not profiting by taking interest on loans and investments, most Muslims do not invest in the stock market; they still prefer to keep hard cash under the mattress.

Now as you will observe dear saint this is no way to prosper in the modern world where instantly, electronically trillions of dollars are moved around the world. The consequence of this conservatism is that there are very few Muslims who are getting really rich and powerful in this new economy. In a world driven by economics this is a serious drawback to the community, without an empowered elite to lead them into the future. The honourable court observed that the Muslim community needs to be represented by and engage with wealthy Muslims/Arabs. It is for this that the idea of a five star hotel right next to the Jama Masjid appealed to the court. This will attract rich Arab sheikhs whose charity, engagement, and business sense will help uplift the Indian Muslim community. It is very unfortunate that this shrine falls within the area designated by the court. The owners of the hotel have promised to rehabilitate all the beggars that live around the shrine by giving them jobs as waiters, car attendants, etc. Anyone who is genuinely involved with the shrine will not suffer a dislocation.

Dear Saint, as you are held with such deep and sacred affection the honourable court has requested that I speak to you first and that this be done with your will and consent. If however you refuse, the court has also directed me to tell you that it is firm in its decision and it has no other stronger means of persuasion than this your humble self and true servant.

An executioner with a gleaming sword in hand takes his place backstage right.

So I request you to wake from your sleep and begin the negotiation

The Commissioner withdraws and in the meantime the entire court of Aurangzeb take their places on stage

Aurangzeb: *leh aayo usey …jaldi karo…. namaz ka vakht honey aa raha hai.* Bring him here fast. Let's get it over with as quickly as we can.

An announcer sounds the entrance of Sarmad Sufi

Sarmad stands upstage. He faces away from Aurangzeb. The trial begins

Maulvi 1: Sarmad Sufi Shahanshah Alamgir Aurangzeb's court of infinite justice makes four clear accusations. Your answer for each charge will be recorded in the royal book for posterity and after the fourth the emperor will give his verdict.

The first accusation is that you sided with the emperor's enemy, his brother Dara going so far as to predict that the throne would be his. As you can see now Dara lies dead in his grave and your prediction has been proved a lie. You are therefore accused of lying and rumour mongering about the emperor's throne. Both are serious and grave crimes. Now say your answer clearly and wisely for it shall surely be your last.

Sarmad speaks again in a strange language (perhaps Persian or Armenian)

Aurangzeb.… *yeh kya keh raha hai* I didn't understand a word of what he said. What language is he speaking? It sounds gibberish to me.

Maulvi 1: Your highness, this was difficult even for me. I think this was pure Persian. Or pure Armenian for that was his place of birth. Certainly not a language of Hindustan. We will need to get a translator. I had anticipated this so he is ready.

Translator: Your highness forgive me but Sarmad Sufi is saying that his prediction indeed has come true. For is not Dara now an emperor of all existence. Of the skies and the stars and the worlds beyond or something to that effect.

Chorus: wah wah Sarmad Sufi. Your answer will surely get you killed. Your head will roll tonight like a football. Your naked body will be bloodied red tonight.

Maulvi 1: Sarmad Sufi this is great. Your answer has been recorded word for word. Now for the next accusation, that in your poetry which you call *rubiayat* you say that the prophet did not ascend to heaven as is believed and is for surely true but that the heavens came and were found inside the prophet. As if the heavens were like a magician's coin that could be whisked away at one end and then out from behind the ear. Speak the answer clearly for it shall be recorded forever for posterity.

Sarmad speaks again in Persian/Armenian

Aurangzeb: *yeh kya keh raha hai* what's he now saying? If he has been living in India why does he speak in this fake ornamented kind of way that no one understands. Speak translator or more precisely, translate.

Translator: *huzoor Sarmad Sufi yeh farma rehey hai* that the truth is there embedded in this *rubaiyat* and that he has nothing more to add

> *They say the prophet went to the heavens*
> *Ahmad says the heavens came inside the prophet*

The Chorus: *wah wah* Sarmad Sufi your every answer is another step towards your doom, your naked body will be bloodied tonight, your curtain shall be drawn forever.

Maulvi 1: Sarmad Sufi you are doing very well. Here is the next accusation that you don't say the *kalma* like all honest Muslims should. That you say the first negation there is no god but god and then stop very cunningly at this point not speaking the rest, denying the existence or at least questioning the existence of the prophet. For the last time you are being given a chance to say what should be said correctly. First I will say the *kalma* and then you will repeat it perfectly without hesitation and without error

> *La illaha illallah Muhammad rasool Allah*
> *Sarmad speaks in Persian/Armenian*

Aurangzeb: This is ridiculous. I just feel like beheading him for talking nonsense, for not making sense to an emperor. Isn't that sufficient ground for his death. That I could not understand what he said and he wasn't bothered. This is ridiculous. Translator!

Translator: Your Highness Sarmad Sufi says that even as he speaks the negation "there is no god but god" he experiences ecstasy and loses consciousness and cannot continue.

Chorus: Wah wah, Sarmad Sufi, what a cunning answer. You had one chance. Your last. And you let it go, it's over. The head is to be cut, the body bloodied, the show is over. Please someone draw the curtain. The final accusation quickly please.

Maulvi 1: Samrad Sufi. Your rebellion is now out in the open, that you will go to any extent to offend and then find a smart answer. Well, between this final accusation and your death is now your last smart answer. Here comes the accusation.

You are accused Sarmad Sufi finally of vulgarity. Just look at you. The creator made clothes for everyone to be dressed in, to be civil but you, like a madman, roam naked, caring for no one, nor child, nor woman, nor mother, nor sister. Do you think of yourself as one of the emperor's garden roses that you are worthy of being looked at! Do you not have even a shred of modesty? Of shame?

Sarmad speaks etc
Aurangzeb just curls up in agony saying nothing

The translator: Your highness Sarmad Sufi is saying that if anyone is offended by his naked body they can close their eyes and he will surely go away, become invisible. And he adds to this a verse

He who stole the evil eye and wine from me
Is the thief that has stolen my clothes too

At this Aurangzeb explodes

Aurangzeb: Now the almighty is a thief for Sarmad. Next, I Alamgir, emperor of Hindustan will be called a common robber. This is blasphemous, inexcusable, he has gone beyond the edge, the abyss, his death is calling him now, call the executioner, let him draw his sword and behead this fraud. Let his curtain be bloodied, let it be drawn, let his own body be his shroud, let this end now.

The executioner steps forward. The chorus leaps forward holding a loin cloth begging Sarmad to cover his nudity and save his life.

Chorus: My dear saint, just wear this brief and save your life.

Sarmad throws it away.

The Chorus: When the executioner came near Sarmad with a gleaming sword in hand he smiled on seeing him, and then lifting his eyes to heaven spoke these historic words.

> May I be sacrificed for you, come for whichever guise you come in I recognize you. There was a commotion and I opened my eyes from the dream of non-existence. I saw that a night of sedition still remained and so went back to sleep.

Then the executioner steps forward.
As the executioner cuts off Sarmad's head there is a blackout
On the curtain we see his naked back all the way to its neck
On the curtain we see the blood slowly dripping down a naked back
Then the image of a face replaces the naked and bloody back
The face speaks the kalma three times

La illaha illAllah Muhammad rasool allah
La illaha illAllah Muhammad rasool allah

The chorus sings Sarmad's verse
In the weight loss room the tummy tuck is over
Zahira draws the curtain
Kalpana is taking her weight

Kalpana: Today I have lost 600 gms.

Zahira: (writing down) From 52.6 Kgs you have come down to 52 Kgs, very good, well done.

Kalpana starts getting dressed

Kalpana: Tonight, can I stay with you? I don't want to go home.

Zahira: Of course, I was thinking about it, that I would ask you. My husband feels very happy to see me with my girlfriends, then he thinks our marriage is safe. If only he knew. Come, you sleep with me tonight. Tomorrow morning we will go see Sarmad's shrine. It will be fun. Shall we go?

Kalpana: After you.

Zahira: No, after you you're still our customer.

They both laugh they leave the stage
Sufi music

THE END

ECDYSIS: THE SNAKE SHEDS ITS SKIN

Characters

Priya: A young Punjabi woman

Kuldip: A young Punjabi man

Chachaji (Uncle): A middle aged Austrian man of Indian heritage

Playwright: Forty year old Indian man

Set

Upstage left, a door with a curtain draping its entrance. The curtain is made from the same material that Priya's saree is made of.

A video screen in the middle of the stage.

To its right is the 'Altar of Grief,' a wall with a number of stuffed birds.

In front of the wall, and downstage, are seven garden dwarfs-the seven miners of the Fairy tale Snow White and Seven Dwarfs. A wall connects the door, the video screen, and the stuffed bird wall, working as a back wall, suggesting the space in front is a large room.

The stage is in the dark.

Voice over: Once upon a time in the ancient and beautiful city of Linz that lay like a sweet lover by the side of the blue Danube, there lived in a Snowy White castle on a hill, a strange man who they said lived alone with no one except his seven garden dwarfs.

The man it was said was haunted by his past, a past that lay right over the other side of the hill. A past no one ever talked about. Not the man. Nor the garden dwarves that lived with him.

The castle was built with its back to the past and looked out to the river and on through the magnificent Hauptplatz and the grand Strandstrasse, past the central Hauptbahnhof, all the way down to the end of town where all the poor people lived.

The poor people never dreamed of ever going to the castle but sometimes at the end of a long day, they whispered to each other that perhaps one day one of them might enter the castle and return to tell the story of the strange man who lived there, alone, with his seven garden dwarf.

Priya enters through a door on stage right. Her face is covered by a red veil.
Lights on Priya

Priya: My Name is Priya Thakur. I come from a mountain village in India. Above my village, beyond the mountain tops is the House of God. The House of a Million Gods. Male Gods and female Gods. Big Gods and small Gods, brown Gods and black Gods, ugly Gods and beautiful Gods, Gods with horns and Gods with tails, goat Gods and pig Gods, rain Gods and wind Gods, hairy Gods and naked Gods. All kinds of Gods.

They all live and breathe and dance joyously in the skies.

At night they get dressed in diamonds and pearls and gold and silver and emeralds and rubies. We believe this is why the stars shine bright at night. For they are God's jewels. A million Gods' jewels.

Of course, in other parts of the world, I know people think and feel differently about the stars and the skies and the house of the Gods but from where I come from everyone believes that Gods live and yes, strangely, once in a while, they die too.

The death of a God is considered a terribly sad thing.

The night I was born a God died. And a star fell from the skies to its grave in the deep and dark ocean. I know, here, people call it a shooting star but in my mountain village people believe that when a star falls from the skies a God dies.

A female God died the night I was born. A Girl God.

It's a curse to be born on such a night. Especially for a girl child. For it is cursed that when she grows up and marries she will lose her husband, that her husband will die young, that soon after her marriage she will become a widow.

No one wants to marry a girl born on such a night. For everyone in the village, life is hard but for a young widow it can be terrible.

In the village I was prepared to stay single my entire life. Childless. Unloved. Poor.

Then my uncle, my mother's brother, made an offer. In a marriage advertisement in a newspaper. Whoever agrees to marry his niece he will help come to Austria?

That is how Kuldip came into my life.

That is how we came to live here in Linz.

Lights fade

On the video screen we see a door, Priya's bathroom door. We see her opening it and entering her bathroom. She closes the door behind her. We notice she is wearing the same red veil that she was wearing in the previous scene.

We hear her pull the flush.

Light on a spot in front of the video screen.

Kuldip walks in, he is in a hurry and is agitated. He addresses the video screen.

Kuldip: Priya, Priya how long is it going to take you. Thomas has told me that if I am late another morning he will cut 10 euros from my daily wage. Have I come here to earn money or lose it? Priya, Priya why don't you respond? Have you died? I am warning you for the last time. If like every morning, even for one morning I have to go to the public toilet under the bridge on my way to work, I will make your life miserable in 'Australia.' I swear I will lock you up in the bathroom. You will be there all day till I return late at night, then sense will dawn on you. All the important changes that need to be made you resist and all that is cosmetic and fashionable and helps you feel like a westerner that you adopt without a struggle. I am tired of explaining to you every morning. This is not the village where you have to go before I do. Here if you feel like you can go all day. In the village it all makes sense…where there is no bathroom to go to…and all the women go early in the morning, in the dark, before everyone to avoid being embarrassed. This behaviour can be understood. But you have all the time in the world once I leave for work…you can in fact go any time, any number of times. The bathrooms here shine clean like the marble floors of the Taj Mahal. You could spend hours in this luxury but you insist on holding onto your village habit. In every other instance you want to change yourself into a modern woman. Putting red *sindoor* in the middle part of your hair you have such an objection to that you took the matter to your uncle and made me include your right not to put sindoor in our marriage agreement. But the fact that I get late for work every morning doesn't seem to bother you.

Priya, Priya I swear this is the last time this drama is going to happen. I am warning you…don't force me.

Leaves the apartment angry. We hear a door shutting.
Once again we hear the flush.
Priya, wearing a red veil, walks out through the curtained door.
Lights on Priya

Priya: So that was my husband Kuldip leaving for work at 4.30 in the morning.

This is Kuldip with Hector and Fifi. They are Thomas' dogs.

We see a photo of Kuldip with Hector and Fifi

Thomas works for my uncle. Every morning Kuldip has to take them out for a walk in the park.

Then he has to go and open the newspaper kiosk.

Late in the evening he works at a restaurant as a waiter.

Thomas is getting old. And has gout in his ankle. It was he who first received us, taught Kuldip his job, when we first arrived in Linz. Thomas has been our link to reality here.

We've never met our uncle you see. Since our arrival. In fact Kuldip has never seen him. Even after working for him for a year.

On the video screen, we see a large leather boot.

My uncle has a sense of humour. He has his own way of encouraging us. Kuldip hates it but Thomas says it's a system with all his employees. They get to see only photos of him, one body part at a time.

This photograph is what we saw put up in our room the first day we arrived.

Thomas told us that it was our uncle shoe. And if we worked hard and made profit for the company then one day the photograph would be changed to be that of his hand.

We would still not be able to see uncle of course but if we worked even harder and made even better profits for the company we would finally get to see his face.

We knew uncle watched us. Somehow. Whenever we left the flat empty there would be a message from us on the answering machine. Just encouraging us to work harder. And to stay out of trouble. They were always there each time we went out and returned.

He sounded completely Austrian. A stranger. It was frightening.

It seemed like he was watching us all the time

Lights on stage
Enter Uncle. He is talking on the phone.
He speaks in English adjusting his accent according to the person he is talking to.
He is wearing the boots we see in the photograph.

Uncle: Yes, Henri. Thank you, my French accent has improved. Speak in France as the Frenchmen do and the French are happy. Ha-ha, yes indeed.

Yes, Henri. That is wonderful. Yes, we can't ignore India anymore for the 3T's, tourism, technology and terrorism,yes,exactly. For the first time in all my years in Austria I am excited about India.

Yes,exactly. My slogan is

The past is dead

The future too far away

Long live the Present.

Well, let me explain my role to you with a story.

Once upon a time just outside an Indian village there lived a terrible monster. Every day the villagers would find one of them killed by this monster. And a few buffalo, sheep, a horse etc. The monster would eat only a small portion of what he killed. Well the villagers were very tired of this terrible killing. But they were afraid, very afraid of the monster and didn't know how to fight him. So they gathered one day in the village square and after much debate and discussion and argument came up with an idea. That once a month, one of the men from the village would take a cart full of food personally to the monster. This would mean that the village would lose only one man every month.

So, you had on the one hand a hungry crazy monster living on the edges of a village, and on the other you had the village people, with their fears and families and their lives to protect.

And in between them you had a facilitator. A man who could go and talk to the monster, who could face both the terror of the monster and his own fears, who could go and negotiate, who could present the villager's case and try and get them the best deal.

And this is what he got. The monster wanted a man and a cart full of food everyday, the villagers every month. So the facilitator helped settle the deal to a week.

And that is how the story has played out through history.

And the man who helped settle the deal was my ancestor, and so I continue to play my traditional role in the modern world. All I ask is, if you have a monster at the edge of your city it's time for you to call 'The Facilitator.'

ArcelorMittal!!!Mittal the Monster hahaha you said it not I. I don't want my neck guillotined as they say in your country. Sure Henri I will research it more for you. At the moment all I know is that the majority shareholders of the Voest Alpine Co are

Austria 43 %

Employees 10.7%

Yes. That's right. The Austrian Takeover Commission.

Yes and an important detail, they very proudly feed the workers 1500 pigs a year at the Voest Alpine plant in Linz. So if Mittal took over and made all meals in the workplace vegetarian then at least someone would be happy, the Linzer pigs would celebrate hahaha he'd become a ShweineGott ha ha The Pigs God!!!haha.

Yes, Mittal spent seventy million euro for his daughter's wedding....haha...same as the entire European Culture Capital budget for one city...hahaha....

My mind is a flea market Henri, every idea is up for sale, haha. You know my charges.

Pleasure Henri, see you in Paris on the 6th au revoir.

To the audience

That was my friend Henri from Paris. Inquiries about VoestAlpine shareholder and ownership. Who knows what's up? VoestAlpine ownership.10.7% workers and 43 % the state of Austria. That gives the people of this city a majority.

But you know, it is terrible but true. You don't know who at what time needs money more than his or her own pride.

Like the Vienna Woods are to Vienna the VoestAlpine Steel Mill is to Linz a natural heritage. I feel very strongly we need to protect it at all cost. If there are any VoestAlpine workers here, please, I beg you to stay together. Your 10.7 share is critical....

Another phone rings

I have a phone for every country/language I need to speak in

Ah Peter. My British customer.

Speaks in a very British Accent.

Hello Peter

Very good to hear back from you.

Yes exactly, India is happening. As my slogan goes, the past is dead, the future far away, long live the present.

Yes I am getting very good feedback for my website. So I am glad you have some information on my work already, well let me explain what I have to offer you with a story, not a story exactly but a fact of nature.

You know every winter a snake needs to shed its skin, to transform itself, revitalise, have a new being, image. Well you know how it goes about doing it, it rubs its forehead against a stone, breaking its skin, and then it slides out of its old skin from this rupture.

The stone facilitates this violent, delicate act of skin tearing.

In India, we worship this stone as a god, a god of facilitation. When something very difficult needs change, transformation we pray to this God.

That is what I offer. The facilitators sacred stone. If you need change to happen just call my number.

Haha... Vijay Mallaya. Yes of course I know him, he is the beer man, Kingfisher beer. Yes he is a very interesting man,very interesting. And interesting too that he has such a drive to acquire excellent English things. And an English football club that is brilliant. English Scotch whiskey, that is even better.

What next? Very good question.

Well, Tata acquired Corus Steel of course. A seventy year old bachelor with two dogs and a hunger to rule the world. Yes, I hear the Jaguar too is in the bag, brilliant.

And Tata and Mittal may be getting together to acquire even more, perhaps the entire steel industry, hahaha, that will be amazing. That's a good one, the new Indian war epic the Tatabharaata...excellent!

It's really a global hunt now, the Indians are coming, hahaha. And 2009, the year of the Culture Capital in Linz is turning out to be the year of the Hindu Vegetarian Vulture Capitalists, hahaha excellent. The Vegetarian Vultures. Hahaha.

Yes, I'll get back to you. Thanks, thanks for calling.

Addressing the audience

You know I could live anywhere in the world today but there is a very simple reason I want to continue living and doing business in Austria. You know why? Because it is only here in Austria that I can still smoke a cigarette in public without being made to feel guilty or paying a fine or even getting arrested. It was bad enough to have this terrible culture in America but now in India too they have banned smoking in public. I mean that is ridiculous. In India you can piss in public, you can crap openly on railway tracks, I mean you can even die on the street and no one bothers your corpse. But smoking a cigarette, that is a crime, is prohibited. It is terrible but here in Austria, thankfully it's still, Civilised.

During this speech, on the video screen we see a young Austrian woman walking the streets, she then turns into a restaurant. We see her sitting down and being served by an Indian waiter. This is Kuldip. The screen freezes with the young woman sitting at the table. The Uncle addresses the screen.

Ok great, I have to interview this lady for a job. Just see how I screw this asshole. Herr Ober, Herr Ober…

Kuldip comes on the screen.

(in Punjabi) you don't look Austrian where are you from?

Kuldip: Ah (*lying*)…er…Pakistan sir.

Uncle: Aha Pakistan I see, and what is the Capital of Pakistan?

Kuldip: er… Lahore…sir.

Uncle: Wrong Herr Ober, it is Islamabad. Where these shoes come from. Do you like them?

Kuldip looks shocked as he seems to recognize the shoes

Uncle: And where do you think I come from?

Kuldip: From India sir…

Uncle: Wrong again. I am Austrian hahaha. You look worried and confused and so you should be! Please make sure you bring my beer cold and coffee warm, not the other way around.

Speaking to the audience

My strategy worked. He recognized the shoes but not me. I know this bastard very well! He's lying, he's not from Pakistan, he is from India. Why do these people lie? I hate liars.

Addresses the young woman for the first time. Seems she has come to him looking for a job.

So let's see your CV.
Your name is….Christina Meyer right?
And you are wanting work in India. Very good. My organisation will set everything up for you.

As if addressing a group and making a presentation on India.

I like to prepare people for their journey to India with a power point presentation I have made specially for this purpose. India may be the great global business destination, but I don't want anyone to have a false idea. There are many ways to do this I am sure but one way to show the reality of

India, specially to warn a lady about its dangers, is through the lives of its street dogs.

We see on the screen a series of photographs of India street dogs. We see starved, miserable, diseased, frightened dogs on the one end of the spectrum and angry, snarling, wolfish and wild dogs on the other.

The presentation leaves Christina looking wary and worried. She does not say a word during the interview. Uncle does all the talking.

Lights fade.

Lights come up on Priya, wearing her red veil, walking out of the curtained door. She speaks in German.

Priya: After our arrival in Linz, Kuldip refused to let me step out of the house. He was afraid I would walk straight into the ocean. He had been told 'Australia' was surrounded by water on all sides.

It took me weeks to make him understand we were not in Australia.

It was a month before I got to see the town.

I insisted, threw a fit, raged, and finally he agreed to show me the town for a day, ordinarily, like any other tourist. He had only one condition. That I would have to keep my face covered.

I agreed but was so angry about it that I swore before the God of Oaths that sits guarding the gates of my heart that not only would the Austrian men never see my face but that my husband too would never see my face, ever again. In fact I would keep my face covered. Always. In the street outside. And at home too. At all times.

I thought he would feel remorse, wanting to see the face that he had said was like the beautiful moon above the Taj Mahal!

However I was wrong.

It only bothered him for a day, my faceless being, but then I think he grew to like it. At night when he made love to me he could fantasise more easily that I was one of the naked white women whose photos he had put up all over our bedroom walls.

On the video screen we see a wall full of photographs of naked white women.

I know it is every Indian man's greatest desire to conquer a white woman. It's there in their psyche. As revenge. For being slaves of white British men for two hundred years.

I understood Kuldip and this made me forgive most of his weaknesses. Until of course that one morning when he finally did what he had been threatening to do, lock me in. That morning I knew I had a long day to spend before he finally came back late at night.

It was very tough to be locked inside a toilet for an entire day.

Switching the light on and off every five minutes, and pulling the flush every half hour to remind myself of where I was. It was hard but as in India where ordinary life itself is hard for millions of people, Bollywood movies become the only source of escape...of fantasy. I too watched movie after movie in my mind, all day long, projecting the scenes onto the veil in front of my eyes. The scenes I like most were those in *Kabhi Alvida Na Kahna*

I loved imagining dancing with Amitabh Bachchan and fighting with Shah Rukh Khan

On the scene we see Priya with her face covered by a veil projected onto which is a scene from Kabhi Alvida Na Kahna with Sharukh Khan and Amitabh Bachchan dancing and singing in typical Bollywood style. The joy and fun of the movie's dance sequence contrasts with the sad situation Priya finds herself in, locked for a day in a toilet.

At this point the play, the performance and storytelling stops and the playwright walks on stage. In a very direct, matter of fact way, he addresses the audience.

The Playwright: Hi, thanks for coming to watch my play. I have been around a number of places on this earth but one place that interests me, with reference to understanding the lives and issues of migrants like Kuldip and Priya, is Australia, not only because someone like Kuldip confuses it with Austria, which a lot of people do, but because it is one of the seven continents and consequently is a very large physical part of the earth. Of course I know there is a vast desert there but then why should all the desert people in India and Afrika not go there instead of being displaced from their traditional lives into big city slums. However, in the context of my speaking with you here in Austria, there is a more significant difference: Austrians belong to Austria, you are native to this land, while all the twenty million people in Australia are migrants, and so it follows that they should welcome a lot more of the earth's population. In the context of human migration I speak of Australia instead of directly addressing the Austrian context, to give you some space to reflect.

On the first evening in Australia I had an interesting experience. I was watching TV and the first channel I tuned into had a very interesting discussion between a group of white Australian professionals and intellectuals, college professors, lawyers etc. It was about the invasion of privacy by technology. Video cameras watching you everywhere, at airports, railways stations, inside shops. And with the public use of mobile phones, no conversation being private anymore, being forced to listen in to other people's intimate lives, a constant threat to one's intimate and most private self. It was a very esoteric conversation

And then I switched channels and quite serendipitously the very next channel was a news story about fifty two illegal immigrants held in a well guarded detention centre. These immigrants had escaped and had got back into 'Australia' by belly crawling through the sewers of the detention centre.

Imagine fifty two men and women on their hands and knees…crawling….through….its gutters.

The Police were out searching for them. The TV was broadcasting a nation wide alert. They were Iranian immigrants but could have been from anywhere else, Phillipino, Indian, Mexican, Somalian.

Through sewers, hanging onto aeroplanes, locked in boxes and sometimes dying in the back of small trucks.

The stories of migrants are similar from all around the earth.

As this one is… a news article …about the Alps

On the video screen we see the scene of an Austrian news studio. The evening news slot has been announced. A presenter announces the news in German. The story is about a group of illegal immigrants frozen to death in the back of a truck as they were trying to cross over the Alps into Europe. Seven of them were sikh migrants from the northern Indian state of Punjab. All of them were under seventeen years old.

T.V presenter: *Sieben von ihnen waren unter 17 Jahre alt-Vom nördlichen indischen bundesstaat Punjab*

The Playwright: Each time I think of the line *Sieben von ihnen waren unter seventeen jahre alt*, I think of seven young Punjabi Sikh boys all less than seventeen years old.

We see on the back wall, next to the wall of the stuffed dead birds, a curtain. The Playwright moves to open the curtain. Behind the curtain, on the wall, are seven hand painted portraits of young sikh men from Punjab. The Playwright identifies each.

Surindar Prakash from Bhatinda

Rajindar Pal from Patiala

Gurdas Singh from Jalandhar

Malkiat Singh Saini from Ambala

Jagjit from Phagwara

Jogindar Singh from Chandigarh

Ajit Pal Singh from Amritsar

All the portraits are painted with the young men wearing red turbans and blue or yellow bright kurtas matching the colours of the garden dwarfs. They look like the seven garden dwarfs.

For me they remind me of the seven little miners of the German fairy tale Snow White and the Seven Dwarfs. The dwarfs too went out to work in inhumane working conditions.

I keep imagining Snow White's Seven Dwarfs packed into a truck full of illegal immigrants. Rocking, rolling along in a claustrophobic crush of illegal humanity till the air-conditioning vents get clogged shut, till the air gets suffocating, as it does so often.

And the seven dwarfs die as so many immigrants do, suffocated in the back of a small truck, somewhere, crossing the Alps, the snowy white Alps.

Buried in the snow.

The death of seven dwarfs, like the death of a god, like the death of fantasy itself is a terribly sad thing.

I would like everyone to observe a minute's silence for all those that have died and suffered terribly crossing borders in search of a better life.

The Playwright stands quiet on stage.
The minute ends.
The Playwright exits
A chair and table is brought out on stage.
A decanter of whiskey and glass is placed on the table.
The Uncle enters.
He pours himself a whiskey.

Uncle:(*looking across at the wall of dead birds*) A wall full of stuffed dead birds

In my childhood home there was a wall full of stuffed dead birds. It's an interesting story I'd like to tell you.

One of my ancestors had been a soldier in the British Indian army during British rule in India, a loyal and brave soldier, trained to do his duty and obey orders. He had been there on that terrible day of the Jallianwala massacre in Punjab, on duty, an innocent young man of eighteen years old when he had been ordered to fire his rifle by a British

Officer, fire at innocent Indians gathering to raise their voice for freedom. He had only observed orders as he had been trained to, killing three hundred and ninety five of his own Indian brothers and sisters.

He had been court-martialed for his crime.

He had fired his rifle with one eye shut. For the rest of his life he went blind in that eye and with the other, he cried tears of terrible pain.

You know, when cannibals experience terrible grief, like the death of a brother, they cannibalise, go out on a human hunt, to find catharsis for their pain.

My ancestor did this by hunting birds for the rest of his life, eating them and then stuffing them and keeping them on a wall. Making for himself a grotesque altar of grief. Exactly as I have done in my home…here in Linz.

This is what I brought my niece for, to show her, to share my life, not its surface success, not the Mercedes car that I own but the stories underneath, the hidden stories of my first nine years, when I couldn't return to my home land, to the people, to the home I had loved and left

Each bird has a story to tell.

Like this bird, the first one I bought from a flea market, the day my younger brother died in India.

My younger brother you see was mentally disturbed… *pagal*…we call him in my village and only I could feed him. He would eat only from my hands.

When I left the village there was none to care for him, he starved to death.

The day he died I got a phone call, I cried all day, and then something took me to the flea market, where I saw this bird, and I brought it home and put it on this wall, and prayed, and strangely felt at peace.

Who knows, maybe it was my grandfather's spirit that made me buy a stuffed dead bird each time I felt deeply sad.

There are so many stories here that I can't really share with anyone, except I hope one day with Priya, for she of all others, is my own blood, from my own homeland.

One day I hope she will be happy enough to take on the grief, the sorrow, the pain and loss, not just of her uncle, or of her great grandfather, but even I hope, of all her ancestors.

I must go now to her home to liberate her. I pray to Ecdysis...the god of transformation...may the change be for the better

The uncle stands praying in front of the altar of grief-the wall full of stuffed birds.

Lights fade

On the video screen we see the uncle dressed in a traditional Punjabi attire, with a turban, walking through the streets of Linz. We see him enter an apartment block. He has a key to Priya's apartment. He opens her front door and enters her room.

The video freezes showing Priya's toilet door.

Lights on stage. The uncle stands addressing the toilet door.

He speaks in Punjabi.

Uncle: My dear Niece,

You can't imagine how sad I feel coming to your house for the first time and finding you locked inside the toilet. It just breaks my heart to see you like this.

I had thought I would come one day with my beard grown to look like your proud Indian ancestors but this fool that you have brought with you has changed all plans and timetables. I come to you today unfortunately dressed like a Punjabi but looking more like your Austrian uncle.

Forgive my saying so but what kind of idiot is this husband of yours.

Here is what he has been up to over the past year.

He works in a restaurant against my orders. An Indian restaurant. How dumb can that be? I was bound to visit it. Or did he do it because he was sure I would visit it. To challenge me.

So I ask my employees to be creative. To work a little harder and come up with creative ideas to sell, to make profit. And what does that fool of a husband do? He sells his newspapers at a red light like an Indian hawker selling his wares. But he is wearing a Burqa. He says he thought people could be frightened into buying newspapers. What a fantastic idea, only this is not India he could be arrested for creating a public nuisance, deported back to India, and I, his employer, blacklisted forever, and my dreams of a business empire, drowned in the Danube.

He is a man lost in his own world, lost in his own fantasies.

Even after a year he still thinks the Church in Postlingberg is a Castle where a King lives. He greets him by bowing low to him every morning. Doesn't he know that Austria is a Republic, where aristocrats are not even allowed to keep their titles.

You know that beggar who stands in the niche of Karmelitenkirche next to Harrachstraße. The man has stood there silently for about fifteen years now. He does not even speak to beg. Well Kuldip walks up to him one day, starts arguing with him telling him to go home, start a family, work instead of begging. I mean the man who has not spoken to anyone for fifteen years starts yelling at Kuldip to leave him alone and Kuldip yells back. They fight till the police car pulls up. I mean it was sheer luck that Thomas was able to pull Kuldip away in time or the game was up.

He may not know how to do many things but he sure knows how to fight. I sent him along to Mauthausen as a tourist guide with one of Mr.Mittal's men. Just an ordinary day of sightseeing. But no, he starts fighting there too, over the audio guides, starts screaming at the officer "Why is the audio guide for the Electric crematorium missing? Why is the audio guide for the gas chamber not there, and most importantly, why is there no audio for the staircase of death?" He starts screaming he wants his money back. I mean what money. Those audio guides are for free. Can this man never keep his mouth shut?

I had hoped in bringing him here I would have an honest, hardworking, loyal, capable and committed employee but instead I find him crazy, unstable and dangerous.

So this is about your husband and now look at you. You keep your face covered from your own husband in your own home. Which country in the world is that a tradition of?

And now, sitting on a pot pulling the flush every half hour to hold onto your sanity, to hold onto the fact, the reality that you are locked in a toilet, by your own husband!

Dear niece, I see my dear sister's, your dead mother's face in front of me when she was a little girl of five and my mother gave me an extra piece of bread because boys need to grow up strong and take care of girls. And she cried and said she wanted to be strong too. I can see her crying then and looking at you now I can see she is still crying.

The day she died I felt so terrible, helpless. I had been able to do nothing for her. And I was her elder brother. I should have been there to protect her…yes…even from death itself.

I could go on about how sad and terrible I feel about all of this but here is the deal. I will not under any condition go against any agreement that I have made. At heart I am an Indian and never help break a marriage, this is very hard for me and I will not ask you to walk out of your home and start a life for yourself to live and work on your own. But when you find me gone from here you will see the toilet door unlocked and you will see the apartment door left open. It is your choice, if you want to stay here and flush your life away…or…step out and begin a new life for yourself leaving your idiot husband in my hands, and to his own fate.

The choice, unfortunately my dear, from now on, is entirely your own.

Silence. Uncle exits.

Lights fade

On the screen we see Kuldip walking back from work. It's late in the evening. From his walk we can see he is drunk. He continues to drink from a bottle.

Lights on stage

Kuldip enters singing the Austrian national anthem. He is messing the anthem up with his Punjabi accent changing "land" to "lund." "Lund" is prick in Punjabi.

Lund der Berge, Lund am Strome,
Lund der Äcker, Lund der Dome,
Lund der Hämmer, zukunftreich:
Heimat bist du großer Söhne,
vielgeprüftes Österreich.

He is drunk and in a happy mood. He is carrying a red leather ladies hand bag. It's a present for Priya.

In India there is real freedom, wherever you want you can stand and piss, at least the poison doesn't stay in the system, here all the time on the street you have to hold it in, the poison. Sometimes I fear I will die of internal poisoning.

Sings

Saare jahan se ganda Hindustan hamara
Hum bulbuley hain iske yeh gulistan hamara....

Translates for audience in English

In all the world our dear India is dirtiest
And still we are happy birds singing in our happy garden
National song
Sorry, please. I, not offended, not disrespectful, very sorry, please forgive me.
Please forgive me, Priya dear. I am very ashamed, I can't meet you eye to eye, please forgive me.
Whatever punishment you want to give I am happy. If you say I will cut off this hand I will die here. But I love you very much, you are my sweetheart.
See I got this for you from a shop in Strandesrasse.

Shows her a red, leather bag

You have been wanting this for a long time. See I got this for you. Today was a great day for me, I sold one hundred papers. Thomas was very happy. He gave me fifty Europes for this month. He said this is for the morning. I told him no no they are my children, for children we don't take money. What will Fifi think if she knows I get paid to take her for a walk in the morning. But then I thought if Thomas wants to give then he should also not feel hurt. So I took the money and for 2 euro I bought myself the magazine that gives me extra strength, as you well know it. And for 34 Europe I bought this bag bag. And with the rest of the money I bought sausages.

You remember Priya in India when I passed the computer exam how happy you were. How many dreams did we had seen together about coming to Europe? Now they are being completed. See this bag for 2000 rupees for you.

I feel very bad, Priya please forgive me.

Promise, I change from today, from today I will become German. Talking like you tell me.

I will eat all things Uncle says, all wurst, all sausages, big one, small one, Frankfurt one, bloody one, all kinds. Apple noodles also.

I love Australia, promise.

He draws open the curtain of his pornographic wall.
He sees photos of nude white women.
*He prays to them...*Victory be to you Goddesses, give me strength!
He starts taking his clothes off

I will make love to you all night for what you have suffered all day. This is my promise.

You will have thousand happy birds singing in your happy garden. This is my dream.

He sees the flowers left behind by Uncle

See, I got flowers also, 6 Europes.
All day I think only of you.
Please, please forgive me.
Priya…Priya…open the door Priya….I love u
Priya…….Ich liebe dich

As he takes off his underwear he steps through the curtained door.
We hear a flush being pulled.
On the video screen we see a sign 'Departure' followed by a scene of
the Linz Airport Departure Terminal. Two immigration officers hold
Kuldip by the arms and lead him into the airport. He is being deported.
Before the airport door Kuldip turns around and addresses the camera.

Kuldip: I am going back to India, on a free ticket!

The scene on the video screen changes to Priya, now wearing a western
dress, taking the seven garden dwarfs for an evening ride, on a cart.
Music from local Bulgarian street musicians plays in the background.
Uncle enters while talking on the phone. He speaks with an Italian
accent.
The video of Priya and the dwarfs plays on, silently.

Uncle: Hello Tony
How goes it in Verona?
Yes, thank you very much. She is finally settled. Yes,
much problem but now she is working for a crazy Austrian…
ha-ha,yes, he lives on top of a mountain in a Castle and he
has no family. He lives with seven garden dwarves as his
children. Yes, my niece is their nanny and my niece has to

take them out for a walk everyday through town. Yes after lunch and after dinner walk, ha-ha, crazy. But she is happy. She is making almost the same money as I am ha-ha walking dwarves. It's a crazy world, people here have so much money to spend.

Yes, I was thinking about our talk.

Ok, you get it, Tony you are too slow and the world is moving too fast...tourism,technology,terrorism so many business opportunities in India ...remember my words Tony...you need a facilitator....

Tony thinks he has a great idea selling Pizzas in India. Pizza hut and Dominos got there fifteen years ago. These Italians, they don't know what is happening in the world, are they sleeping...Mama Mia.

On the video screen we see Priya and the garden dwarfs now sitting beside the Danube river.

The sun is setting.

Music fades.

THE END

'I AM NO FEEBLE RICE EATER

Cast

Director: Middle aged Austrian man

Writer: A young German man

Actress: A young German woman

Ramachandra: A fifty year old Malayali male actor

TV Presenter: Played by the same actor as the director

Mr. Kapoor: Played by same actor who plays the writer

Mrs. Kapoor: Played by the same actor who plays the actress

Monkey Men: 7 young Indian men

The Leader: Middle aged Indian man

Lights fade in the theatre

Voice over (*in the Director's voice*): A theatre director of an Austrian theatre is creating *The New Taj Mahal*. A multi styled performance *The New Taj Mahal* uses contemporary as well as traditional texts like the Ramayana and Goethe's Faustus.

During the course of this production the Director falls in love with the German actress/singer who plays Gretchen and who works in his theatre, but she rejects his love. Condemned by her for loving the money his theatre earns more than the Art it creates, and hurt by this rejection the Director plots revenge. He plans to persuade the actor playing the demon King Ravanna to cross boundaries of fiction and make 'real' the abduction of Sita. The Director works to manipulate the innocence of the actor whose own ambition to perform a role never performed before, to cross boundaries never crossed leads him to play his Faustian part in the plot. The actress, too seduced by her attraction to the sacred dancer and in love with his pure innocence, allows herself to be taken to the edge and beyond.

This play about two separate worlds, about multiple points of inter-cultural perception, combined with the fact that the Theater Director is a Jew and the woman who he loves and is rejected by is German makes this 21st century story of rejection and revenge a specially relevant political story told under the shadow of many dark histories.

Lights on stage
Prelude (inspired by the opening scene of Goethe's Faust)
Enter Director, Writer, Actress.
All speak English with a German accent

Director
Say dear ones in these times of financial backbreaking
Say what you think of our new undertaking
The New Taj Mahal an original piece I've had commissioned
How will it meet with, then, our audiences in Europe and India?

I know how to make the people happy
But I've never been so unsure: you see,
They've all here read such a lot
How can we make it all seem fresh and new,
Weighty, but entertaining too?
We have to mix and match the old and new
A bit if this a bit of that and something else too
I know it hurts for a purist like you it's insane
To mix Goethe's Faust with the Ramayana is profane
To chop these texts and slice the characters is inane
But the world has not heard of him, known, or seen him
What goes well in Germany may not in Timbuktu
And wherever we go around the world
I'd love to see a joyful crowd, that's certain,
When the waves drive them to our place,
Pushing, till they've reached the window,
As if they're at the baker's, starving, nearly
Breaking their necks: just for a ticket. Oh!
Only I know how much I need to get those tickets sold
To pay the bills, the actors, dramaturgs
Lights men and the technicians too
To run a theatre is no joke
With no audiences you are surely broke

Actress
O, don't speak to me of people filling theatres
The sight of who makes my inspiration fade.
Hide from me the surging numbers,
Whose noise will drive my art away.
I would be as happy to play with no one there
Only a heavenly silence listening to me

Where my art for its own sake thrives
Where beauty and joy grace our lives
Not bums on seats and the sale of tickets
Crowds come to be entertained now
And very soon forget what they saw before
What dazzles is a momentary act
What's true is left for posterity, intact.

Writer
Don't speak about posterity to me!
If I went on about posterity,
Where would you get your worldly fun?
Folks want it, and they'll still have some.
The presence of a mix of things
Is nice, I think, for everyone.
Be brave, and show them what you've got,
The contemporary with the classical, thrown in together
The oriental and occidental all burning boiling in one pot

Director
Yes we must make sure,
Above all, plenty's happening there!
They come to look, and then they want to stare.
Spin endlessly before their faces,
So the people gape amazed,
You've won them by your many paces,
You'll be the man most praised.
The mass are only moved by things *en masse*,
Each one, himself, will choose the bit he needs:
Who brings a lot, brings something that will pass:
And everyone goes home contentedly.

Actress

You don't see how badly such work will do!
How little it suits the genuine creator!
Already, I see, it's a principle with you
The finest master is a sloppy worker
Your scenes have no continuity of character feeling or of
sense
Each is there to please a part of your audience
A scene you have where I play
This Indian woman hanging from the roof
All covered in ash while her husband cleans the floor
All on a TV program titled A Moment of a family's Truth
Worldwide
Seeing families and their secrets worldwide
So Germans in their own tongue can hear and know
What's happening around the world that's going to and fro.
In another scene you want me to be poor Gretchen
Betrayed by her lover Faustus tricked by the devil
Slowly carrying her illegitimate love child
To the top of a bridge below which the blue waters run
And from there from that great height throw
Down into the river this new born baby boy must go
Before he has even grown to be a glorious German man
And then you have me play a sacred Queen
Sita wife of Rama the Hindu God
Even as she is abducted by Ravanna the demon King
How are these scenes connected to each other?
A story weaved not into one but broken into many
Will not work as Art nor earn you even a penny
I know this world is fast and furious
And things are changing even as we speak

Our lives have a new shape and size
And no one cares who lives who dies
And it is for this the chaos of our times
That I say Art must hold its centre
Do Goethe in purity exactly and in fullness too
Not a bit of this, that and a scene of swine flu too

Director
Such a reproach leaves me unmoved
The man who seeks to be approved
Must stick to the best tools for it
Think, is not soft wood the best to split
And have a look for whom you play
See, this one boredom brings here
Another's come from some overloaded work-table,
Or, worst of all, he arrives,
Like most, fresh from an afternoon nap
They rush here mindlessly, as to a market fair,
And curiosity inspires their hurry
The ladies bring themselves, and in their best,
Come here to play their part even before the start.
What dream of yours is this, to play?
This pure exalted German verse
To a house empty except for that sour critic
Who must write a review and sourly too
Doesn't a full house make you happy?
Have a good look at your patrons first!
After the show *he* hopes for card-play:
He hopes for a wild night, and a woman's kiss.
I tell you, just give them more and more,
So they leave well fed, happy, contented and in bliss

Writer
I must say for once I must agree
And not only because he pays my writer's fee
When two worlds meet there is a double game
A little from that world and a little from this
In that I agree there is no shame
Like mirror images shadowing each other
Things must multiply not simplify
Sita with Gretchen hand in hand must go
As Ravanna the demon King and Mephistopheles
Both in one boat on one river row
I am all for weaving a tale not of one but many
And of course in these times of global recession
I could do with more than just a penny

Actress
I must be frank with you
I am disappointed in your Art and you
I thought I could love your work and maybe you
I thought I dreamt and I had feelings too
But now I realise and see clearly too
Money is your power and so you must have more of it
And so you manipulate and work your way to get it
I need the work I need the money too
But my Art my soul my being is mine
I am contracted to this work it's all written there
I am a professional and will do my job and listen
To what you have to say and the writer make me do
But let me make myself heard loud and clear
To treat Goethe's Faust the way you do
Makes me conclude you are the devil too

You are that I repeat it too, The Devil
You have my work but not my Art
You have my body but not my heart
This money obsession I am afraid it is not new
You are after all an Austrian Jew

Leaves stage

Director
That's enough words for the moment

Speaks to the writer and technicians, stagehands etc

Now let me see some action!
Make sure that you let nothing go,
Don't fail to show me, I'm your man,
Your trap-doors and your scenery.
Use heavenly lights, the big and small,
Squander stars in any number,
Rocky cliffs, and fire, and water,
Birds and creatures use them all.
So in our narrow playhouse waken
The whole wide circle of creation,
And stride, deliberately, as well,
From Heaven, through the world, to Hell

Writer exits stage
Activity of stage hands, lights changing curtain etc
Director is alone on stage

Director: And so now I have no choice

And now I must take revenge it's true
For she has rejected my love saying
I am an Austrian Jew
After all that's past in World War 2
For such prejudice to exists even now
How dare she, how dare she that German Cow?
There is a wound here so deep and wide
That opens right here, between me and my pride
For while I have great powers to make magic on this stage
Yet, in real life, I am powerless to make another love me
For I am cursed to live unloved unliked disliked detested
Called The Manager, Mephistopheles or very simply
As she I loved called me The Devil.
You are that, the devil.
And so you know
Of why I feel as I feel and why I hate
As I do hate her now the one I loved before
For I had loved her and wanted her
As any good man would to make her his noble wife
To be the queen of this theatre in which she acts and sings
But she had said that she could not love a man
Who counts silver coins even as she sang
How else do you run such a grand and beautiful theatre!
Who placed profit before Art, money before beauty
A man who counted every penny earned in the theatre he ran
And gave one singer less another actor more and a third
well almost none
And so while she did love every note in the song she sung
She could never love such a man as I, nor ever marry me.
And this rejection is why I hate and hurt for I have
feelings too.

And so I must revenge

And so I plan now to make her travel far to a dark land

To find a dark man costumed in sacred robes

A savage man who dances a sacred temple dance

Unaware of the silver coin, of money unconcerned, a pure artist

And I will ask this man this dancer actor

To tell a story I once saw on my travels

Through the many worlds I do

The story of a woman's abduction and worse

The sacred Story of Sita and Ravanna

And I will cast both this godlike being, this spirit actor

And this beautiful woman I love who rejects me now

As abductor and abducted

And then I will let my spirit free, my real feelings take charge

And I will plot and plan and influence this innocent man

To let him truly become the evil he performs

Become what he pretends to be, be the abductor and more

And in his innocence ignorance powerlessness be controlled manipulated by me

And this shall be my revenge

And this shall heal the wound that hurts my heart

For I had loved her as any good man does

And wanted to make her my wife as any good man would.

And yet I failed despite my powers to make her love me

For while I have great power to make magic happen on the stage

In real life I do not have the power to make another person love me.

For I am condemned to be cursed detested disliked unloved

Called The Manager Mephistopholes, The Baron or very simply
As she I loved called me The Devil.
You are that The Devil

He walks off stage
Lights do down
The stage hands now raise as a backdrop a very Indian rural scene
painted on canvas, a theatre space in South India, a Kaleri, where Rama
the great actor has just finished a rehearsal of a traditional performance.
His powerful athletic body is sweaty with effort and energy spent. He is
a very handsome, beautiful man.
The scene is played in front of the backdrop.
Lights come on Rama, the sacred dancer

Rama: They say at the age of fifty years a sacred dancer
Is at the height of his powers
All secrets of his ancient art lie here
At the the centre of the forehead
And the 3rd eye opens to reveal worlds beyond the present one
To see beyond this veil of illusion, of Maya, the material world
Beyond the real world, to the world of spirit, of being, the true world
I am fifty years old now
I have played all great roles to be played
Felt all nine emotions burn my being with a passion unknown to the ordinary
I have been both god and man and beast and monster
Lover and tyrant half beast half human half man half woman

A bird, a fish, a mountain, a stream, and even the cool breeze on a hot summer day
I have not just played at but become all these things
I have been baby Krishna even as he sucks
At the poisoned breast of the monstress Putana
Breasts poisoned to kill a baby god
Instead the god sucks the very life out of the Monstress
I have been the Monstress too, feeling not just my poisoned milk but even my blood, my being sucked out
I have been the great Bhima transformed to a lion tearing at the chest of a Dushasanna
Quenching his thirst at the hot gushing fountain of blood rushing out
My mouth has tasted human blood even as I have kissed my Draupadi with the same lips
Felt sweet blood rush to lips locked in an embrace of true *shringar,*
I have become the dancing peacock thrilled by a spring awakening
I have been both the forest as well as Nakratundi
The black untouchable woman who lives in the forest
Dancing her lonely dance of solitude even as nearby Hanuman the monkey god
Meditates detached from her, from the forest, from the world, and from all Maya
I have been the monkey god as well as Narasimha half lion half human
I have taken all forms the god Vishnu has appeared on this earth in
I have been the fish, the tortoise, the wild boar and the dwarf
I have been as truthful as Lord Rama, as conscious as

Lord Krishna

And enlightened as Lord Buddha

I have felt all beings, all feelings as real as a child feels a toy in his hand

And of course there has been a price I have had to pay

To gain the highest glories of a sacred dancer

To remain pure untouched unsullied and uncorrupted by Maya

I have been a Brahmacharya, staying ignorant of a woman's touch

Of her hair, her lips, her thighs and that sweet heaven between her legs

This is what I have offered into the great fire of my sacred Art

My lonely being, nights spent tossing and turning in bed

For years and years and years till now I am a golden fifty

The gifts, the glory in return, too have been as great

I have been honoured by the Temple High priest

Awarded scholarships, grants, a home, land, all material comfort

I have all a dancer actor could hope or dream for

What more could I ask for without being ungrateful to the lord for what he has given me?

Of course I desire to have a true vision of my lord a true darshan

It is true I have only played and like a child believed what has been shown

I want to look beyond this veil of illusion, this Maya,this game, this play

I want to feel the real, become the real, open my heart out to become even for a moment

Truly become a Shiva absorbed in meditation, a Nala in love, or even a Keechaka in an act of lust.

I do not want to play at Ravanna any more, offering his ten heads to the sacrificial fire, cutting one head off at a time.

I have one head, I am willing to behead it, to not play at but cut it off and offer it to the sacred fire for real, to feel, to go beyond, to experience the real.

Exits stage
Lights go down
A new backdrop replaces the Indian rural scene. It's the Director's library/office.
Lights come on the Director. He has a Ramayana in his hand.

The Director

As a spider weaves its web with its spit
I with my words a net so fine
To be invisible to the ordinary eye
To catch a singer with a song as sweet as a lover's serenade
The song of Sita the pure innocent beautiful wife of the Lord Rama
A baby found innocently cradled by the earth
Now grown into the wife of a God
A King, the Glory of the Hindu race
The glory of the Aryans lord Rama
Ah! Why does the word Aryan burn my being?
Is no place on this earth untouched?
Uncorrupted pure free from the source of my pain
I must stay calm through this, control my passion, my heart
Learn to keep the sweet face of a lover desperate for love
Even as I draw this woman into the web that I weave

Even as I hold her rejection at the very heart of my being
The Aryan Race!!!

Referring to the book in his hand

India, where the original inhabitants the Dravidians were
driven south
By the conquering Aryans who now occupy the North
The fair skinned Aryans the upper caste Brahmins, the
Kshatriyas, the warriors
And the dark skinned Dravidians driven out of the fertile
Northern plains
Into the hot south. Rama was an Aryan King
And Rama is also my sacred dancer, the hero of the plot
I plan to weave, a Dravidian
Enacting the stories of Rama, Rama playing Rama
The Ramayana, the episode I have selected is sweet and
simple
Sita, Rama's wife has been kidnapped by Ravanna the
demon King of Lanka
She sits kidnapped in a forest even as Ravanna tries to
woo her and seduce her
The wife of an Aryan King being abducted and seduced
by a Dravidian king
What an opportunity to take revenge on the Aryans
To get the Demon king to succeed in this seduction, to
change the script
To persuade Sita to be attracted to, to submit, to be
ravaged by the Dravadian
To get both the actors playing Ravanna and Sita to agree
The Indian actor and the German actress!

For this to happen for real, I must persuade the actor playing Ravanna to go beyond the illusion, beyond Maya, to make it real.

To persuade a Dravidian actor playing the role of a Dravidian King

To succeed in seducing not only the wife of an Aryan King

But even further, a white German actress playing the role of Sita

And which European woman would resist such a persuasion

To go to India to learn the part of Sita

To learn to play the pure woman

To discover what it means to be an actor in a sacred theatre

To understand the pure, the unsullied, the uncorrupted

And then to be a part of a grand corruption I plan

To learn to get seduced by a Dravidian demon King

To become a part of the plot I weave

Even this woman who has rejected my love

Will not be able to resist this offer to travel to India

To learn from a great master the role of Sita

To experience the exotic, the magic, the power of sacred India

I failed to seduce her to my bed

But I will not fail to seduce her to the bed of the demon King

For I have powers that can make magic happen on the stage

For I have powers that go beyond the four walls of any space

Now I must sit down and write a letter to this great actor
Persuade him to be a part of my story, reveal to him
enough of my plot
To make him step out of his sacred theatre
To begin to cross boundaries never crossed
To include a white German woman in his sacred theatre
To teach her to play that part of Sita and him to play
Ravanna
To make him believe in the change, the turn, the twisted end
Slowly surely to begin to take control of him, his art, his
life, etc

Starts writing a letter

Dear Ravanna, Dear Demon King…

A curtain comes down mid stage.
The following scenes are performed in front of the curtain.
Lights slowly come on to reveal the interiors of an Indian home.
It's a large multipurpose room. On one side a ladder is placed. It goes
up to the ceiling. The actress playing an Indian woman Mrs. Kapoor
walks slowly ritualistically around the stage. Her naked body is covered
entirely in Ash. She climbs the ladder as if it's her daily business. She
hangs upside down from the ceiling. On the floor a man (the writer
playing Mr. Kapoor) is sweeping, crouched low, he is cleaning the floor.
The TV is on. A German TV channel is making a program on India.
It's called A Moment of a Family's Truth Worldwide

Presenter: Welcome to *A Moment of a Family's Truth Worldwide*.
A program that helps you get to see different cultures and
how they work. The inner truths of people's lives around the

world that no tourist trip could provide. As Goethe wrote "To get to know the world is to get to know yourself better, and to stay ignorant of the world is to stay ignorant of your own humanity."

So with that spirit of adventure, today's focus is on that ancient and yet very contemporary and happening world of India. Welcome to the Kapoor family, a successful middle class Indian family.

This is Mrs. Kapoor. Vice President of Siemens and Sons, the makers of low cost test tubes used to make babies for childless couples. Mrs. Kapoor was educated in the U.S. of A but returned to her country so that she and her children could grow up with traditional family life and values.

This is Mr. Kapoor. He is a progressive Indian male. He has been laid off from work and he has consequently laid off the domestic help and is doing all the housework.

The rules of the game allow any member of the family to answer the question. Our Truth Meter here checks if the answer is true or false.

Unveils a Truth Meter. It looks like a space age contraption, a Time Machine capsule.

Another twist to the game is there are questions for you too, the audience, and depending on your answers you too could win prizes.

So let's get on with a big welcome to you, the Kapoors, the great clan of the Kapoors. By the way, are you related to the first family of Bollywood? Are you by any chance Aunt and Uncle of Kareena Kapoor the great film actress.

The man stops sweeping. Stares back at the Presenter.

Ok sorry, sorry dumb question, not every Kapoor has to be related. Ok,peace. Let's get on with the game.

First question for ten thousand rupees.

Does Mr. Kapoor know exactly what Mrs. Kapoor is doing?

There is silence. Mrs. Kapoor hanging/ swinging. Mr. Kapoor continues sweeping the floor.

You have thirty seconds left to answer the question.

Mr. Kapoor stops sweeping.

Mr. Kapoor: Could you ask the question again please?

Presenter: Does Mr. Kapoor know exactly what Mrs. Kapoor is doing?

Mr. Kapoor: Did you say exactly?

Presenter: Yes, exactly what Mrs.Kapoor is doing?

Mr. Kapoor: Well, do I know exactly what my wife is doing? The answer is no I don't.

Presenter: That's great. Thank you for the answer and now ladies and gentleman for the first moment of truth for the Kapoor family here is our Truth Meter.

Switches on the 'Truth Meter' which starts whirring with a mechanical noise

Presenter: And for you ... *(to the audience)*

While our Truth Meter checks whether Mr. Kapoor has spoken the truth or not here is our first question for you. Is Mrs. Kapoor hanging there exercising and trying to lose weight? Please tick the appropriate column. By the end of the program if all the audience questions are ticked correctly you could win a trip to India to see 'The Taj Mahal' for yourself and your family.

And now, let's get back to check what our truth metre has decided

The Truth Meter makes a final sound.

Mr. Kapoor your answer is correct. You do not in fact know *exactly* what Mrs. Kapoor is doing. In fact you have no idea at all!

Of course this question could have been answered by Mrs. Kapoor who would have known exactly what she is doing. But, she chose to keep quiet, and your answer has been found correct, so you are now a winner of ten thousand rupees.

Mr. Kapoor, what may I ask, will you do with the money you win today?

Mr. Kapoor: Well I hope to go down to the local store and buy some Swedish wall to wall carpeting and then buy a German Vacuum cleaner and make this job of mine easier.

Presenter: ha-ha, that is very good Mr. Kapoor. I say thank you on behalf of the European Union, for keeping us alive, ha-ha..Quite literally. Now for the next question.

Is Mr. Kapoor exercising and trying to lose weight?

Mr. Kapoor *(laughs)* That is an easy one. I am not sweeping the floor to lose weight, though that may be a consequence. I am actually trying to save money by doing the job done by our domestic help. I lost my job you see and so have time,while my wife is a very busy woman, she works very hard as Vice President of Siemens Corporation. We have three children. They are all studying in their air-conditioned rooms. It's terribly hot and then there are power cuts. So we have inverters and it all costs a lot. As my wife brings in all the lolly...so....

Presenter: So to summarise, your answer is that you are not trying to lose weight but trying to save money and our Truth Meter tells us your answer is correct and you have won for yourself fifty thousand rupees. Congratulations! You are on the march, as it were. Well done.

Fake studio audience applause sound.

With two more correct answers you will win ten lakh rupees with which Mr. Kapoor wants to carpet his entire apartment and buy the finest vacuum cleaner from Europe. So all the best to Mr. Kapoor as here comes the next question.

Mrs. Kapoor gives an anguished groan from above.

Presenter: Did you say something Mrs. Kapoor?

Silence

I thought I heard some sound from above. Were you trying to communicate to us Mrs. Kapoor?

Silence

I guess not. Did you understand what she just said, Mr. Kapoor?

Mr. Kapoor does not answer instead continues sweeping the floor.

Your next question for five lakh rupees is the following. If I was to say that Mrs.Kapoor is only trying to relax herself in however bizarre a way would that be a correct answer. Your time starts now.

Mr. Kapoor stops sweeping. He looks up at Mrs.Kapoor

Mr. Kapoor: I wish you'd answer for yourself. Why am I put on a spot each time, you know yourself better than I do. In fact you know me better than I do. That's why you are the boss, at work and at home. I am not sure of each answer. If I get it wrong I will lose the chance of buying that wall to wall carpet and vacuum cleaner. I will have to clean floors for the rest of my life. I will be miserable. I am a qualified man from a well to do family. I cannot spend my whole life sweeping dirty floors, please, I beg you to answer this question. It's so easy for you, and then one more answer and we will have won ten lakhs. I promise to let you decide the colour of the carpet. Whatever you want. I promise I will not ask you to speak again, you can do as you please only this time I beg you, please answer.

Silence

Presenter: Mr. Kapoor?

Mr. Kapoor looks lost, broken. He looks like the rag he is sweeping with.

Mr. Kapoor: This damn thing stinks, smells. Can I have the question again?

Presenter: Right. For five lakh rupees your question is the following. But before we go to the question, here is a commercial break.

The lights go down
The commercial break has an advertisement of a German lingerie company selling their goods. Long legged German women walking/displaying all kinds of lingerie. Very sexy, attractive and very commercial.
The ad ends.
When the lights come on Mrs.Kapoor is slowly being lowered by a stagehand to the ground
She is alone on stage.
She speaks directly to the audience.

Mrs. Kapoor: You fucking grandson of a Nazi. Who the fuck gave you the right to ask so many questions. Where did you learned this from. The SS. Don't think I am ignorant of your history. We Indians are awake now, awake and aware of everything, past, present and future. You foreigners, you are in Modern India now. Never forget that. It's we who ask the questions and you answer. This is not a fucking TV program. This is real life now, your time is up.

Suddenly softening, changing tone.

You got a light?

The Director gives her a light.
She stands smoking.

This ash is memory. It keeps me alive, human, beautiful.
It hides all my scars, keeps the spirit within, alive, burning.
What would you know, you asshole of a beautiful spirit?
What have you got for me?

The Director runs to get a suitcase full of gifts
She picks out a gstring and a bra, stilettos
Dress me
The Director looks shocked

Don't worry, my husband is putting the children to sleep.
He loves them a lot, he falls off to sleep with them.

The Director dresses her, puts on her stilettos.
She walks around enjoying herself.
She turns to him
What shall I call you?
Before he can answer she says

I don't care whatever your fucking name is I am going to
call you Hanz
I like what you give me Hanz, this feels good (*touching her*
g string). Makes me feel alive, free, makes me like my body.
Nice work Hanz.
This will sell here. Your goods will sell well in this country.
Your goods are good Hanz. Maybe I will sell them for

you. Maybe if you are nice to me I will market them for you all over India. Would you like that Hanz. Would you like me to do that for you?

Of course, in exchange I would like you to do something for me.

I would like to see your goods Hanz, I mean your real goods

I am waiting, Hanz, to see what you've got for me?

Silence

I am waiting

She is now in a tight spotlight.

I was in Germany once. And I met this man, in a hotel, a German, almost twice my age. I was thirty then. We spent a night in a hotel room. It was the first time he had been with an Indian woman. He held me, kissed me, touched me but only till my waist, below my waist he refused to go. I felt halved, I felt diseased in my lower half.

I couldn't help remembering, Ubermensch, above the waist, Untermensch, below the waist

I have stayed halved since then.

His name was Hanz. Are any of you there Hanz? Or his brother or son.

This ash is memory, it keeps me burning inside, keeps me alive, I have a beautiful spirit you see.

Would you like some of this ash Hanz. Would you like me to rub it all over your body, it will make you feel beautiful inside Hanz like a warm breath inside the flute before it becomes music. Would you like me to do that. Of course there is a condition Hanz. While I rub ash all over you, your willie should stay a willie and not rise to salute your fatherland!

Could you control that Hanz, could you control your willie from rising? Could you control yourself from breaking me again in half Hanz. If you can, then I'll rub ash all over your body. It will make you feel beautiful inside. I will work for you then Hanz, sell all the goods you bring. There are millions of women out there wanting to buy these things, wanting to walk as I did now, and feel the bodies free as I did now.

I like the way I feel when I walk in these stilettos,the way my hips sway

But you Hanz?

This ash is memory you see Hanz

I hang myself each day to forget things Hanz, the ash keeps in what's worth remembering. Would you like to learn how to hang Hanz?

Then we can go out and sell things together, we'd be such a great team.My husband? Oh don't worry about him. He cares too much about the children to worry about me and then he does want that carpet and vacuum cleaner. He does want to stop working like a poor sweeper. He'll be fine Hanz, thanks for your concern.

It's you I am worried about, it's your breath you see

It smells of....Ash

Lights fade

When they come on the German actress is alone on stage. She is naked and covered with ash.

A tub is brought.

She steps into it and begins a bath.

The Director comes in with more hot water and a towel.
He dries her body with the towel

Director: My darling Gretchen you were wonderful

You, hanging from that ceiling, and that groan at that precise moment that was perfect, brilliant. I thought the whole piece held with a crackling tension. For the next rehearsal we will give you a baby to hold, a doll, Gretchen's baby that she drowns in the river. Then I am sure you will connect deeper with the emotion. I am really happy with the way the scene is going.

And you, you my darling Gretchen, were you satisfied? Oh what a question.

You are never satisfied right? Always looking to make the scene better. That is what I love about you as an actress, your restlessness, your creativity, your courage, your desire for danger, your desire to cross boundaries never crossed before. I mean to hang there like that with ash covering you. That was your idea, that was brilliant, no safe actress would have dreamed of doing that. That's what makes this piece such a complete success, this is what is going to make our India piece such a success at that festival. It's really going to be your show. I mean you will be the star of *The New Taj Mahal*. We have a piece here of contemporary India told from our perspective, in our style of theatre making, through a game show, but I have another idea which I wanted to share with you. I mean I know you don't like me talking about it but I have decided to increase the budget, not spare any cash for this production. What I think this work needs besides this contemporary stuff is something of the tension between the old and new, the ancient and modern, the sacred and profane. I mean when I went to India I felt it truly, the sacred does exist there, the power of faith and belief. It's all there. It may be a cliche but we have to use it.

So here is the plan. We need to include a traditional sacred story, the Ramayana and give it a twist, change it to what we like, what makes sense to us. And I have the perfect story for this: the story of Sita and Ravanna. Do you know at the end of the Ramayana Sita too like Gretchen is shamed, humiliated, and is swallowed back into the earth. So that moment when you are hanging and groaning can be a moment for both, for Gretchen before she throws her baby into the earth and for Sita, before she jumps into the holy fire and the earth swallows her. We can create a real moment of intercultural tension. It will be amazing.

And I have a perfect actor to play Ravanna, the demon King who abducts Sita. A Ramannatam actor, an ancient dance form that tells the story of the Aryan King God Hero Rama. I have written to him and I want you my dear to travel to India and work with him on the part of Sita, to learn to play it traditionally. And then, here is the twist, you will then bring him here, and over the next three months we will transform him, corrupt him with our European ways. Show him the sins of the modern world and use his corruption to liberate him, free him from a false consciousness of the sacred and divine that his culture has trapped him in, and use this freedom to transform the traditional story to that which will suit our appetite, change the end to something more juicy, real, sexy, passionate, of the body, of blood.

So my darling Gretchen I want you to put on a mask, pretend, go in disguise as this beautiful obedient student out there to learn this old sacred dance, and then I want you to bring him back, make this great Artist come across the oceans to be at the mercy of my direction, of my plot, of my ways.

We together will create a work of Art never before seen in this theatre, in this city, country...in our time.

Do we have a pact my darling Gretchen? Do I take that faraway look in your eyes to mean you are already travelling. I knew you'd love to go to India my darling. I knew you'd want to cross that boundary. See I know you my dear one

My Gretchen.

My darling Gretchen, My beautiful Sita.

Wear this robe and by my magical powers

You'll be transported to a world more beautiful

Than you had ever imagined

A world of purity,art,beauty

A world untouched by what you detest

That silver coin that slippery note

I want you to experience this world

And I will wait for you here even as you transform

To the wife of an Aryan God, to Rama's wife

To Sita, oh my darling Gretchen what a role

I can already see the glory that will be yours

This Robe shall transport you know

To a place of true divinity

Exits

The Actress walks stylistically, slowly around the stage wearing the robe. It feels as if she is travelling a long distance

She then takes off the robe

She slowly begins an Indian dance with a Salutation

Very slowly step by step through a process of learning, with musical

instructions heard over the speakers a dance of Sita emerges
It ends with her sitting peacefully in a meditative pose
Through her dance we can hear the teacher singing the song in Sanskrit
And beating the rhythm
We can't see the teacher.
Then with a burst of theatrical energy a wild ten headed demon king
Ravana comes dancing, seducing, threatening, cajoling wanting Sita
He dances wildly to the beating of drums
He presents her with a box of jewels
He sings an ancient keening song

Ravanna: O beautiful Sita of Rama it hurts me to see
You sit here dressed in white like a widow
I have here jewels for you to wear
Gold and pearls and diamonds and emeralds
For you to adorn and I promise I will not remove
As naked you come to me to make love
Like a queen to his king in gold and silver

He laughs an evil laugh
He leaves threatening to be back. Next time he will force her to
submit to him.
Sita sits staring at the box of jewels
She starts getting dressed in the jewels and at the same time tells the
story of Faustus

Actress: I am sorry but I insist, this great story, this great piece of German literature cannot be just sliced up and swallowed like a piece of pizza. I insist on at least, in brief, telling you, telling the world, the entire story of Goethe's Faust. I will tell the story in German and the translator will translate it into your language.

She tells the story

This section does not have to run smoothly. It works with all the trials and errors made when a 'live' translation process is being rehearsed.

In this and the next section the play seems to be faltering, losing its theatricality, as the struggle to tell the two stories of Faust and the Ramayana make it a little too realistic, prosaic and boring. Too many words and too little action, is the stylistic mode of this section.

Actress speaks German.

Translator: *Goethe's Faust* begins with a prologue in heaven
Where the Lord challenges Mephistopheles, the Devil,
To lead astray the Lord's favourite scholar, Dr. Faust.
When the play opens we see Faust in his study, attempting and failing
To gain knowledge of the universe by magic means.
The dejected Faust contemplates suicide, but is held back by the sounds of Easter celebrations.
He joins his assistant Wagner for an Easter walk in the countryside,
And after much celebration, is followed home by a dog.
Back in the study, the dog transforms itself into Mephistopheles, the devil,
Who offers Faust a contract: he will do Faust's bidding on earth,
and Faust will do the same for him in hell if Mephistopheles can get him to be satisfied and want a moment to last forever.
Faust signs the contract in blood.
He is then transformed into a young man by a witch,

Faust encounters Gretchen and she excites his desires.

Mephistopheles brings about Faust's and Gretchen's liaison.

After a period of separation, Faust seduces Gretchen even as she

Accidentally kills her mother with a potion Faust had given her.

Gretchen gets pregnant and gives birth to Faust's illegitimate child. Fearing societal shame and rejection she drowns her child.

Gretchen is given the death sentence for this crime.

In the dungeon, Faust in vain tries to persuade Gretchen to follow him to freedom.

At the end of the drama, as Faust and Mephisto flee the dungeon,

A voice from heaven announces Gretchen's salvation.

A stage hand comes and places a baby in the Actresses hands

The actress is naked and while holding a baby in her hands sings a sad lullaby.

She walks slowly around the stage

A stage hand comes and places a ladder

The actress climbs the ladder while singing to her baby

On top of the ladder she waits

There is silence

The actor playing Ravanna walks on stage. He is taking his costume off

He speaks in Malayalam, a translator translates.

In this section too the play seems to be faltering, losing its theatricality, as the struggle to tell the story of the Ramayana makes it a little too realistic, prosaic and boring. The play at this point is meant to falter.

Translator: If she can tell the story of Faustus then I must tell the entire story of the Ramayana. Please have patience.

Dasharatha, King of Ayodhya, has three wives and four sons. Rama is the eldest. His mother is Kaushalya. In a neighbouring city the ruler's daughter is named Sita. At a ceremony called a swayamvara, she chooses Rama as her husband. King Dasharatha, Rama's father, decides it is time to give his throne to his eldest son Rama. Rama's step-mother, the king's second wife, is not pleased. She wants her son, Bharata, to rule. Because of an oath Dasharatha had made to her years before by which she could ask for anything she wished and he would grant it, she gets the king to agree to banish Rama to the forest for fourteen years and to crown Bharata as King. Rama, always the obedient son, is content to go into banishment in the forest. Sita and his brother Laxman too join him.

Years pass and Rama, Sita and Lakshman are very happy in the forest. One day a rakshasi or monstress tries to seduce Rama, and Lakshmana wounds her by cutting off her nose and drives her away. She returns to her brother Ravana, the ten-headed ruler of Lanka, and tells her brother about the lovely Sita.

Ravana devises a plan to abduct Sita. He sends a magical golden deer which Sita sees and desires. Rama and Lakshman go off to hunt the deer, first drawing a protective circle around Sita and warning her she will be safe as long as she does not step outside the circle. As they go off, Ravana (who can transform himself into any shape) appears as a holy man begging alms. The moment Sita steps outside the circle to give him food, Ravana grabs her and carries her off to his kingdom in Lanka.

Rama is broken-hearted when he returns to the empty hut. A band of monkeys however offer to help him find Sita. Ravana has carried Sita to his palace in Lanka, but he cannot force her to be his wife so he puts her in a grove and alternately sweet-talks her and threatens her in an attempt to get her to agree to marry him. Now Hanuman, the chief of the monkeys can fly through the skies since his father is the God of the wind, and so Hanuman flies to Lanka and, finding Sita in the grove, comforts her and tells her Rama will soon come and save her.

Rama, Lakshman and the monkey army build a causeway from the tip of India to Lanka and cross over to Lanka. A mighty battle follows in which Rama kills Ravana.

But the Ramayana does not end here. The fact that Sita lived in another man's palace causes disparaging rumours about her chastity. She is obliged to take a fire test in which she sits in a fire but comes out unharmed and therefore purified from all charges.

After Rama and Sita return to Ayodhya, the rumours about Sita's adultery in Ravan's captivity continue and therefore the people disrespect her. Eventually Sita insists on proving her loyalty to Rama by asking Mother Earth to swallow her if she was loyal to Rama and so Mother Earth to testify her loyalty, opens up and swallows her and Sita disappears into earth.

The story telling by now has gotten very tedious, dull and boring. It is meant to be so. No attempt should be made to make the above sections entertaining.

Enter Writer. He injects some energy into the performance.

Writer: So you have two stories: Goethe's Faustus and the

Ramayana and you have perhaps two similar endings possible for this play, the New Taj Mahal about two women both shamed by the world, suspected of adultery and both paying a price for it with their lives.

Dear audience, you can see Gretchen hanging there with a baby in her arms. If she lets go of the baby and the baby falls into the river that would be from Faustus. If then she herself jumps to the ground and the earth swallows her up it will be Sita from the Ramayana. Of course we would have the stage designed to open and swallow her up the moment she lands, it will be all quite dramatic.

As a dramaturgical choice, we could end with one, or both, with one following the other, but which one? Of these two which one do you think is a more effective ending? Of course when the baby falls we can have a scream recorded in the background for effect, in the same way with the Sita swallowing the earth up scene we could have wonderful thunder and lightning effects.

Waits for the audience to respond.
Director steps in a little angry and upset.

Director: Enough of this question and answer session
 For me the end is very simple very clear
 Faustus illegitimate child must drown in the river
 Or else it'll grow to be a grandfather of a Nazi
 For all who do not know world History
 Goethe wrote in 1832, a hundred years previous to World War 2
 And we all know what happened in World War 2
 Some things in this show I must insist

You all have seen how prejudice against my race still exists
Even now sixty years on in the German mind
There are things thought about us that are unkind
And as I pay your bills I have the power to decide
The end must be Faust, this baby must die
And there is an end.

Suddenly from out of the shadows appear seven men dressed in shorts wearing monkey masks
They take aggressive postures
Everyone freezes
Then their leader comes in. He rides a huge black wooden dog

The leader: Jai Bajrang Bali victory to Lord Hanuman the monkey God

The seven men: Jai Bajrang Bali-victory to Lord Hanuman the monkey God

The leader: So what's happening here? You English motherfuckers still think you own this country and can do whatever you want? Who gave you the right to play with our Ramayana? This is our sacred story? This is our soul, you have no right to do anything with it. How dare you make a white woman play our sacred Sita Mata. Like our God Hanuman ji went to protect her from the demon Ravana we have come here to protect our sacred story from you foreign demons. Do you want us to sort you foreigners out in the same way as we have sorted these people, these *katuas*. If you really want to make a story, tell my story, make me the hero. I am the true hero of Hindustan. You want to hear my story. It is the story of courage and bravery. The story of a true Indian, a patriot.

So listen to my story.

> I was the first to start the Naroda Patiya operation. We and the local residents were all together. Patiya is just half a kilometre away from my home. I had gone to Godhra when it happened. I could not bear what I saw. I just came back to Naroda and we took revenge. We organised everything that night itself. We mobilised a team of 29 or 30 people. Those who had guns, we went to them that night itself and told them to give us their guns, we collected 23 guns. But nobody died of gunshots. What happened was this: in Patiya, there is a State Transport workshop with a huge wall beside it; next to this wall, Patiya begins. Opposite Patiya, there is a Masjid and beside it is a sprawling *khadda*. That's where we killed them all. It was a huge pit. You could enter it from one side but you couldn't climb out at the other end. They were all there together. They started clinging to each other. Even while they were dying, they told each other, "you die too, what are you going to be saved for, you die too," so the number of deaths increased.

> They were hacked to pieces,hacked, burnt, set on fire, many things were done… many. We believe in setting them on fire because these bastards say they don't want to be cremated, they're afraid of it, they say this and that will happen to them. I have just one wish, one last wish. Let me be sentenced to

death. Give me two days before my hanging and I will go and have a field day in Juhapura where seven or eight lakh of these people stay. I will finish them off. Let a few more of them die. At least 25-50,000 should die. It has been written in my FIR there was this pregnant woman, I slit her open, sister f****r. Showed them what kind of revenge we can take if our people are killed. **I am no feeble rice-eater.** I didn't spare anyone… they shouldn't even be allowed to breed.

That day, it was like what happened between Pakistan and India. There were bodies everywhere. I came back after I killed them, called up the home minister and went to sleep. I felt like Rana Pratap, that I had done something like Maharana Pratap. I'd heard stories about him, but that day I did what he did myself.

This is a real play you white asshole. As for this play of yours, if you try anything dirty with our Sita Mata, we'll do to you firangis what we did to these people. So I suggest you just pack your bags and leave.

The earth opened and swallowed Sita up. That's how it ends in the Ramayana and that's how it'll end here. Or we bury you alive, here on this earth.

Just remember, never forget.
I am no feeble rice eater.

Exits
Silence

The actress slowly comes down
The writer joins her on stage

Epilogue

Director to the Actress and Writer and to the audience

Director: So my friends as you can see
This man who did such terrible crimes is walking free
Spending his time bragging merrily
About what he did to my friends, my human family

A long pause follows.

You may think my words strange, coming from one who
began the show
Seeking revenge for a wound from a lover's blow
Plotting like Mephistopheles' a real abduction
In revenge for a failed seduction
But that was all a setup to surprise you into a story
Of terrible prejudice that ends in things more gory
Of course I am an Austrian jew
And one who cares a lot for his money too
But I come from a race that's been hunted down
By those who think they wear the crown
And now its my arts violent endeavour
To ring a warning bell wherever
Prejudice and Power combine to hide
The early signs of a Genocide
You may argue defend it saying it's not true
All because to your country I am new

You may be right and I grant you this I grant you that
But one thing inescapable is the fact
What happened in 1939
Came ten years after a terrible time
Which is why this story starts with the line
Say dear ones in these times of financial backbreaking
Say what you think of our new undertaking
It all began when times went bad
And what followed were things terribly sad
But for now this story of doom and gloom I must end

The lights begin to fade

I thank you for buying tickets and coming here
I hope with all this my warning is clear
I will now settle down with a bottle of wine
And enjoy the feel of each silver coin
Stay alert, awake god forbid what I predict, in your
country, come true
So goodnight to you all from this Austrian Jew

A stage hand walks in

Stagehand: *Please rise for the national anthem of the two countries
Indian and Austria to be played one after the other.*
As everyone stands and waits
Darkness

THE END

THE COLONIAL THE CONVICT AND THE COCKATOO

Characters

The Convict: A middle aged white Australian man

The Cockatoo: A young white working class Australian man

The Colonial: A middle aged white British man pretending to be upper class

Singer/Musician: An Australian folk singer/musician

Narrator/Playwright: Middle aged Indian man

There is a video screen upstage centre

Singer sits downstage left

Darkness

Cockatoo on video (*cursing*):

Pox on this house

Pox on this house

Pox on this house

Whip the slave

Whip the slave

Whip the slave

Red plague on you

Red plague on you

Red plague on you

Lights on singer

Singer sings a song

Singer: My name is Vince

And I ain't no Prince

All I ever want to be is a man who is free

And I am proud of my convict history

The Convict enters

He is wearing a red suit with a white hat

Convict: My grandpa's pa

    Stole a sweet girl's heart

    And for this crime

    For a seven year time

    First on the high seas he sailed

    Then far away in the penal colony was he jailed

    All for stealing a sweet girl's heart

    Now this is how it all began in that merry month of May

    Now this is how it all happened on a sunny English day

    Well my grandpa's pa saw this girl carrying hay

And as he stepped up stopping her way

And then took all on his shoulders before a word she could say

Lightening her step and brightening her heart

Lightening her step and winning her heart

Lightening her step and stealing her heart

Yes! Lightning her step and stealing her heart

O my grandpa's pa stole a sweet girl's heart

And for this crime

For a seven year time

On the high seas he sailed

And far away in the penal colony was he jailed

Now I ask you good people was this such a crime

That deserved taking seven years of my grand pa's pa's time

Was it a crime for a poor man to love?

To call a sweet girl his Mrs, his dove

And for calling her his Mrs

And for a few stolen kisses

Once the girl's father's anger was spent

To a trail in a courtroom was my grandpa's pa sent

For the girl's father had ranted and raved and threatened to kill

And chased the young lovers over meadow and hill

Now the good judge god bless him was old and grey

Had long forgotten the bliss of a love filled day

And so keenly to the girl's father he gave an ear

Then turned to the girl who was wiping a tear

And from this her wet eyes he did surmise

That the boy was a rogue his heart full of lies

Who planned first stealing her heart

And then dumping her as if she were a tart

And so the old judge called my grand pa's pa's love a crime
And ordered him transported for a seven years time
And so on a ship was he sailed
And in Van Diemen's land jailed
All for stealing a sweet girl's heart

Lights fade on Convict on stage
On the video we see that the Cockatoo is very agitated.

Cockatoo: Pox on this house
Pox on this house
Pox on this house
The Red Plague on you
The Red Plague on you
Whip the slave
Whip the slave
Whip the slave

Lights on Cockatoo on stage. The two Cockatoo's CS (stage) and
CV (video) start interacting, reciting text one line at a time. The actor
playing the Cockatoo embodies the movements and form of a Cockatoo.

CS: I am a wild Cockatoo I was not born in a zoo
    CV: To be here encaged makes me enraged
    CS: I am an original Aussie creature that's right
    CV: And to top it all my colour is white
    CS: I am a wild Cockatoo I was not born in a zoo
    CV: To be here encaged makes me enraged
    CS: All day I sit and curse rhyming out my curses in verse
    CS: Bangs like a dunny door
    CV: Well what you expect from a bloody whore

CS: Bowling from the pavilion end

CV: Is a man who likes to make his backside bend

CS: For the curses and the noise I make they shoot me as a pest

CV: But to lie dead under the sun is no jest

CS: I am a wild Cockatoo

CV: I was not born in the zoo

CS: To be here encaged

CV: Makes me enraged

CS: All day I sit and curse

CV: Rhyming out the curses into verse

CS: A man with a big Donga

CV: Thinks he can stay inside a woman much longer

CS: Now a Fuck muppet a Fuck tard and a Fuckwit

CV: Are really three different names for the same twit

CS: Good day cock features

CV: What fucking ugly creatures

CS: I could eat the arse end out of a low flying duck

CV: With no food to eat and only a thumb to suck

CS: A vagina decliner, an arse monkey and a vegemite driller

CV: Are all a man who with another man gets a thriller

CS: A carpet muncher and a plate licker

CV: Are two women attached together one to another like a sticker

CS: A Barnard

CV: Is a retard

CS: Get on your knees and smile like a doughnut

CV: Well take my donga in your mouth you slut

Cockatoo on video completes the text

CV: I am a wild Cockatoo
I was not born in the zoo
To be here encaged
Makes me enraged
All day I sit and curse
Rhyming out the curse into verse

Video switches off.
Lights go down.
Only a central spot is left.
The Colonial walks into the spot.
On the video screen we see the title of the scene as 'His Lordship's Trial'
He is dressed as a 19th century gentleman

The Colonial: Once upon a time in the year 1834
An ordinary trickster really no more
To all convicts who had been recently freed
Pretended he was a British lord indeed
Calling himself Edward Viscount Lascelles he arrived
And on the gullibility of newly freed Convicts he thrived
He bought three horses from a Mr. Roberts for fifty pounds
Then just quietly vanished and was nowhere to be found
He lodged with a Mr. Pendergast and drank his wine
Ate his turkeys, geese, chickens, goats and swine
But when the time came for him to pay
The great lord just ran away
And just as the word of this fraud was noted in the Lawman's diary
The trickster transformed himself into a Commissioner of Inquiry

Now about the treatment of convicts there was indeed a
hue and a cry
Their condition was often so terrible that some preferred
to die
One Monster Magistrate Murdie so often would a convict
flog
That the man would rather die than live the life of a dog
Now this man Murdie was the one who coined the term
Felonry
To give to the convict colony well a certain dignity
A big landlord was he of a property
That used convict labour very successfully
He made the men work very hard but if by chance he
found them slack
He whipped them hard and left them with a bloody back
Now it was rumoured that the trickster-Commissioner of
Inquiry went from farm to farm
Checking if the property owners, like Murdie, were doing
the convict servants any harm
But this Commissioner was no Commissioner was indeed
a fraud
So the local Police finally decided to use the Iron Rod
And so this nobleman arrived at Penrith Jail
With no chance of course of being granted bail
In the trial he insisted he was in truth an Earl
Who had indeed been once of London society a pearl
But since for a long time the Earl had not been heard of
(a fact that was indeed true)
For where the 'real' earl was, well, no one really knew
So in court this was the trickster's main argument
On which a considerable amount of time was spent

That if anywhere else in the world the lord had been
He would by now have been in the newspapers seen
It was only possible to be unheard of for this length of
time
If he was in penal colony, well, spending time
For in the penal colony it was possible your past to hide
Which is why he could take a lot of people for a ride
Now even though this part of his argument was true
The good judge wasn't mistaking red for blue
And so to the gallows the fraudster was sent
And hung by the ropes till his neck was bent
For friends if there is one thing true in the penal colony
Indeed there is one thing no one can take
It is a two faced man, a man who is fake
What you see here indeed is what you get
And more than that you needn't fret
And so to introduce my self

Indicates towards the Singer who now takes over.
Lights fade on The Colonial.
Lights on Singer.

Singer

My name is Vince
And I ain't no Prince
And all I ever want to be
Is a man who is free
And proud of his convict history
I am who I am
And my name is Vince
And I ain't no Prince

All I ever want to be
Is a man who is free
And proud of his convict history
My grandpa's pa
Stole a sweet girl's heart
And for this crime
For a seven year time
First on the high seas he sailed
Then far away in the penal colony was he was jailed
All for stealing a sweet girl's heart.

Enter the playwright/narrator dressed in a black suit and white shirt.

Narrator: Now here is another tragic tale of a woman transported for life

The sad story of young Master Abel and Eliza his wife
Turned out of their lodgings for not paying their rent
Out on the street the poor family of three was sent
Cold and miserable on that wintery English night
The young family huddled making a pitable sight
The baby girl cried and Eliza shivered in fear
For she knew how Abel felt about her sweet little dear
For Abel he never wanted a child
And since the baby's birth had often gone wild
Threatening to throw her into the river
And this is what made the mother shiver
For no mother wants to part
With something dearer than her heart
Now Able was heartless and cruel indeed
And grabbing the bundle and gathering speed

He tore the baby out of Eliza's hands
Then disappeared into the fog covered lands
Eliza cried in vain but heard not a sound
As silently into the cold river her baby was drowned
And in the morning cold dead by a farmer found
For days no one asked or came looking worried
And finally in the Church graveyard was the little girl
buried
For many days Eliza pretended her bundle her girl
But soon she sensed her secret unfurl
The neighbours grew suspicious not hearing a sound
And then all was known when nothing in the bundle was
found
The judge sent Able to hang
A different song to Eliza he sang
And so for her crime on the high seas she sailed
And far away in a penal colony was she jailed
And for years after, terrible tears of a guilty heart she wailed

Exit
Singer/musician plays a melancholic tune
We hear trumpets and celebratory sounds.
Enter Playwright/Narrator

Narrator: Hello and Welcome to The Colonial The
Convict and the Cockatoo a pesty zesty show which helps
you understand the wonderful history of this land called
Australia, with episodes from Australian convict history
written by an Internationally celebrated ex-colonized Indian
Playwright now a resident of Gisborne, Victoria, Australia
and recited in a language inspired by the rhyming couplets

of the bush ballad tradition. And so, after stories of how convicts were transported to Australia for crimes as little as stealing a chicken and as terrible as drowning your own baby, let us change track to introduce some 'High Culture' into this evening's performance by adding a scene from that famous Pommie Playwright William Shakespeare. To put it across more colourfully lets add some Shakespearean Spice to this evening's Indian Curry.

So now ladies and gentlemen let's begin with an episode from the Tempest.

In the following scene produced by the BBC for their Shakespeare series, you will see Prospero, the Colonial Master, his daughter Miranda, and their slave Caliban, an original inhabitant of the island. Prospero has Caliban as his servant treating him well till one day Caliban tries to rape his daughter. Caliban, as he is the child of Sycorax a native of this island, considers himself the rightful owner of this island. However, now he has to work as a slave to the more powerful Prospero. A set of relationships brilliantly constructed by Shakespeare in the year 1605 predicting quite prophetically the exact set of relationship almost two hundred years later between the Colonizing master and the Aboriginal slave raising the critical conspiratorial question: how did Shakespeare know so much? Was the Colonial enterprise already in the minds of the Elizabethans? When exactly in time can we say British Colonisation began? Please note at the end of the scene Caliban's curse 'The red plague on you' refers to the smallpox disease that ironically plagued Aboriginal inhabitants as they had no defences against it.

So now ladies and Gentlemen or as the Cockatoo would say

You fuck muppets, fucktards, and fuckwits
Here is a scene from the BBC production of the Tempest

On the video screen we see the the following excerpt

CALIBAN

This island's mine, by Sycorax, my mother,

Which thou takest from me. When thou camest first,

Thou strokedst me and madest much of me, wouldst give me

Water with berries in't, and teach me how

To name the bigger light, and how the less,

That burn by day and night: and then I loved thee

And showed thee all the qualities o' the isle,

The fresh springs, brine-pits, barren place and fertile:

Cursed be I that did so! All the charms

Of Sycorax, toads, beetles, bats, light on you!

For I am all the subjects that you have,

Which first was mine own king: and here you sty me

In this hard rock, whiles you do keep from me

The rest of the island.

PROSPERO

Thou most lying slave,

Whom stripes may move, not kindness! I have used thee,

Filth as thou art, with human care, and lodged thee

In mine own cell, till thou didst seek to violate

The honour of my child.

CALIBAN

O ho, O ho! would't had been done!

Thou didst prevent me; I had peopled else

This isle with Calibans.

PROSPERO

Abhorred slave,

Which any print of goodness wilt not take,

Being capable of all ill! I pitied thee,

Took pains to make thee speak, taught thee each hour

One thing or other: when thou didst not, savage,

Know thine own meaning, but wouldst gabble like

A thing most brutish, I endow'd thy purposes

With words that made them known. But thy vile race,

Though thou didst learn, had that in't which good natures

Could not abide to be with; therefore wast thou

Deservedly confined into this rock,

Who had not deserved more than a prison.

CALIBAN

You taught me language; and my profit on't

Is, I know how to curse. The red plague rid you

For learning me your language!

Exit CALIBAN

The narrator returns repeating a lines from The Tempest

Narrator: Thou most lying slave,

Whom stripes may move, not kindness!

And

You taught me language; and my profit on't

Is, I know how to curse. The red plague rid you

For learning me your language!

He then returns to the narration

Narrator: The flogging of convicts....

Flogging in the Penal Colony was suffered by men rather than by the women and inflicted upon the bond and not the free. But its sights and sounds were part of the bloody reality of every man, woman and child in the colony. The cat of nine tails, a whip made of nine to twelve green hide leather strips sometimes knotted at the end, could skin a man's back in twenty five strokes. It spread gobs of flesh about for ants to carry off and filled the victims shoes with blood so that when released he squelched his way from the triangles where he had been bound. In the summer flies later laid their eggs in the lacerated flesh and one was lucky if a humane companion was on hand to extract the maggots. When prisoners went to receive a flogging they referred to it as going to wear their red shirts.

The performance halts at this point and the narrator/playwright steps up

Narrator/Playwright: Good evening. Besides playing the narrator I am also the writer of this show, and in the midst of reading and researching for these terrible memories of convict servants and their being whipped I thought about, and now would like to share a relatively lighter story about my own school principal in India, an Irish Catholic Missionary. To preserve his anonymity and for the sake of the artistic unity of this performance let us call him Brother Murdie, this in resonance with the evil Magistrate Murdie the one who was known to have treated his convict servants terribly, having them whipped every day. In fact, for the sake of an artistic and thematic unity, you will find in this play all cruel men referred to as Murdie. So here is the story I have written about my school principal Brother Murdie

The Playwright sits down and starts reading from a book

One hot Indian summer afternoon

Brother Murdie sits in his office behind his large desk in his white robes and dark glasses that shade his eyes from the blazing summer sun.

Brother Murdie is the principal of St.Michael School, New Delhi.

Next to him on a rack in his office are placed three canes. He has given them names to help identify them Piggy, ziggy and twiggy. Piggy because it is fat and hard like bacon rind. Ziggy because it is flexible and zigzags its way through the air. And twiggy because it is the thinnest.

Students can choose their own means of punishment. Brother Murdie however decides the number and the viciousness of the cuts.

A little boy of less than ten stands in line behind Rudy Hooligan, the school bad boy. Rudy is the youngest of the infamous Harrigan brothers. It is the teachers that refer to the brothers as the Hooligan brothers. They are Anglo Indian and fair like the Irish Christian missionaries who run the school and who make it a point of being seen free of any negative prejudice towards black skins by giving the Hooligan brothers the severest of punishments each time they commit an offence.

Rudy is standing in line outside the Principal's office because he has been caught whistling love songs to the Convent of Jesus and Mary girls while swinging from the step of a moving school bus. Sister Therese has complained to Brother Murdie personally and Rudy has been called for on the school intercom

'Will that guttersnipe Harrigan boy please glide his way to my office'

No one in the entire school knows what a snipe is but everyone does know what a gutter is and they all know Rudy Harrigan is now neck deep in it. When Brother Murdie calls someone personally on the school intercom then it is usually six of the best with each of the three canes. That is six each with piggy, ziggy, and twiggy.

That is a lot of pain.

From his place by the principal's door the little boy of less than ten can see Rudy with his chewed up tie and dirty muddy keds explaining his position to Brother Murdie who sits behind a large desk with his hands hidden deep within his white robes.

He can also see the three canes shining away on the rack like three prized trophies. One by one the canes are taken down from the rack and Rudy is whipped 18 times.

The little boy of less than ten is next.

> And why are you here sir? Asks Brother Murdie menacingly
>
> I forgot to wear my belt today sir. So my teacher sent me to you.
>
> Aha. You forgot to or you cared not to. You thought you'd just hang your shirt out and hide it from us. We are not blind you know.

And then to show him that he is not blind Brother Murdie takes off his dark glasses. His blue eyes feel cold and brutal.

> So young man, which of these would you like?

For lesser offences you could choose your own. Those who had been there often knew the thickest one Piggy hurt the least.

> Piggy sir.

Three cuts of Piggy is what the little boy of less than ten got that day. For not wearing his school belt. For not being in proper uniform.

A few months after Brother Murdie whipped him eighteen times for whistling at a Convent of Jesus and Mary girl while swinging from the boarding step of a school bus the Harriggan family left India and migrated to Australia.

The next song is dedicated to my childhood friend Rudy
Harrigan

Light on the singer

Singer (*chants/recites the text*)
Where are you now my childhood friend
Where are you Rudy Harrigan
Should I search for you in happy Melbourne town
Or in dark Brisbane where all the lights are down
Or should I take a boat through flooded Toowoomba
How much trouble you got into then
How much trouble are you in now
Eighteen cuts of Brother Murdie's cane
Was just the beginning of your pain
What happened to you Rudy my Friend
After you came down under
Did you learn to walk the straight path
Or did you get yourself into more trouble
I hope you are not spending time
I hope you are free
For I remember you as a brave boy
Not flinching once as you were whipped
Why did they whip us till our skin peeled off
To make better men of us
Did you become a better man, Rudy my friend
I hope you are not in prison spending time
I hope you are free

Hearing the word 'free' the Cockatoo starts singing

O to be h free
Searching from tree to tree
For my dear friend Rudy
Singing merrily
Who the fuck is Murdie
A cruel Magistrate who whipped his servants daily
Who invented the incredible appellative Felonry
To give a certain dignity to the Penal colony

The Colonial enters

The Colonial: Ladies and Gentlemen Introducing to you *The Preface to The Felonry of New South Wales Being a Faithful Picture of the Real Romance of Life in Botany Bay With Anecdotes of Botany Bay Society.* Dated 1836

Very theatrically in a heavy Colonised upper class British Accent he reads out the preface

The object of the writer of the following pages is to lay before the British public and more specially the legislature and the government a new term which should bring both delight and dignity to the body of people it hopes to represent. And that is the term Felonry.

The Colonial appears on video and takes over the narration. On stage the Colonial is joined by an actress dressed in a fancy nineteenth century costume. They are both out on the promenade, they walk, they amble and dance to the singers music throughout the next section while the Colonial continues to read the preamble from the video screen.

The Author has ventured to coin the term Felonry as the appellative of an order or class of persons in New South Wales -an order which happily exists in no other country in the world. The majority of the inhabitants of the colony are felons now undergoing or who have already undergone their sentences. They occupy not only the state of the peasantry and labourers in other civilised societies but many, very many of them are also as respects their wealth or their pursuits in the condition of gentry or of dealers, manufactures, merchants, and lawyers, and other members of the liberal professions. Hitherto there was no single term that could be employed to designate these various descriptions of persons who now bear the denomination of convicts or tickets of leave men as also emancipists (as they are absurdly enough called) who again are subdivided into conditionally pardoned convicts, fully pardoned convicts, and expirees, or transported felons whose sentences have expired: together with runaway convicts subdivided into absentees (a name foolish for its mildness) and the bush rangers. The single term Felonry (which comprehends all these descriptions of the criminal population) though new is evidently a member of the tribe of appellatives distinguished by the same termination as peasantry tenantry yeomanry military chivalry gentry, etc. The author has the honour of specially presenting to the gentleman emancipists, alias, the emancipated felons of the colony by whom he has no doubt it will be received with most peculiar approbation and delight, in so far as it not only expresses but elegantly expresses their place in society but as it also raises their caste with all the beauty and fashion of the felonry at New South Wales, whether sparkling in silks and jewels at the theatre and the ball, or the races at Parramatta, or over the glittering and crowded drive to Bellevue point, on South Heath road, made not more romantic by the magnificence of its natural scenery than by the living splendours of its rich and animated felonry. It raises the true caste of such men and women to the dignity of an "Order of the Commonwealth."

The Colonial and the Actress bow to each other. The Actress leaves the stage.

The Cockatoo appears on the video dressed as a judge, watching the scene below

The narrator enters

Narrator: Mr.Murdie, the inventor of the extraordinary appellative Felonry and a strong votary against any kind of humane reform towards the convict population is here on trial himself under scrutiny for the severity of his control of the convict servant population, a severity that deserves even today, so many years later a careful examination. For is not the severe control of the convict population and the threat that their freedom posed to the colony's newly settled property owners the originator of the severe control that has been the true story of this country's immigration policy. Those first struggles within the colony between the free settlers and the convicts / felons, those struggles for liberty and control, are they not the bedrock of the policies that exist even today?

And Mr.Murdie the big property landowner and free settler, the model citizen, whose mindset, was, has been, and is the dominant mindset that has, and continues to rule this land. A mindset that still dictates a language that often describes homes as properties and big landlords quite unashamedly as squatters.

Well his story in brief…

Reading from a book

Through the benevolence of the Colonial Office in Britain Mr.Murdie (with a mild criminal background) arrived at Sydney in July 1822 with an order for a land grant and was given 2150 acres (870 hectares) on the Hunter River. Later in 1825 Mr.Murdie acquired another 2000 adjoining acres boasting that his homestead was a fortress guarded by Newfoundland dogs and that his servants were severely disciplined under exacting rules. In November 1833 six convict servants mutinied but an attempt to shoot Mr.Murdie failed and he escaped. The mutineers were arrested and remanded to Sydney, where they were found guilty;

After passing the sentence of death by hanging on each of the accused the judge asked the men if they knew of any reason why the sentence of death should not be passed upon them. Mr. Hitchcock, one of Mr.Murdie's convict servants and sentenced to death by hanging rose with dignity to his feet.

In Mr. Hitchcocks words

Mr. Hitchcock enters. He speaks with a broad working class Australian accent.

Mr. Hitchcock: It was to the unfortunate circumstance of my being assigned to the service of Mr. Murdie that I attribute all my subsequent misfortune and present unhappiness. I had possessed an exemplary character before I worked for Mr. Murdie, since then I have been repeatedly flogged by which and by the unwholesome food I have subsisted on my health has been ruined and life itself rendered burdensome. I denounce the system of the infliction of the lash throughout the district of the Hunter river. I call for justice and urge your lordship if the court would but look at my back to see my statement was not exaggerated.

Please your honour I do but beg you to give permission for me to show you my back.

Narrator: Even as he stood pleading begging for permission to show the court his back the court in its wisdom chose not to look at Mr. Hitchcock's back.

The singer now chants an Ode to Mr. Hitchcock...

You were hung by the neck Mr. Hitchcock
For no one cared to see your back
What would they have seen if you had turned your back?
We cannot bring you back from the grave Mr. Hitchcock
We cannot give you back what was taken away from you
Your dignity and your life
But we can see what you wanted the world to see
Turn around Mr. Hitchock turn around
Turn around

Mr. Hitchcock takes off his jacket revealing a white shirt underneath. He then turns his back and stands to block the projection. An image of a bloody and lacerated back is projected onto the back of his shirt.

Then the image blurs revealing another image of a body covered with smallpox.

The image of another body with small pox follows. Then another. And another

With the turning of Mr. Hitchcock's back and with images of bodies infected with smallpox the play in effect turns to another page of Australian history

The narrator: So Ladies and Gentleman these images you now see (*pointing to the images of small pox covered bodies which can now be seen on the screen*)

Are images of that terrible disease called pox
That forces us to take this convict story and place it in another box
I know some of you are a little puzzled at the plot
That moves this play from Mr. Hitchcock's lacerated back to an even darker blot

The consequences to the natives of this island of establishing a Felonry
Are now of course well known in history
But let me tell you an old Indian saying that goes thus
Once the wound is scratched out pours the pus
So here is a song from this Indian Man's tongue
Riding on air that he breathes out from an ancient lung
A sad prayer this is for those that of smallpox died
Sounds from an earth still wet with tears that have not yet dried

A sad keening native American Indian song is heard

Now my friends let us not create a mystery
Of this land's sad history
We all know that within four years of the first convict ships that arrived
Half of the Aboriginal tribes around Sydney harbour had died
Now of course the question is this
Was this because of the Convict's kiss?
Or had the smallpox been brought
Wrapped in trader's goods that the aborigines had sought
So who is really to blame?
For this terrible shame
To answer this it is necessary to step outside
Of this island within which these stories reside
To North America in the year 1763 I'd like you to go
And for this I introduce another British war hero
Though his name was General Amherst I'll have you know

We'll call him General Murdie for the artistic unity of this show

So here from some History books I read some prose

Narrator reads from a book. The singer too joins in and shares this narration.

> General Murdie was commanding general of British forces in North America during the final battles of the so-called French & Indian war (1754-1763). He won victories against the French to acquire Canada for England and helped make England the world's chief coloniser at the conclusion of the Seven Years War among the colonial powers (1756-1763).
>
> The town of Murdie, Massachusetts, was named for Lord Jeff
>
> Despite his fame, Jeffrey Murdie's name became tarnished by stories of smallpox-infected blankets used as germ warfare against American Indians. These stories are reported, for example, in Carl Waldman's *Atlas of the North American Indian* (NY: Facts on File, 1985). Waldman writes 'Captain Simeon Ecuyer had bought time by sending smallpox-infected blankets and handkerchiefs to the Indians surrounding the fort-an early example of biological warfare-which started an epidemic among them. Murdie himself had encouraged this tactic in a letter to Ecuyer.'

Now here is my point for turning to this prose
To answer the question that first arose

Who was to blame

For the shame

Of the hundreds of thousands that died by the pox

Here is my simple argument

And I hope you will find my logic straight, not bent

The fact that native tribes were defenceless against the disease was not unknown to the European invaders of the Americas in 1763

And what follows after this is a simple exercise of chronology

1763 smallpox deaths recorded in Native American tribes

1771 till this year British Convicts are sent to the Americas

1776 After winning the war of Independence the American Govt puts an end to British Convicts being sent to the Americas following which the British Government decides to send them to 'Australia'

1788 the first British Convict ships arrive in Sydney Harbor

1792 tribes in and around Sydney Harbor are reduced by half their numbers due to smallpox deaths

Collateral damage or germ warfare

The truth to find is always rare

However the fact remains that soon after the first Convicts arrived many native Australians died of smallpox

Now ladies and gentlemen we all know that an

acknowledgement of guilt is the beginning of the process of healing

As it was for the aboriginal children that the Australian governments had been stealing

It is for this that I propose another apology, this time to the dead, to those who died of smallpox....

I say "Sorry"

The Cockatoo enters

Cockatoo

O fuck you curry

O fuck you curry

O fuck you curry

I am a moody Cockatoo

And now I am feeling blue.

And I won't say sorry

I won't say sorry

I won't say sorry

With floods and bushfires and cyclones that daily this island blast

Who the fucking hell has time to go digging up the past

Shit happens

Shit happens

Shit happens and that's the end of that

As it was well said in Afghanistan by my friend Prime Minister Tony A bat (sic)

I am a Moody Cockatoo

And now I am feeling blue

Fuck this political shit

This is what this fucking multiculturalism leads to

Fucking curries telling us what to do

These fuckwits should stick to staring at tits if you know what I mean

Bollywood dancing is what your culture is you fucktard

Learn the Aussie way of life you arse monkey

And so let me introduce you fucking currys to some true blue Aussie culture

Waltzing Matilda! It's no waltz you fuckwit. Aussies are not about some high brow Shakespearen culture stuff you chicken shit.

Aussies are about real people, real rough and ready people, real people, real culture.

Matilda is no woman you dimwit. It's a bedroll. The song is about a lonely man dancing with his bedroll.

It's about a hobo or a swagman dancing with his bedroll

Here are some terms that will help you understand the song

A jumbuck is a sheep

A tucker bag is a knapsack

A billabong is a deep pool of water

A squatter is a larger property owner

The narrator and the singer now sing

Once a jolly swagman camped by a billabong
Under the shade of the Coolibah tree
And he sang as he watched and waited for his billy boil
You'll come a waltzing Matilda with me

Refrain

Waltzing Matilda, waltzing Matilda you'll come a waltzing Matilda with me

Then down came a Jumbuck to drink from the billabong
Up jumped the swagman and grabbed him with glee
And he sang as he shoved the Jumbuck in his tucker-bag
You'll come a waltzing Matilda with me

Refrain

Waltzing Matilda, waltzing Matilda you'll come a waltzing Matilda with me

Then down came the squatter mounted on his thoroughbred
Down came the troopers One Two Three
Right! Where is that Jolly Jumbuck that you've got in your tucker-bag
You'll come a waltzing Matilda with me

Refrain

Waltzing Matilda, waltzing Matilda you'll come waltzing Matilda with me...

So up jumped the swagman
And he sprang into that billabong
You'll never take me alive said he
And his ghost maybe heard as you pass by that billabong
You'll come a waltzing Matilda with me

Narrator
Now ladies and gentlemen I'd like to thank the crazy Cockatoo

For introducing me to a song that is both joyous and blue

For while the song has the swagger of a swagman

In the end he kills himself rather than go to prison

And this confirms the fact that the swagman was a convict too

For who else would rather die than go to prison for another year or two

Now, with this song while I would like to end this show there is one issue that troubles me- it is the part of the song that goes

"The swagman shoved the Jumbuck into his Tucker Bag"

I imagine the Jumbuck being stuffed kicking and screaming into the bag and then slowly suffocating and dying in the sack

I apologise. I cannot continue to try and rhyme sentences even as the Jumbuck suffocates to death in the Tucker-bag.

That's a terribly cruel way to die

The swagman couldn't care less I know, however, what an uncivil and uncultured way to kill an animal. On the other hand, is there a civil and cultured way to kill an animal?

Allow me to introduce to you the Islamic tradition of *zibah* or slaughtering a goat by first cutting its jugular vein (Let me clarify I am not a Muslim in case you think I am promoting my own culture, this is all objective stuff here)

When the 'swagmen' of the desert wanted to eat camel meat they would kill the camel in all kinds of brutal ways and because the animal was so large often they would take chunks of meat off its body even as it was dying, leaving the animal to die a terribly slow painful death.

This is why the Prophet Mohammed (peace be upon him) suggested *zibah* or cutting the jugular to bleed the animal to death, making sure the animal is dead, clean, and peaceful before it is cut up and eaten.

Now isn't that a civil cultured way to kill an animal.

Unlike the Jumbuck in the Tucker-bag which must have died a terribly slow suffocating death.

Of course the Swagman too, to escape the cop jumped into the billabong and drowned to his own death.

At least with that drowning we know that the Jumbuck too must have drowned and died and there come to a final end

Sad. All very sad (*laughs*)

I hope I haven't spoiled the wonderful song Waltzing Matilda for you. I hope you, unlike me, will be able to forget about the terrible cruelty of the suffocating Jumbuck and enjoy the rest of the song

I think with this we have all had enough

Of this cruelty and culture stuff

So, on this note that culture is a strange beast

With all kinds of dishes that make up the feast

From the Colonial the Convict and the Cockatoo

I say a good night to all of you

Good night and sweet dreams

Of happy Jumbucks dancing over meadows and streams

THE END

STRAIGHT FROM
A HORSE'S HEART

Characters

Paro-a young Indian woman

Mr X- a middle aged Indian man

Andy Marvin- An ageing white Australian man

John Shaw- A young white Australian man

Victoria Shaw- A middle aged white Australian woman

Robert- a middle aged white Australian man

Leslie Johnson-A detective. A middle aged white Australian man

Peter Thomson-A detective. A young white Australian man

General ambient sound: Bird/ nature sounds

The Zoom performance begins with the audience logging in and being allowed to enter into the zoom performance space by the host. As in the theatre while the audience members join in there is a pre-show musical entertainment. A performer plays a raga on the Sitar.

The cue to start the storytelling is the call of a kookaburra.

Entries and exits are made by the performers switching their videos on and off.

The performance on Zoom was played on Speaker view- the character who was speaking occupied the screen space. Other characters were present in a thumbnail screen on the side panel.

Exit Sitar player

Enter narrator

Narrator: Hello everyone, welcome to Straight from a Horse's Heart. I am the narrator or *sutradhaar* of this show. Our story begins one morning at the Om Shanti Healing Center situated somewhere in rural Victoria.

Exit Narrator

Enter Paro

Paro (*singing a lullaby*): My boy doesn't go to sleep unless I sing him a lullaby. It's 10.30 p.m at night at home in India. Wish I could wake up an hour earlier at 3 a.m when it's quieter, the birds here are so loud at this time. But I just can't, I am so tired.

She then calls a number on her mobile phone

Paro: Hello Mr. Mahalingam. This is Paro calling from the Om Shanti Holistic Healing Center. Madam Victoria has asked me to call you. Please call her when it is convenient. She is concerned that you did not come here the last two weekends. Please call her. Thank you, bye.

Sound: Buzzer

Paro (*Curses*):

Ah that damn bell! Who is ringing it at four o'clock, wanting me so early in the morning? They never let you rest, the forever restless.

She takes out her robot suit and starts wearing it.

It's so hot in this suit. I am afraid one day I will get caught out because of my terrible sweating!!! But this robot suit fools everyone. They are all so wrapped in themselves, in their own illnesses, in their own stress, no one notices this is a Halloween costume.

Acts like a robot

And of course my excellent acting!

I am an automated care provider. My name is Paro. Cya later.

Exit Paro
Music from Mr X's room
Enter Mr X
Enter Andy

Andy: He never says a word. Just sits listening to songs, in Indian, all the time. I've tried asking things about his life but he never answers. The little I know about him is from his son who brought him in. He comes once a week to see him. He doesn't speak much to his son either, speaks to no one. I've been trying to connect with bits and pieces of my life. I once even tried enticing him with a sensational story, telling him of my wife, a nurse's murder on night duty, by a burglar, while I was away from home on a business trip. I thought he might express some empathy or at least want to hear the story in greater detail. Nope. Not a word of interest. Silence. Dead heart is what I thought to myself, dead fucking heart, no point trying to make it beat. That's depressing huh having to live your final days with a dead heart! Fucking shit, I need a whiskey, got to keep it hidden, it's not allowed this poison here. This is a place for holistic healing. Luckily most of the time Paro the robotic nurse is the only one looking after this place, doing all the work, she has a video camera embedded in her heart. It sends images to the big screen in the office where Victoria sits. So all I have to make sure is that the whiskey is not in line with her vision.

Cheers old man, here's to your health. Would you like a whiskey? A small one?

Looking surprised

He did a thumbs up? Did you see that? Fucking hell let me try again. Would you like a small whiskey, sir? It's excellent scotch.

It's a thumbs up again. Whoopiee. The dead heart is beating again at a whiff of whisky. He wants a whiskey and he is going to get a whiskey. We are communicating, we are finally mates, cellmates, we are finally doing things together, this is going to be a party, and life is fucking good.

Drinks his whiskey

Wonder what Paro is cooking up for tonight eh? Wouldn't

mind some meat, dreamt of eating a roast leg of pork last night. In the dream it was Easter, my wife had cooked this wonderful leg of ham, my son and daughter were home, we were all sitting around a fire and both my horses were looking in through the windows. It was a complete family portrait, couldn't have been more perfect, and the meat was just so tender and dripping with fat, just the way I like it. I don't see how this vegetarian stuff is helping us die better, Father Christmas.

Maybe it's just the stress of having to face another bowl of that terrible pumpkin soup. It's the fucking color that depresses me.

Gets a book out

Here, see this, my masterpiece about Dressage. I was one of the first horsemen to do the entire dressage routine not riding the horse but walking besides it. The secret art of leading by earning a horse's respect. All the techniques are in here. This chapter is about making the horse do an elegant canter. Like this…

Performs a canter

I love doing this canter, it makes me feel one with the horse, as if I am back in the paddock training my horse, it feels so elegant,but … my lungs.

Ah … I can't breathe, it hurts … I could do with a pain killer. Hey, hide that glass. Paro is here

Enter Paro

Hello and welcome Paro, I need you, desperately.

Paro: Hello Andy, I have told you not to canter around the room. It always leads you to pain. Luckily I have a painkiller here. You will get relief in a minute or two.

Andy: You're an angel, a sweet singing nightingale. Bless you my dear. May I call you Florence.

Paro: No. My name is Paro, PARO Paro. With an equal emphasis on both syllables. Pa Ro.

Turning to Mr. X

Hello Mr. X. I am an automated care provider. All my interactions are recorded in order for my superiors to study the effects of the interaction. I work for Victoria. She is my boss. Using the video recordings Victoria examines the psychological condition of seniors interacting with me. This is done by telling me a story.

Everyday you need to tell me a story. Till the first story is recorded I will not be able to move onto the next module. Please tell me a story today.

Andy, Victoria says you need to tell us the story of your wife's murder. You keep mentioning it, dwelling on it but you have never spoken about it in detail. We've heard enough about your horses, we need to hear about your wife, about her murder. Were you really away on a business trip? We need the truth. I am sure you will find the courage to tell us. Victoria says she is praying for you, you know that, you know we are all praying for you Andy. Give me a hug.

And now Mr. X. Victoria says till you start talking I am not to call you by your name. No hugs for you till you start talking. I am waiting for you to talk Mr. X

Exit Paro, Andy, Mr X
Sound: Bird/ nature sound
Enter Narrator

Narrator: In Victoria Shaw's office, on the upper floor of the healing centre, Victoria is in an agitated state. Her son John is becoming what she phrases as a "pain in mum's bum".

Exit Narrator
Enter John and Victoria

John: No mum, no, that's not true, I did not set up Fredrick to ask for a salary, why would I do that, though I do believe he needs to be compensated in some way for the work he's been doing.

Victoria (*on phone*): Tell Freddie to suck it up his arse, you heard me, tell him to suck it up his arse. Tell him you don't get a salary for sitting on a trust, I will never let that happen, how dare he ask? If it's not you, who else has been plugging his ears? So lawyers for this urban developer turn up out of the blue, with a proposal to subdivide the property and Freddie says we should consider it. I know you're behind that, I'm not blind. I know what you are up to, John Shaw, you want to bring it all on the agenda, so that next year when you are on the trust you can take your crazy schemes forward.

John: No mum, that's a ridiculous accusation, I am not plotting anything against you. Why would I need Freddie to put things forward when I can talk directly to you? I am afraid you're getting paranoid. These are all ideas, suggestions for the future. You don't have to be threatened by new ideas mum.

Victoria: Goddamn you John Shaw! I will never let you change this god inspired work I am doing into some urban nightmare! You heard me never, ever. You've turned out even more devious than your father. At least he had the decency never to lie to my face. Goodbye, I've had enough of you.

Exit John Shaw
He gives me the one thing I don't need, Stress!
Makes a phone call

Hello, is that the Macedonian Gazette, yes, I have a poem for you, it's called I WILL NOT DIE OF CANCER. Here is how it goes.
Every morning I wake up and pray to the rising sun
And tell myself this life's for living and to have some fun
Then I bathe and wear a bright coloured dress
And repeat to myself the cause of cancer is stress
The cause of cancer is stress
The cause of cancer is stress
I repeat to myself the cause of cancer is stress
Now, the next stanza
Here is a simple way to stay Cancer free
Breakfast, lunch, and dinner all three
All freshly cooked hot vegetarian meals must be

And yoga meditation to be done daily
And yoga meditation to be done daily
Every morning I wake and pray to the rising sun
And tell myself this life's for living and to have some fun
Then I bathe
What? Yes,that's right you just repeat the verse, right.
When is it coming out? Sunday, that's good, very good.

Enter Paro

Paro: Hello Victoria. Good Morning.

Victoria: Hello Paro my dear. It's a relief to see you. Lucky you're a robot and don't have a monstrous family to deal with like I do. It's my son John, he's paid some lawyer and urban developer hundreds of thousands of dollars and they have come up with this bloody report. It's a conspiracy. As if I will allow him to turn this beautiful rural property into some miserable little housing blocks. I mean he is crazy. The only problem is, he turns forty-five the next month and then according to his grandfather's wishes he has an equal say in the trust. So his balls are getting bigger with every passing day and the noise they make clangier. What he does not realise is that his mother's breasts from which he sucked so desperately buckets and buckets full of milk are really made of iron, are iron hard. I will crush him to powder if I need to. I will destroy him.

What an awful life! Anyway, thanks for the offload, whose story do you have today?

Paro: Yes Victoria. It's Andy's. I am afraid it is another one of his horse stories. Here it is.

She plays Andy's video

> **Andy:** I had a mare once, went old and blind, just stood there in the field, like a beautiful white marble spectre, till the wind and the rain stripped all the skin off her back. I returned home from a trip overseas to find her carcass right there in the field. I had loved her so dearly when she was young but could do so little for her in her final years. We are such carcasses by the end of our lives. A friend of mine loved a sow, a pig, he...

Victoria: No, no, stop this. I have had enough of his horse stories. That man is in pain. He keeps bringing up his wife's murder but never tells the story in detail. Maybe we need to be tougher on him? Be a little cruel only to be kind? Deny him his tranquilliser when he has one of his attacks! You have my permission. We have to get to him. And that Indian man, he too is a time bomb ticking away. Keep a special eye on both of them, we have to solve this problem.

Maybe you need Robert too, to help in this? Perhaps a man could help. Get him to befriend these two, spend time with them. He is coming here tomorrow anyway, to shoot rabbits.

And Paro, let's not tell him you are a robot. Let's see if you can pass yourself off for real. Get out of this robotic costume and wear a normal Indian woman's dress. Your company promised me you could adapt your role to perfection in three weeks. Well, let's try it out. Let's see how successful an experiment you really are. I'll inform all the residents to expect Paro the Housekeeper so they don't have a heart attack when they see you. It'll be a relief to see you get out of this ugly Halloween nightmare.

Exit Victoria

Paro: Damn now I have to change out of this robot suit and into a normal Indian dress and cook rabbit stew for that terrible man who kills these sweet bunny rabbits. I have tried all day to call my son, but the Internet is down, Telstra is so incompetent especially in the country.

My little boy has broken his arm. He was telling me about it when the connection broke. All I want to do is to sing him a sweet lullaby, my mother used to put us to sleep with it.

I am so fucking tired of all this acting.

I am tired of filling my heart with other people's stories. I am tired of listening to their guilt, their trauma and misery. I don't care a fuck. I hate listening to their soggy stale sad stories about their hollow and unfulfilled lives

I don't care for Victoria and her mean and selfish children.

I don't care for Andy and his horses and his dead wife

All I want is to talk to my boy all night, I want to hear his pain, I want to sing him a song and put him to sleep. It hurts deep inside this separation.

And now to make things worse the boss says I have to cook a rabbit stew tomorrow. I hate the smell of meat. I am a vegetarian.

I won't be able to sleep tonight thinking of those sweet rabbits. And my poor boy

Exit Paro
Sound: Gun Shots
Enter Narrator

Narrator: The next day the tranquillity and peace of the Om Shanti healing centre was disturbed by Robert the Rabbit Ridder's gun shots.

Sound: Gun Shots (x2)

He has had a successful day of shooting rabbits. In the kitchen Paro is cooking rabbit stew while Mr. X waits at the table for his dinner. Robert comes into the kitchen to amuse him and make him talk.

Exit Narrator
Enter Peter and Mr X

Robert: No touching this. Keep it loaded, I always do. Never know when I might need it. Ah, the kitchen smells as it should, of a hot-blooded animal, of meat. That was the condition I put in my contract with Victoria, to shoot rabbits. A hundred dollars for the day's shoot, all the rabbits I shoot are mine and I don't go home hungry. I get a free cooked dinner and my dishes all washed up, that's right. I told her straight no hunter ends a day's hunt with eating carrots and pumpkin soup. What I kill I eat or you can find yourself another fucking rabbit ridder for all I care.

When you shoot a rabbit it flips over like a high jumper doing the Fosbury flop. By the time it lands it's dead, flopped out.

Hey Godfather. Good evening. How's it going mate? I hear you have some problems talking. No worries. I am here to cheer you up mate. I am sure you have never heard this one before.

> A Chinaman arranges for a hooker to come to his room for the evening. Once in the room they undress, climb into bed, and go at it. When finished, the Chinaman jumps up, runs over to the window, takes a deep breath, dives under the bed, climbs out the other side, jumps back into bed with the hooker and commences a repeat performance.

Enter Paro

> The hooker is impressed with the gusto of the second encounter. When finished, the Chinaman jumps up, runs over to the window, takes a deep breath, dives under the bed, climbs out the other side, jumps back into bed with the hooker and starts again. The hooker is amazed as this sequence is repeated four times. During the fifth encore, she decides to try it herself. So when they are done she jumps up, goes to the window and takes a deep breath of fresh air, dives under the bed and finds four Chinaman.

No one laughs

Huh, it seems I am the only one with a sense of humour here. No worries.

Sorry lady (*looks at Paro*) this tongue's a bit rough, the jokes rougher. Nice to have a lady cooking for me tonight, feels like you are my wife for this evening. You look straightforward, cook a man his stew, and feed him and then some rock and roll. You from India? I guessed that right, didn't I. Never been there, never been out of Victoria really. My wife wanted to go to New Zealand but we got divorced before we could. Doesn't mean I haven't had my fun after that, life gets lonely you know and after a day of firing the gun you feel like bang, bang. Ah, this whiskey tastes even better now!

Hey lady, why are you sitting so far away, you wont join us? Come on. Aha, I see. I've heard of this. Asian women don't eat till their men have. Is that it...aw...that is sexy. I like that. But this is Australia, we are all equal here. I need you to eat with me. Honey, here, I'll get you a bowl of stew, here.

Here it is served for you, on the table. Now come and eat with us. I mean I insist. I fucking insist my darling you eat with us, all together like a family. You, grandfather, and me here.

Paro: No, I like to eat on my stool here, this is my place. I am happy here.

Enter Andy

Robert: What, my beautiful wife? You're not going to obey your husband, a disobedient wife. That is even more sexy and attractive. You want me to do a dance for you, see, here.

Paro: Please stop. It's a horrible dance.

Robert: Hey I love your Bollywood dances. Here see this. What beautiful hair do you have my dear?

Paro: No I don't have beautiful hair. Please go away

Robert: What beautiful lips you have my dear? All the better to kiss you my dear!

Paro: I am an automated care provider. I work for Victoria. You smell of Alcohol. You are drunk.

Mr.Varma: Leave her you bastard, or I will shoot you.

Andy: What are you trying to do, you pervert? She is not real. She is a robot. An automated service provider. A robotic nurse. She's just taken off her robotic suit and you are fucking drunk.

Robert: If she's a robot then I am a fucking joey and my mother's a kangaroo. I've never had it harder in my life. She's for real, she's fucking for real.

Enter Victoria

Victoria: I saw that you bastard. I have cameras everywhere, I see everything that happens here. You're an animal, Robert. A pervert. I could have you arrested for this. Get off my property before I come down and kick you out myself. I never want to see your face again, get out.

Exit Robert, Paro, Mr. X and Andy

Whoopee, what a triumph!

Makes a phone call

Hello, Mr.Mahalingam. Where the hell are you? We've been leaving one voice message after another. Anyway, just wanted to tell you that the experiment has been a success, in fact our very own Robert the Rabbit Ridder as we like to call him, got fooled and confused enough to make a pass at dear Paro. He was a bit drunk I am afraid and well sort of grabbed at her but there were others around to protect your dear invention. She did seem a bit in shock though, she may need some attention. You need to program a self-defence reflex for her, for all kinds of emergencies that may come her way, so that when we keep her artificial identity a secret there are no mishaps. That will be the ultimate success. I am so excited by this. I am even looking for you to design my trustees now, in fact a whole board of robot directors! It will just be so wonderful to have everything ordered, in control, organised, predictable and I do look forward to seeing you to discuss this very soon indeed. Please call me back.

Exit Victoria
Sound: Music playing at pub
Enter Narrator

Narrator: That same night a very revengeful Robert the Rabbit Ridder is having a dark conversation with John Shaw. They are both at the pub drinking beer and plotting Victoria Shaw's downfall.

Exit Narrator
Enter John and Robert

John: Are you sure, she is not a robot? You know I've heard of these things before. Can't imagine mum's messing with illegal immigrants? I mean she is getting all nutty with this spiritual stuff, but she's still screwed on tight. Your story better be believable or else we will be in trouble.

Robert: No way John, no way from fucking hell that she is a robot. She is as real as all the rabbits that I shoot on your mum's estate. Well, I go in there today and as usual I am shooting the rabbits and swigging my whiskey when I get one. I mean it becomes like a game, shoot one, swig one, shoot one, swig one. And so by the time I finally go into the kitchen I am like warm and happy inside, and there she is all small and pretty with beautiful black eyes and she's there cooking rabbit stew for me like my wife used to, all warm and homely, and I swig another whiskey and like you know I get hard real hard for her. So I politely ask her if she's interested and suddenly she's all offended and running and the guys there are shouting at me calling me a pervert, saying I got a thing for a robot, screaming she's a robot. I mean you can hang me for all you want but I was real hard and she is no fucking robot and then your mum like shouts at me, abuses me and tells me to get out of her property. This makes me mad, so - I have these friends. My sister in law's brother who works for this private detective agency. So I call him and they want to know if I am sure about all this. And so I say of course I am sure, as sure as death, she is no fucking robot I say and so they plan this whole charade to come in as insurance agents dressed as border control officials. They are in there now! I thought I would let you know because we all know what's happening between your mum, and you with the trust, and I am on your side mate. I am all for the little people with their little blocks of land and not these fucking squatters with their estates. One call from you and the press would come running.

John:All sounds a little crazy to me mate, especially the bit about the two detectives going in as funeral cover insurance agents but dressed as border control officials. Why the double camouflage?

Robert:…to frighten her into handing over her papers to them. Why would she hand over her passport to insurance agents?

John: Well that makes sense. If it's true she is an illegal immigrant then there is more in it for you than just a beer I assure you. All I can say is that I don't think my mum is that stupid, but you never know what she's up to in that wild den of hers. Keep me in the loop mate best of luck.

Robert: Best of luck to you too, John Shaw

Exit John and Robert
Enter Narrator

Narrator: While Robert plans his revenge by hiring a detective agency we have a brief five minute interval. Enjoy music in the foyer played by our inhouse musicians.

Exit Narrator
Interval action – variations of the Pink Panther title track
Sound: kookaburra calls
Sound: Bird/nature sounds
Enter Narrator

Narrator: Welcome back to the Om Shanti Healing Center. The two detectives, sent by Robert to find out the truth about Paro are now at the gates of the centre practising their routine. Allowed inside by Victoria to sell a new life insurance policy to the ageing residents, they are dressed, unknown to her, as border control officials.

Exit Narrator
Enter Leslie and Peter

Leslie: G'Day. My name is Leslie Johnson

    Peter: G' Day. My name is Peter Thomson

    Leslie: We may look like border control officials but we are not

    Peter: We may dress like border control officials but we are not

    Leslie: We are JTFCI

    Peter: Johnson and Thomson Funeral Cover Insurers *(drum sounds)*

    Leslie: If you love your loved ones

    Peter: As we are sure you do

    Leslie: You wouldn't want to leave the burden

    Peter: Of your funeral on them

    Leslie: They will already be burdened

    Peter: With a house loan

Leslie: A car loan

Peter: A second house loan

Leslie: A second car loan

Peter: Student loans

Leslie: Travel loans

Peter: And credit card debit

Leslie: The last thing they will want

Peter: Or more correctly

Leslie: The last thing you would want for them

Peter: Is for them to have to take another loan

Leslie: Mum and dad's funeral loan

Peter: No never, you couldn't do that

Leslie: We would not let you do that.

Peter: That's why were are here

Leslie: Dressed as were in the theme of border control agents

Peter: Or maybe we are that, we are border control agents

Leslie: Haha fooled you we did, but we are

Peter: At JTFCI we are really just that aren't we

Leslie: Checking if you have got everything right

Peter: Before you cross over to that glorious land

Leslie: Leaving no debts behind

Peter: *(musically)* All for just a few dollars a week

Leslie: That's it, it's as simple as that

Peter: *(musically)* For just a few dollars a week

Leslie: Why would you not free your family of that final burden?

Peter: We guarantee to renew your policy every year until your 120th birthday, unless your cover stops earlier

Leslie: You're good Peter

Peter: You're excellent Leslie

Leslie: What a routine,

Peter: Let's go swing it!

Leslie: Shall I Dutton up now

Peter: Beam me up Scottie I am ready to go fly

Leslie and Peter wear face masks of Peter Dutton (the immigration minister) and Scott Morrison (the prime minister).

Enter Paro

Leslie: Hey Lady carrying all this wood, let us help you? Are you the cook here? You're dressed like a cooking nurse! It's a little odd a cooking nurse, isn't it, or is it your goose that shall soon be cooked haha!

Paro:Who are the two of you? How did you come in? Who let you in through the gate? Who do you want to meet?

Leslie: Good day lady. TJFCI at your service. Good to see a young face among all the old folks here.

Peter: And a pretty one at that, I say, very pretty.

Leslie: It's you we're after

Peter: Sweet sunshine and laughter

Leslie: Before we offer advice on the funeral cover package for you, not that we think you need one, not in a hurry anyway, we would like to ask a few questions?

Peter: You would be having your passport on you wouldn't you?

Paro: Why, why do you want my passport?

Leslie: What is your real name?

Peter: When did you first come to Australia?

Leslie: Can we see your passport please?

Peter: What is your visa status?

Leslie: Since when have you been working here?

Peter: Do you have a valid work permit?

Leslie: How much did you get paid?

Peter: Who is your employer?

Paro: I am an automated service provider. I am not programmed to answer immigration questions. Why are you trying to frighten me? Leave me alone. I am an expensive robot. I am protected by a security system that gets activated when I press this button.

Presses a button on her watch
Exit Leslie, Peter and Paro
Enter Mr Varma

Mr. Varma: Mr. Mahalingam, Good morning sir, this is Varma reporting from the Om Shanti Healing Center. There is a crisis here. I just received an SOS message from Paro with a photo of two border control agents questioning her. As you know sir Paro performed perfectly, too perfectly. She was almost raped by one drunken man here. I had to step in to protect her. Luckily I had his gun.

Enter Andy

Victoria ma'am was very angry. She asked the man to get out of the property but I think he is very angry, he is reporting Paro to the police or something because there are two men dressed as immigration control police. I am sure they are after Paro. Sir they may arrest her very soon then I will be in big trouble also. Sir, I am putting exit plan 34 2B into place, please note I am putting exit plan 34 2B in place, please take appropriate action. I repeat please take appropriate action immediately. Time is short, time is in fact running out. I am signing out now.

Andy: What the fuck is going on here? I heard all that! Who are you? Who is Mr. Mahalingam? What is plan 34 2B? What is this you are getting out of your suitcase? What are you doing with this dummy robot? Christ in heaven, it looks exactly like Paro. A mannequin named Paro. What's up mate? Here I thought you were just a sad old blind Indian man, and you turn out to be a secret service guy on a secret mission with hundreds of plans under your belt? I mean I did suspect you were mafia. You do look dangerous in those dark glasses pretending to be fucking blind. Sucking up all that sympathy. What the fuck is going on? You drank half my bottle of whiskey, you owe me an explanation. I demand it.

Mr. Varma: Sir very briefly sir I must apologise. This is not a time for long talk but for action. It's true you have been very kind, very friendly to me with all your horse stories and real life stories and sad wife stories and also I have drunk your whiskey so I must speak the truth. Ms. Paro is no robot but she is really Ms. Paro. Mr. Robert was absolutely right. She is real. No one is knowing this. Ms. Paro is playing her part perfectly, as a robot. It is all acting, fantastic. Our company Mahalingam Robotics' chief Mr.Mahalingam, he is the young man visiting me like my son but he is not my son, he is my boss. He is away on a business trip. He is so busy but I know he is listening to voicemail. Mahalingam Robotics is getting so many orders, so many demands for robots that we are over booked but we do not want to lose customers so we are supplying some real Ms. Paros. After excellent training of course to become robots. Our products are so excellent that no one is suspecting. My job is security officer to protect Ms. Paro if trouble happens. Please sir this is a secret now between you and me otherwise I will lose my job, go to prison. You are a good Aussie mate, you are not wanting me to go to prison right? I only tell you because of whiskey. By your beloved horse's heart pleasure promise you will keep my secret. This stays in your heart only.

Exit Andy

Now I must activate plan 34 2B to save the situation. I must replace the real Paro with this dummy Paro. Then announce that these men have destroyed the robot.

Exit Mr. Varma
Enter Paro, Peter, and Leslie
The two detectives continue their investigation of Paro

Leslie: Are you from India?
　　Peter: When did you first come to Australia?
　　Leslie: Did you come by boat?
　　Peter: Who got you a job at this centre?
　　Leslie: Since when have you been working here?
　　Peter: Where did you train for your nursing skills?
　　Leslie: How much did you get paid?
　　Peter: Who is your real boss?
　　Leslie: How come you speak such good English?

Paro replies like an agitated robot

Paro: Hello my name is Paro. I am an automated care provider. I am programmed to provide all help required by seniors in a nursing environment. I work for Victoria. She is my boss. I am now switching on this camera so my boss Victoria can see the two of you. Here it is on. Now you will be in trouble.

Presses a button on her phone
Exit Paro
Enter Victoria

Victoria: What in hell is happening down there? I can see what the two of you are up to. How dare you? How dare you?

moving to her balcony

Get out, get out of my kitchen you two morons. Come out in front so I can see your sick faces.

Exit Leslie and Peter

It's all because of that demented son of mine, he is desperate, desperate to defame me. Where are the two of you? Come on out before I call the police to arrest you. GET OUT OF MY KITCHEN! Ah there you are you scoundrels. Just wait there till I come down and sort you out.

Exit Victoria
Enter Mr. Varma and Paro

Mr. Varma: Here's my chance, while the two men are out of the kitchen - I will replace Paro with this dummy. There it's placed. Hey Paro go hide at the back and wait till I call you.

Exit Paro

In the meantime, let me go out and speak to these two bastards, let me sort them out. I will threaten to sue them for damages.

Enter Peter and Leslie

Gentlemen please come into the kitchen, and see for yourself

Leslie and Peter remove masks

See here (*showing them the dummy Paro*). Sir, gentlemen, your aggressiveness has so disturbed her that she has had a breakdown, a technical breakdown I mean. You can see sir she is neither talking, nor walking. Only the camera here in her heart is still working. This is a tragedy. Sir, she is a very expensive robot, her repairs will cost hundreds of thousands of dollars, there is all recorded proof here, my company will sue your company.

Enter Victoria

Victoria: What's happening down here? She's conked off has she? I knew it. Look what you've gone and fucking done. You know this is bloody ridiculous, go ahead, ask your questions, she can't even talk now, see? She's just a fucking robot, and now you've destroyed her. Please get out of here before I call in the real cops and have you arrested. Out, get out of my property you morons, leave, now.

Exit Leslie and Peter
Sound: Bird/nature sounds

Mr. Varma: Madam, see they are running away as fast as the rabbits in your driveway. I wish Mr. Roberts was here with his gun, he would have gone bang bang and we would have seen a fine pair of high jumpers doing some Fosbury flops. I must apologise. I too have been part of charade. I am not the father of Indian migrant who recently come (sic) from India. I have been keeping silent, like angry suffering old Indian man, as part of a strategy to convince you that I am depressed and angry old Indian migrant man. I am not madam. I am as matter of factly senior security official of Mahalingam robotics, the company that is mostly making sophisticated robotic nurses. It is my duty to protect this very expensive product especially in the phase when the robot is adapting to the real environment. It needs very special protection, as you are well knowing madam. Nowadays you see madam there are so many demands for our robots, so much shortage of labour is there that sometimes our company is short on supply side. I mean so we are using all strategies to provide excellent service to the customer's benefit madam. Our product is so excellent, so perfect, so real that we are using product that is fooling even immigration agent into thinking she is an illegal migrant. But all our devices are only for customer satisfaction madam. We are sincerely apologising for keeping madam in the dark so to speak.

Victoria: (*aside to the audience*) What in heaven is he trying to say. Do they all sound mechanical like those telemarketing robots? Well, Mr.Mahalingam's man Friday I don't know what in god's heaven you are blubbering about. All I know is that I have lost this wonderful worker and I have an entire nursing home to run. I need a replacement as soon as possible. I can't wait even a day, you have to solve this problem for me right now.

Mr. Varma: O no problem madam. We have every solution for every emergency problem.

Enter Paro

Very quick madam our customer service is

Shouts

O Paro ithay aayeen.

Paro: Namaste ji, hello ji, how may I help you?

Mr. Varma: At your service madam this is an Indian lady you may also call her Paro, no problem. She already knows all the jobs, cooking, cutting, nursing, excellent service, minimum wage also, low cost high efficiency. We have one, two, ten, twenty, one hundred, two hundred, one thousand, two thousand. However many workers you are wanting, very obedient workers also, see here madam, Paro please touch her feet first.

Victoria looks shocked

She is seeking your blessings Madam. See Madam, she can even speak exactly like a Robot. Paro speak.

Paro: Hello Madam I am Paro, I have a request. Can you please upgrade to a better internet service plan? We are living in the 21st century. Uninterrupted internet service is not rocket science. Conditions of service have to improve so I can talk to my child in India. It is inhuman immigration policy to separate a mother from her child. You are a mother also. You must have a heart. Do you have a heart Ms. Victoria Shaw?

Victoria: Paro? Excuse me?

Mr. Varma: (embarrassed) Ok, ok enough, *itna drama kyon kar rahi hai* now please take this robot outside immediately.

Paro:*Drama mai, asli drama queen toh yeh hai, kutti*

Exit Paro

See madam, perfect replacement. Mahalingam and sons immigration department at your service madam.

Exit Mr Varma

Victoria: Whatever it takes, Mr. Friday. Whatever it takes.

Exit Victoria
Sound: Bird/nature sounds
Enter Narrator

Narrator: Despite Victoria Shaw's best efforts the story is there in the morning newspapers. It is not the story Robert the Rabbit ridder and John Shaw wanted, but if someone is happy it is Andrew Marvin, who finally finds his name somewhere in the fine print.

Exit Narrator
Enter Andy

Andy: Whoopee, I have my name in the newspaper, I am finally famous, I can now die in peace. Mahalingam Robotics sues Sherlock's Shadows Pvt detective agency. Two men from Sherlock's Shadows with support and encouragement from one of John Shaw's men entered his mother Victoria Shaw's Om Shanti Healing Center attempting to expose an illegal migrant workers network etc etc, yes here it is. When asked by the press Andrew Marvin, an inmate of the healing centre, and a man dying of Cancer stated that it was typical prejudice amounting to racism to suspect an Indian Company of using an illegal migrant worker pretending to be a robot. When asked further if he thought John Shaw would run the trust better than Victoria Shaw he had no comments to make except to say "Mum's the word". Whoopee! Andrew Marvin on the front-page, finally! I am so happy I feel like doing a canter, and when I feel like doing a canter I fucking well just do one....Whopeeeeeeeeeeee

Ah....my lungs...what an idiot I am....please please Paro give me the painkiller

Enter Paro

Paro: Hello Andy, I have your injection here, but I have orders not to give it to you till you tell us the truth about your wife's murder? How did your wife really die? Where were you that night? Were you on a business trip or were you overseas for some other reason? We need the truth Andy, the whole truth and nothing but the truth. Here is a glass of whiskey. Maybe this will help. Please know I am pushing you to the edge for your own sake. Victoria says this is what you will carry you through to your next life, these final lies are what cloud your shining beam of light.

Andy:(*in agony*) Yes you fucking bitch that burglar story was a lie. I made up that story because I could not deal with the truth. I was away from home but not on a business trip. I was in another town fucking another woman while my wife was busy tying a rope around her neck, to hang herself from the fan. I cooked up the burglar story because I couldn't deal with the fact that my wife committed suicide. The police showed me photographs of her, when I got there the next day she had shaved her head bald and her blonde hair lay scattered on the floor like so many strings of broken sunlight. I had no idea she had found out about me and Jessica, if I had known I would never have carried on the affair, yes, you fucking bitch I was having an affair with her sister Jessica and it was no ones bloody business to know. She loved me, trusted me completely, someone betrayed us and told her, and she killed herself. But in truth it wasn't she who killed herself, it was I who fucking killed my wife, my darling wife. I killed her with my betrayal, murdered her. It's the guilt, the terrible guilt that makes me lie each time I think of her death.

The guilt burns still like wild fire here in my chest, all the time and that's why I have fucking Cancer.

Breaks down crying, shaking, shivering with pain

Paro: Thank you Andy I am sorry to see you in such pain. As you can hear I have stopped the Truth Meter. Before we find out whether you were speaking the truth or not, here is a video I would like to show you. After the detectives left destroying our company's precious robot, Victoria got an idea. She hired them to find out about your wife's murder. We were surprised by what they found. Watch.

Paro plays Sarah's video

Sarah: Hello everyone, so lovely to be here, my name is Sarah Hall, previously Sarah Marvin married to Andy Marvin. This video is to certify that I am alive, well, and kicking. While it is true I was a nurse, I can assure you, no attempt was ever made by a burglar to kill me. It took me years to realise that Andy was a compulsive yarn spinner, that he enjoyed a story, a lie, more than the truth. I loved him dearly, but when I realised he loved his horses, especially his mare appropriately named 'Sheila' more than he loved me I decided to leave him. The last Christmas eve we spent together we were in the house, while he was in the stable with his horses feeding them plum pudding. The children were grown up enough to see what was happening. It was humiliating. Anyway, it's all in the past now, I am married to a lovely man, and have put behind me my life with Andy. I wish him luck with his cancer. Merry Christmas Andy.

Sound: Bach Music

Andy: haha no way I loved Sheila more than I loved Jessica. Go figure that one Sarah. Anyway, it all doesn't matter anymore, it's the end of the road for me. Go away Paro, I can bear my pain on my own and with a little help from this whisky. You've made it all legal now.

Pours himself a whisky

And with some fine Bach to heal my soul

Sound: Bach Music fades as singing starts
Paro sings a lullaby
Enter: Entire cast

Narrator: (Narrator ends the show) And with that sweet lullaby sung this time to Andy we end this Zoom drama. Good day, good afternoon and good night to all of you, we hope you stay safe and stay well.

Cast waves goodbye
Exit

THE END

HAWKING THE BARD
IN THE HEART OF WHITENESS

Characters

Nitin Sethi: A young Indian man

Dr. Harry Singh: A middle aged Australian man of Indian heritage

Sir Barnaby Higgenbottom: An ageing white Australian man

Hawker: Middle aged Indian/ Punjabi man

Barbara: An ageing white Australian woman

Author: A middle aged Indian /on video

A video screen upstage centre

A small oriental carpet lies in the centre. Most of the dramatic action happens within the limited area of the carpet.

The show opens with a fun Punjabi folk/ bhangra song to which Nitin Sethi is seen dancing while doing his morning chores, taking the garbage out, hanging the clothes for washing, and cleaning the floors.

An ABC video is projected on the screen. The narrator describes a funeral of a hawker he remembers from his childhood.

Another video plays out. The year is 2018.

The video shows a car going through the streets of contemporary Melbourne. The voice over is a letter, a young Indian man Nitin has written to his mother in India. The letter goes as the following:

Dear Mother

Sat Sri Akal and Pranam. By guru ji's blessings I finally have some good news for you. Last so many times I have called you, you have been crying continuously. Now you can stop. I found a very good job. It's with the Telstra company. My work will take me all over Melbourne and in the surrounding villages also. Every day I meet many *phirangis*. It's a very important job. Now I will work hard and make you proud. Please don't be concerned about me. Sometimes the news you hear about Australia is very sensational. There is no negative feeling here for Indians. Everyone loves India specially Bollywood films. People in Melbourne are very happy. They are like us Punjabi people also. They work hard and on the weekends they do the bhangra. So don't worry about me. I will not marry an Australian girl, I will marry only the girl you will choose for me.

Lights fade
Lights on the carpet
Dr. Harry (Hari) Singh the historian enters, is dressed in a flamboyant yellow suit, with a yellow hat, and speaks with a broad Australian accent.

Dr. Harry: Good evening, good evening welcome to Hawking the Bard

A show designed to hit you folks right there where it hurts you hard

My burden as the narrator of this theatrical show

Is tell you a little more than what you already know

While the bard of Avon is a familiar character in these parts

The story of Indian hawkers in Australia may need a bit of a kick start

The late nineteenth century saw a wave of Indians here arrive

Working as hawkers many of them did greatly thrive

With an increase in their numbers came rumours about the strangers

More humorous than dark were some of these perceived dangers

Imagine a horse and a rider trotting along a country road

Used to being challenged by no more than well a country toad

Now from around a bend out looms a man and a turban

A piece of cloth as long as Melbourne is from Durban

The startled horse in fear bolts right across the meadow

Leaving behind on his behind the poor wounded fellow

Now these Indian hawkers and their turbans were often seen in rural spaces

Or in city court rooms accused in many a criminal cases

The arrival of male Indian bodies at the doorsteps of lone women residents was a source of intense anxiety

Accused as they were of staring with feelings very different to piety

This narrative of Indian men as prone to prey on young girls
Though profoundly untrue emerged from a dark political twirl
The late nineteenth century saw an intensified governmental move
To create a "White Australia"all the other colours to remove
However, any attempt to mitigate Indian immigration was legally doomed
For unlike the Chinese, Afghans, and Syrians, Indians were as
British subjects, groomed
As part of a multiracial, multicultural, and multilingual empire
Any legislation against the Indians would raise the British government's ire
Under the British empire's Indian Emigration Act of 1883
Indians could not legally immigrate under a contract "to labour"
but must be "free."
It was then that free movement of many a turbaned face
That raised a cry to protect white women in their domestic space
The control of their sexuality, and of the borders of the nation-to-be
Were matters for the Australian federation of high priority.
It is then to honour the hawker's queen
That I raise a toast to the British empire
Leaving aside for the moment
Its history as a vampire
I request you all to rise and honour the British queen
The one who I prophesize has not very long left to be seen

Lights fade
We hear the national song 'God Save the Queen'
On the video screen we see images of Queen Elizabeth
A slide show follows.
Melbourne, 1895. General Sessions Court.
A court announcement is heard for a case of an abetment to a robbery.
Sir Barnaby Higgenbottom enters. He is dressed as a 19th Century lawyer, wearing an artificial wig.

Sir Higgenbottom: My lord and members of the Jury (*addressing the audience*). The case before us today is one of an abetment to a robbery. The victim Hardayal Singh the Hindu Hawker, accuses Henry James Down, a horse carriage driver of being an accessory to a robbery. As the victim Hardyal Singh suffers from the same infirmity that plagues all the free migrants that are ravaging the country, that is to say an inability to speak the English language, I have for the consideration of a small fee of course, used a translation service to help translate his testimony which I shall now proceed to read out.

Reads out from his dairy, mocking an Indian accent

I am a Hawker of 24 Little Lonsdale street Melbourne. On the 24th of May I was travelling from Echuca to Melbourne by rail. At Lansfield station four men got into the second class compartment and attacked me and robbed me of my money. At Footscray station the four men got off the train, crossed the tracks and entered into the buggy driven by the accused Henry James Down. I ran after them shouting 'these men have robbed me' but the man refused to stop, almost killing me along the way. I stood on the road shouting 'police, police' but no one came to my help.

My Lord, with your permission of course, could I request the Hindu Hawker recite a brief section of his complaint in his own language. The reason for inflicting on your ears what shall only seem like gibberish is to hear the man's particular emotion, specially in those bits where he curses the horse carriage driver. You will sense an anger my lord, which in the interest of the law and the wider social world we live in, I mean the country, where our women are often alone when these men arrive, we must take into account especially while delivering justice. Members of the jury (*addressing the audience*) imagine for example a widow named Barbara, living alone in the country, and this man, together as it were.

Makes a disgusted face
I leave the rest to your imaginations.
The Hindu Hawker

The Hawker enters

The Hawker: *(in Punjabi)* Your lordship, I am a hawker of 24 Casseldon Street off Little Lonsdale Street Melbourne. On the 14th of this month I was travelling from Echuca to Melbourne by rail. When I got to Lancefield Station, four men got into the second class compartment with me. On the journey to Melbourne a conversation took place between me and the four men about money and where I was going. After this conversation I was seized by three of the men and thrown down on the seat and the fourth man put his hand in my pocket and took ten five pound notes and four one pound notes out of it. I struggled with them and called out but they beat me and stopped my mouth. When we came to the next Station the four men left the compartment and went into another compartment and I followed them there, at the same time I kept calling that I was robbed and I told the Guard so. Every time the train stopped I complained about it. When the train got to Footscray two of the four men left the train. I could not say whether one of the two men that left at Footscray was the one that took the notes from me. They went from the railway platform to the road and then they got out and I followed them. I caught hold of the front of the cab. That son of a bitch, now in court, Henry James Down, was the driver of the cab. When the two men got onto the front of the cab the driver was sitting in his seat. I called out to the driver " you bastard I said don't take that man he robbed me, don't take that man in your car" I called out in this manner several times. I tried to get into the cab but the driver would not allow me. The two men in the cab cursed me in English saying **"you bloody Indian dog"*** and told the cab driver to drive on. When I caught hold of the cab I was on the driver's side close to him. As I was getting on to the cab and had my foot on the step this mother fucker whipped the horse and if I had not got out of the road I must have been run over. As the accused drove on I called out "Police" and said to him I would tell the Police. The driver whipped the horse and went on at a quick pace and I followed, calling out in a loud tone "those men have robbed me." The cabman (the accused) could hear me calling out at first, but he kept whipping his horse. I kept shouting these men had robbed me but (*in a repressed rage*) no mother fucker, son of a bitch, no bastard bastard came to my help.

*This is the only line in English
Walks off stage

Dr. Harry: Ladies and Gentleman before I continue with the story I would like to apologise to some of you here
In case I offended you by what I said earlier
I do appreciate that some of you might think highly of the British empire
And be upset at my suggestion that it was a blood sucking vampire
In my defence I have to say it was said in the spirit of a satire
Of course the old adage is also true where there is smoke, there is fire
Let me explain how clouds form and from the rain
These Hindu Hawkers were from the kingdom of the Punjab
A land of five rivers Jhelum, Sutlej, Beas, Rabi and the Chenab
In the great mutiny of 1857 when the Indian soldiers attacked the officers of the empire
The fate of British rule in India was indeed dire
It was the loyalty of the Punjabi soldiers that helped turned the tide
A decision that offered our Hawkers here in Australia a royal ride
However when in 1947 the British India in a hurry left
They partitioned the Punjab through a violent cleft
The west was declared Pakistan, the east India, and in between flowed a bloody river of terrible fear
Brother butchered brother sister raped and killed

With the dead and dying were the gruesome trenches filled

The moral of the gory story I would like to make clear

When empires are forced to leave they make the land pay a price that's dear

I don't want to create panic but I prophecy

When Elizabeth the second of natural causes does die

For multicultural Australia critical times ahead of us lie

Insecure and without their queen I suspect the new order may return to its Anglo Saxon core

As it had done with the White Australia Policy in the days of yore

As a backdrop to what are perhaps my irrational fears

Of the coming new order of Australia

And as a welcoming gift to the new King Charles and his queen Camelia

For those not already familia

Here is a vision of the empires gruesome exit from India

On the screen are projected excerpts from a BBC documentary on the Partition of India. Scenes of refugees fleeing, arson and looting. Voice over:

It is a battleground, people have gone mad, trains from, and to Pakistan are being looted and occupants slaughtered. We all knew that carnage was in the offering, so did Mountbatten. The British empire that was trying to build India over centuries can never live down this great tragedy.

Ten million are displaced in the partition of India, one million are dead.

Lights fade
On screen: 2018. The Widow. Country Victoria
Lights on Carpet

Barbara: Hello my name is Barbara Hogg. This urn has my husband John's ashes. After a four year struggle with kidney disease his body finally gave in. I was there holding his hand. We were together, as close in death as we had been in life. From college sweethearts to old dying farts, as John liked to put it.

We've been living in this little estate, our paradise, our own little island of green, for many years now. Our horses, our dogs, our chooks have all lived and died here.

John wanted his ashes buried here, under the cockatoo tree, where he liked to sit, singing a song that went something like this

> I like to sit each arvo at three
>
> Under the cockatoo tree
>
> Singing a song merrily
>
> With words meaning nothing particularly
>
> Now this it what it means to be a retiree
>
> Living like a true blue Aussie
>
> Generally feeling lazy
>
> Sipping a cuppa tea

Reading a book of poetry

Or just watching over Dorothy

Sitting under the cockatoo tree

Our friends Alan and Leslie helped me dig this spot, here under the Cockatoo tree. Then I told them to go, go home to their families, that's where I wanted them to be. I told them I wanted to do this on my own, I needed to be with John alone for one last time.

This being alone stuff is a complicated business isn't it. One is never really alone. There is always a dog around, or a bird in the bush, or a Kookaburras cackle in the distance, never really alone.

Even now all of you are here too, as presences, breathing, alive.

Recently an old Kangaroo has come here to live with us, does nothing most of the time just lies around, well like most old men do in any case. Not very imaginatively, I've named him Roger Roo.

I really need to do this alone. I really do. But then I thought about my friends and their feelings, and so I decided to call them over for tea, next Saturday. Most of them are actors, from the theatre company John and I loved working with. They are rehearsing Romeo and Juliet these days, I thought maybe they could do a scene from the play or something. John would have liked that, the show must go on as he always said. I tried sending everyone an email to invite them but the internet is down, so I must call everyone separately. That's a bummer. I've called Telstra for repairs, they said they'll send someone over but I am still waiting. They are so slow and incompetent.

(*looking at the spot for the ashes*) John and I used to go to a mantra workshop. We both really enjoyed it. He wanted me to recite this specific mantra. Sorry I don't sing very well. But here goes

Buries the ashes while chanting

Om bhoor bhuva swaha

Tat savitoor varenium

Bhargo devasya dhi mahi

Dhiyo yona prachodaya

Walk off stage

Lights fade

Projected on the screen is a video of the author now 'hawking' his voice and speech coaching skills. He speaks directly to the audience.

Ladies and Gentlemen I hope you don't consider it rude

For me to bung in here, in the midst of a serious story, what may seem a comic interlude

But I would like to pause this story that moves between fact and fiction

With a brief plug, as it were, for my skills of enunciation and diction

You will all appreciate that while a story of Indian

migration to Australia is enjoyable to tell

To survive here in Australia one needs something that is a richer sell

So I offer here my voice and speech coaching skills

Promising to make your spoken ability like lark trill

At the table on the way out you will see my visiting card

That sells a voice coach trained in mastering verses of the bard

As Hamlet says I will help you speak the language trippingly on the tongue

Making your voice ride your breath from a powerful lung

With fun exercises like playing with a tongue twister

This course is open for all for the Mrs and the Mr

So please come join my course helping my coffers grow

By learning how to use your voice from a real pro

With the business of hawking my skill over

Let us now return to the story of John and Barbara

Who is preparing for her party by bringing out the Candelabra

The scene moves to the widows party

The video shows a scene from a BBC production of Macbeth. It's the witches, a gathering of poor old white women, who are preparing a potent brew. They sense Macbeth approaching:

Witch: By the twitching of my thumbs something wicked this way comes

All the witches laugh

Macbeth: How now you secret black and midnight hags, what is it you do?

Witch: A deed without a name

The rest of the witches chant

Double, double toil and trouble;

Fire burn and caldron bubble.

Fillet of a fenny snake,

In the caldron boil and bake;

Eye of newt and toe of frog,

Wool of bat and tongue of dog,

Adder's fork and blind-worm's sting,

Lizard's leg and howlet's wing,

For a charm of powerful trouble,

Like a hell-broth boil and bubble.

All the witches cackle and laugh
Video ends.
Lights on carpet. For a brief while nothing happens.
Barbara enters. She is in a fluster, preparing all things needed for the party. Her face is covered in a black veil, a sign of her recent widowhood. She is carrying a bowl to feed Roger roo.

Barbara: Sorry, sorry, sorry I am late, the I.T guy has finally arrived, come to fix the internet. They're just so slow these Telstra guys, it's pathetic. Anyway I am happy Roger has started eating from the bowl I keep for him out here in the driveway. He has not been looking well at all. I feed him Kangaroo muesli and straw, though it's not very good to feed wild Kangaroos. Did you know that Kangaroos are matriarchal, who knows I may have been a Kangaroo matriarch in my past life. Not that I believe in all this past life nonsense but you know, that's the wonderful thing about death, nobody knows anything really and everyone is free to make up whatever they want.

Did you enjoy the video of Macbeth's witches? That excerpt was from one of John's productions. He choreographed this wonderful witches dance, I am going to perform it for everyone this evening. I better practise the routine because I am a bit rusty. All you professionals huh, keep your judgements to yourself, this is strictly amateur stuff.

Starts performing a very amateur witches dance, making the hands shiver to the rhythm of the witches chant

> Double, double toil and trouble;
> Fire burn and caldron bubble.
> Fillet of a fenny snake,
> In the caldron boil and bake;

Forgets the movement, checks herself.

> I think it went something like this from here…

Performs with an increased shiver of hands which ends in a violent tremble above the head. By the end Barbara looks possessed.

Eye of newt and toe of frog,

Wool of bat and tongue of dog,

Adder's fork and blind-worm's sting,

Lizard's leg and howlet's wing,

For a charm of powerful trouble,

Like a hell-broth boil and bubble.

With the word bubble her body seems to tremble and shake
She laughs herself out of this possession

Barbara: I think I am going to enjoy myself tonight. Finally after a week's grieving I am feeling a little wild and free, it's the party mood eh. Maybe it's been helped a little bit by John's favourite whiskey (*takes a flask out of the coat pocket and swigs from behind the veil*). I don't know if it's appropriate for a widow to swig away, but I have to do it, you know, I can't grieve forever.

She's standing under the Cockatoo tree.

I love coming here every evening to recite the mantra. Who knows, maybe if I add the witches choreography to the mantra John may just enjoy it more, wherever he is.

She dances the witches choreography and recites the mantra

Om bhoor bhuva swa

Tat savitoor varenium

Bhargodevasya dhi mahi

Dhiyo yona prachodaya sw ha

Once again she seems to be in a possessed state with her hands shivering and body trembling.
Breaks out of the state

(*laughing*) I hope that's not blasphemous or something, this whiskey is making me do things, making me drop my mask.

Takes out a perfume and starts spraying herself

You know, it's been a week, and time passes, and I am really excited about this party because you never know who you might meet, and life might just take an unexpected turn. Death does not always have to be such an anal thing, I may just meet someone nice tonight.

Barbara hears the actors rehearsing a dance sequence for the party

Did you hear that? They are rehearsing a dance sequence from Romeo and Juliet. I love it that everyone is taking it so seriously, that's John's spirit working here for sure. This is going to be such a wonderful party.

Seems to remember something, goes in search of it

I better put up this sign, you know, because everyone is going to be drinking this evening, it's a sign warning everyone that there is a Kangaroo here in the driveway, don't drink and drive.

Puts up the sign in the driveway

Well that's done. Anyway, I insist on having a lot of fun tonight

Lights fade as Barbara exits
On the screen we see a video of a group of masked white men and women all dancing and singing, rehearsing a sequence from Romeo and Juliet. All except one are wearing Venetian party masks. The exception is wearing a ghost mask with ugly teeth sticking out. He is also dancing clumsily. At first glance he is barely noticeable.
The video fades. A court announcement follows

Melbourne general sessions court. The Queen versus Telstra Mobile company. General sessions court, Melbourne, first of May 2018. The barrister at the bar Mr. Barnaby Higgenbottom please present your case.

Barnaby Higgenbottom enters, wearing a contemporary lawyers suit

Mr. Higgenbottom: My Lord and members of the Jury. The case before us today is one of Criminal Trespass. Criminal Trespass involves the transpassing of someone's private property, without proper authorisation or permission. In the case of criminal trespass before us today the trespasser is accused of trespassing a widow's party being held on her private property. The trespasser is further accused of drinking her alcohol, eating her ham sandwiches without using any mustard and singing and dancing with the members of the Mountview Theatre company.

In his defence the trespasser argues that he as an I.T worker was invited as it were to be on the property, to fix a defective internet line and connection. Seeing a party in progress, he very innocently decided to join in by wearing a mask and costume.

The trespasser is further accused this time by the female members of the party of repeatedly asking to be kissed. Which they obliged, thinking that he was one of their own. In his defence the trespasser argues that when he entered the party he heard everyone talking in a very Shakespearean language, and he being an Indian, having read Shakespeare in school decided to join in, to try and assimilate as it were, by reciting the one and only line he still remembered, a line from (*opening and reading from a diary*) The Taming of the Shrew, which went something like this COME ON AND KISS ME KATE. To his surprise he found everytime he uttered the line someone or the other obliged him with a kiss, they of course thinking that he was one of their own.

The final acquisition is made by the widow herself. At the end of the party when everyone had left, as it so happens she found herself alone with the trespasser and as it so happens she found herself receiving a very intimate shoulder massage, which she acknowledges very honestly it is to be noted, she did enjoy a lot. However when she wanted to thank the trespasser, she insisted he remove his mask. It was when she saw his face, she was horrified to discover it was not one of her friends but Nitin Sethi, the I.T worker come to fix the internet.

My lord, as evidence I have for you here a video recording of the party. You will see a masked dance sequence. After forty seconds or so, you will see the trespasser wearing a very ugly ghost mask, different to all the other venetian party masks, revealing his ignorance of wearing an appropriate mask for the occasion. You will also notice his very clumsy unrehearsed movements, showing he is not an actor at all.

As a final point of order, members of the jury, before we see the video evidence, I would like you to deliberate on this matter. After all these unsober shenanigans, this man drove his car all the way from the country back into the city. We didn't get him then, but we have him now. I leave the rest to your fair judgement.

The evidence please

On the screen we see projected once again the video of a group of masked white men and women all dancing and singing, a sequence from Romeo and Juliet. All except one are wearing Venetian party masks. The exception is wearing a ghost mask with ugly teeth sticking out. He is also dancing clumsily.

The audience as jury searches for the imposter from within this group of white men and women.

After forty seconds, he is identified.

The video ends

The light fades

It's dark and quiet

Lights on carpet

Barbara enters pulling behind her a garbage bin. It's heavy, making it a difficult exercise for Barbara. It's a long driveway to the gate of the

*estate. She walks in a circle around the carpet. She stops to address the
audience, resting her weight on the garbage bin.*

Barbara: You know I am feeling very sad. I thought I would
end this story on a happy note, but I have some bad news to
share. This morning Roger died. I hadn't seen him for a week,
I was worried someone had driven into him or knocked him
over or something. Then I went out for a walk this morning
and there he was lying on the dirt track, desperately breathing
his last. I sat down next to him, his eyes were glazed, but for a
moment they seemed to clear, and he looked at me, then they
closed and he was gone forever. You know when John had
passed away I had seen his slow decline over many months of
his illness, and of course I grieved at his passing. But to see this
ancient creature lying on that dirt track desperately breathing
his last and then just so quietly slipping away I couldn't hold
back the tears. It just broke me up, it felt so sad.

You know I feel sad about another matter, about that
I.T. boy. My heart is wracked with guilt, perhaps wracked
is overdoing it a bit but I feel terribly sorry for him. I don't
know what got into me, I was so angry, I picked up the phone
and called Mr. Higgenbottom, he is one of the oldest patrons
of the Mountview theatre company. He too was very upset
and he immediately decided to file a case on the company
for using all these Asians and Muslims, as a part of some
bumbling plan of his, some Final Solution to rid Australia
of all these unsavoury characters as he referred to them. I
don't know, I really didn't want this boy to lose his job or
worse get thrown out of the country or something. I did
try to tell Mr. Higgenbottom that I had indeed enjoyed the
massage. Do you think that will help his case? I don't know,

this is all making me so stressed, maybe I should just go for a long walk, or just lie in bed all day, I don't know. But then there are all these chores you see. You know the longer the driveway the longer it takes to get rid of garbage. I am not getting younger, you know. I tried telling John to down size but he so loved the place, he refused to leave.

This is such a chore. My back hurts.

Starts dragging the bin.

He was such a selfish bastard sometimes.

Exits
Light fades.
On the screen we see a video of a Melbourne yellow taxi cab. The camera follows the taxi as it drives through the city. A voice over has Nitin writing a letter to his mother.

Dear Mother

Sat Sri Akal and Pranam. By guru ji's blessings I finally have some good news for you. Last so many times I have called you, you have been crying continuously for my losing the job. Now you can stop. I found a very good job. It's much better than that Telstra company. It's a very smart job with Melbourne Smart Taxi Services. My work will take me all over Melbourne and in the surrounding villages also. Every day I meet many *phirangis*. It's a very important job. Now I will work hard and make you proud. Please don't be so concerned about me. Sometimes the news you hear about Australia is very sensational. There is no negative feeling here for Indians. Everyone loves India specially Bollywood films. People in Melbourne are very happy. They are like us Punjabi people also. They work hard through the week, and on the weekends they do the bhangra. So don't worry about me. I will not marry an Australian girl, I will marry only one you will choose for me.

On the video we see a looped image of an Aussie young woman walking. It's a stylised image.

As the young woman walks Punjabi dance/bhangra music plays. Nitin comes out dancing. He shows a placard that says:

If it's all white

It's not quite right

Lights fade

THE END

CAMP DARWIN

Act 1 Sc 1

A quarantine camp at Howard Springs, Darwin.

Characters

Jack Gold: A sixty five year old white British man

Raminder: a thirty five year old Indian/Punjabi man

Chris: A fifty year old white Australian man

Larry: A forty year old white Australian man

Peter: A fifty five year old Chinese Australian man

Dalip: A 30 year old Indian/ Punjabi man

The set

Upstage, at a height, is a pathway working itself across the stage exiting left to the laundry and further to the exit/entry point of the camp.

Centre stage is a pathway to a garbage bin kept down stage.

In two diagonal lines, on each side of the central pathway, are the dongas, the rooms, each with a little porch. Each porch has a work table and a chair.

Six main characters stand on the upstage pathway facing the audience. Each character is holding a trolley with luggage.

A nurse and assistant are recording their temperatures.

A Posse of Security/Cops in PPE suits stand downstage. Everyone is wearing a mask.

Cop One: Welcome home to Australia and to the Center for National Resilience in Howard Springs National Territory.

Cop two: The Center for National Resilience is a Northern Territory Government multi agency effort with NT Health as the lead agency assisted by NT Police, Department of Infrastructure, Planning and Logistics, Department of Corporate and Digital Development, the Australian Federal Police and the Australian Defence Force.

Cop three: As an arrival ritual we give you the opportunity to introduce yourselves and to offer your gratitude to these agencies that have been working hard to bring you back to Australia, back into the community, back to your homes where your loved ones have been waiting for you.

Cop four: To reassure you this is not a prison camp while introducing yourself you are free to express yourself. No consequences for anything you say.

The six shy/awkward, begin this ritual

Jack Gold: I offer my gratitude to The National Territory Police Force. I acknowledge without all that you have done, I wouldn't be standing here today. I am keenly looking forward to returning to my Caravan which waits for me in a small village of Anglewood in the goldfields region of Victoria. I am a gold prospector.(*Takes a piece out of his pocket*). Here is a nugget of gold, I keep it to show people what I do. I predict prices of gold are going to rocket sky high. My real name is Jack Dwyer but I am better known locally as Jack Gold.

Raminder Singh: Thanks mate, thanks to the Australian Federal Police. Raminder Singh here, I am taxi driver, very excellent Chef also, if you like I can cook fine Indian food for the entire camp also. Just give me a big *daegh* vessel...and see how I do Indian magic...I am returning from India after 4 years. I am looking for work, if there is any work in the camp I am happy to stay in Darwin also, otherwise I go to Sydney.

Dalip Singh: No problem, hey Planning and Logistics, thanks buddies. *Sat sri aakal* Dalip here, I drive a truck, all day all night, sometimes for 2 days and 2 nights without sleep, carrying milk from Sheparton cow to Devondale factory in Laverton for baby in China, no problem. Sorry, I don't like to speak more, much.

Peter: G'day, Department of Infrastructure Planning and Logistics. I am very grateful for this opportunity to return to my family in Melbourne. My name is Peter Xu, written as Xu but pronounced as Sheu in Chinese, Sheu not zoo, haha painful joke from my childhood. Many years ago I worked for Rivers Restoration Australia. I first came to India for a project on the holy Ganga in Benares. That's when I found my spiritual guru. He taught me yoga and the secret art of finding inner happiness. Om Shanti. I am planning to hold yoga classes on the porch, everyone is welcome to join, from their own porches of course.

Larry: Thanks Australian Defence Force. Larry's the name. Worked in the force many years ago, I know how you guys think and act. With you there, I know I am in safe hands. Can't trust these politicians though. Like all good veterans I like to live light, live on the run, I live in a car. It's parked somewhere in south Melbourne for the past 18 months while I was stuck in India. That's it, that's what I am returning to, my car.. By the way this whole thing stinks, is illegal making us pay 2,500 dollars for our stay here...I will challenge it in a court of law...where is the legislation, where is the fucking legislation? I refuse to pay a dollar! You're getting nothing out of me.

Chris:(mumbling) This is not going to be easy, its a fucking police state, not sure if I can get through this...which department is left....here goes...though I hate filling digital forms, I would like to offer my gratitude to the Department of Corporate and Digital Development. With your help I have been able to get unstuck from India where I have been stuck for the past 18 months. Three cheers for DCDD, hip hip hooray....hip hip hooray...hip hip...(*He loses steam and no one seems to respond to him.*) Oh sorry I forgot to say my name, not sure if I want to say my name, do I have to? What are my rights here?

Cop One: Thanks gentlemen for your introductions. As you can see, this is not a prison camp, you are free to think and speak your minds as long as you keep your bodies within the prescribed limits. It is your bodies that are a bio security threat, not your minds.

Cop two: Your bodies and your breath is what we have to keep in check. We take social distancing rules very seriously here. There is a 5000 dollar fine for any breach. That's a lot of money as you would know. A lot of money. Five thousand, not hundred, five thousand.

Cop three (*loud and slow*):FIVE THOUSAND AUSTRALIAN DOLLARS. SO PLEASE BE WARNED.

Cop four: Thanks Gentlemen. If today is day zero Day 1 starts tomorrow with your first RTPCR COVID TEST. If you fail the test, that is you are positive, you will be taken out of this zone and be placed in a red zone…you must stay there for another 14 days.

Cop One: To be clear, if you test positive on the first day then you are here for 15 days, if on the 7th then for 21, if on the 12th day then for 26. There was a gentleman here with us for 3 months. We had to keep moving him from block to block to protect the new residents.

Cop two: Thanks for your cooperation and remember -masks on and maintain physical distance at all times.

Cop three: We will now lead you to your rooms where you must stay for the next fourteen days.

Lights fade

ACT 1 SCENE TWO

All six characters stand in front of their dongas with their luggage trolleys. A big burly security woman in a PPE kit is checking their identities before letting them into their rooms. Cops carry guns, Security personnel don't.

Security: Please say your name and date of birth and your room number. I will confirm your room number. Then you can step on your porch. Once you do, you will not be allowed to leave your porch except to get rid of garbage and do your washing every second day. You sir, please begin. You may sit on the porch with your masks on at all times. While eating your meals you may take off your masks.

Chris: Chris Connery. Date of birth 03-10-1965. Room No C4 3D

Security: Chris Connery. Room No C4 3D

Chris steps onto the porch. This process is repeated for all.

Peter: Peter Xu. Date of Birth 04-01-1955. Room C4 3C.

Security: Peter Xu . Room C4 3C.

Larry: Larry Johnson. Date of birth 29-07-1972. Room C4 2D.

Security: Larry Johnson. Room C4 2D.

Raminder: Raminder Singh. Date of birth 22-09-1985. Room C4 2C.

Security: Raminder Singh. Room C4 2C.

Jack: Jack Gold. Date of birth 04-11-1950. Room C4 1D.

Security: Jack Gold. Room C4 1D.

Dalip: Dalip Singh. Date of birth 01-03-1988. Room C4 1C.

Security: Dalip Singh. Room C4 1C.

All the characters stand on their own porches with their luggage. Lights fade.

ACT 1 SCENE THREE

Lights are on the dongas. Chris is reading a newspaper. Larry and Jack sit on their porches.

Chris: (reading aloud) Tourism still suffering because of SLOW-MO VACCINE ROLLOUT. Australia's tourism industry is again being smashed by mass cancellations, all because of Scott Morrison's broken promise on COVID 19 vaccines. Scott Morrison said we'd be at the front of the queue for vaccines, but the reality is our vaccination rate puts us last in the developed world.

(*Looking up*)

I hate Scott Morrison. If he had his way he would have left us in India. He is a narcissist, a sociopath. He doesn't care for no one, for nothing except for what will bring him back to power. I thought I would be in India forever. It felt terrifying. I would go down to the beach each day and just play with the dogs. Healed my pain each day. Don't get me wrong, I love being in India. Always have. Even now a part of me wants to go back. But I was afraid I would never see my family. Especially Maya, my 15 year old lab. Want to see her desperately before she dies.

Larry: After the first few repatriation flights Scott Morrison stopped all flights. For seven months I was locked down in my room, I had only a small staircase to sit on. No balcony, no other space. For the first two months the neighbours were aggressive, the virus you see had been brought in by foreigners, can't blame them of course, there was so much misinformation, suspicion....they locked my room from the outside, and called the cops on me. The cops came in, checked all my papers, saw there was no issue, left me alone, told the neighbours to shut up. There was this shopkeeper who had some family in Melbourne, he would always talk enthusiastically to me, as if I knew them personally, but after the lockdown he refused to sell anything to me, would waive me away most times, or just pull down the shutter when he saw me. It became difficult to even buy spuds. Luckily I had bought a sack of rice. Just ate boiled rice for months. My time with the defence forces had toughened me up but this was testing my limits for sure.

Chris: Yeah, people were terrified of us, the women, before they would smile when they saw me, but then they changed, would bury their faces in their elbows, hide them away in their shawls. You're right, can't blame them though, it was a terrifying time for them. Their government had just locked the whole country down, without any information, everyone was terrified. All these whats app groups they came up later. The first few months there was nothing, no hope. And the virus seemed to be spreading everywhere. No vaccines, nothing.

Jack: I survived on Ivermectin. Been having a pill every week since March last year. It's the best thing against Covid. All the doctors in India have been taking it. Working in the hospitals has kept them safe. But vaccinations are better for business so it's all about vaccinations now. It's big pharma making money, that's it. I refuse to be vaccinated. They change your DNA. I have a heart condition, I am not going to take risks. Unless they force us to be vaccinated to travel. Then I suppose I will have to. Can't spend the summer months in the caravan park. Gets too hot. I need to get out desperately each year. Love being in India. Been going there since the seventies. I was lucky I met the two of you, Larry helped me book my flight, I was just so lost.

Chris: (*A little aggressively*) That doesn't make sense John. Ivermectin also costs so there is money to be made in selling it. Fact is there is no conclusive data that says it works.

Jack: There is data. All the doctors in India use it in hospitals.

Chris:(*dismissive*) That's nonsense, where did you get that fact from? From a whats app group? And this changing DNA bit is nonsense too. There are enough articles on the net to say the vaccines do no such thing.

Jack: (*mumbling*) There are lots of articles that say they do, anyway these academic articles are also paid by big pharma.

Larry: Not sure what to make of all this, all I know is there is a class action waiting to happen against this whole quarantine business...the govt can't be making money off us...if the govt wants us here to protect the community they should be willing to pay for it.

In the meantime Raminder has come out of his room.

Raminder: You guys seemed to be lucky....happily chatting in the shade...we are getting the sun on our side for most of the day, Darwin sun is hot. Seems they have put you together as protection from us coloured folks haha. You guys know each other from before?

Larry: Yes we do, we met each other on a film set in India many months ago before the lockdown, we were British officers or *goras* (winks) fighting the mutineers in a film with Kangana Ranuat as a heroine. After the lock down we connected on whats app. We asked for a south facing room when the guy from the camp called us in India, we told him we wanted to be together so they placed us here. You'll get a nice shade later in the evening. What's with these two guys, haven't seen them since they entered their rooms?

Raminder: No idea, I think this one here is into some kind of prayer and meditation. Maybe they will come out in the evening when it cools off. We should see them tomorrow morning when they come to do our Covid test.

Chris: Three tests in India and now three more here! I am fucking tired of things being poked up my orifices. Next time they come I am going to offer them this.

Bends around showing his backside
Everyone laughs nervously

Chris: It's my porch, I am free to do what I like as long as I don't cross the boundary. Of course if I fart I may just be crossing the boundary, (*playing the Cop*) "it's your body and your breath that is the security risk,"its all so fucking exhausting.

Larry: (*laughing*) Haha you're cracking me up too, it's true though, 3 tests in India and 3 tests now. Not sure if the tests in India were worth anything, they would barely touch the tongue before they pulled it out, just twirled the edge of the nostril each time and it was done. Maybe they wanted all of us to come out negative. I mean the whole flight was negative right? Not even one positive result makes me suspicious…. who knows….they were so incompetent…got my name wrong…I called them, emailed them saying I am not Harry Singh, Larry not Harry, and I can't sing for my life, threatened to sue them. They made sure they changed, and got my name right. The food in the Leela Palace was good though. On the first day I asked for extra helping. After that each meal they provided me with two trays. I lapped it all up. The rooms were also big. I must have got the emperor's room, at the end of three days I thought I could spend another fourteen in there.

Raminder: It's good to be on the porch, to talk with each other. In the hotel room it gets very lonely. I know, I've done a quarantine in the Maldives before this one. Had a very hard time, anyway see you later when the sun's gone down.

Larry: See ya mate

Chris: I am going in to watch some Olympics. We are doing good this time. Ariarne Titmus 200 metres freestyle final is coming up. She's already won a Gold. What a star! I love her (*exits*)

Jack: I hate watching Television. Prefer watching the skies, the stars. The winds are starting up. It's a south wind I predict tomorrow will be cooler. I wonder when they'll come to take our fever, it says the fever will be recorded each day. I've got my own thermometer, want to take my own reading to match with theirs.

Larry: Yes, I have my thermometer too. Take it three times a day. Have my paracetamols ready just in case. They say if you have any symptoms like fever or a sore throat they move you to the red zone.

Is there a porch with the rooms in the red zone?

Jack shrugs his shoulders looking unsure, worried.

Lights fade

ACT 1 SC 4

Lights come on the dongas.

In two brown packets the day's dinner and the next day's breakfast and lunch have been placed on each porch.

Jack opens his door and walks on to the porch.

Mick Jagger is playing from Jack's room.

He settles down to eat his dinner.

One by one all the characters come on stage and sit down to eat their dinner. Dalip is the only one missing, his packets are lying on the porch.

Lights fade

Lights come up again

One by one we see each character take his dinner bag and walk down to the garbage bin.

Lights fade as the last one returns

ACT 1 SC 5

Evening. The porches are lit by a solitary bulb.

Jack is out on the porch. Raminder sits across on his porch.

Jack: Nice cool breeze blowing in from the south eh. The moon is almost full tonight. That's Jupiter next to it. Nothing like being out in the desert and sleeping under the stars. I love photographing the planets with my handy camera. See here I can zoom in and see the craters on the moon. Little pleasures. I used to be a singer songwriter,loved the music of the Rolling Stones, Leonard Cohen, what a genius!

(*Starts singing*)

Suzzanne takes you down
To her place by the river
You can hear the boats go by you can spend the night beside her
And the sun pours down like honey...
It's nice to be here with company. I live alone in my caravan, in a caravan park, no family in Australia, my sister in London died a couple of years ago, didn't get to know until sometime early this year in India, her children didn't inform me. I am getting old, you know. Gold prospecting isn't doing too good either. I called the owner of the park, he seemed suspicious of my returning from India, said a lot of the residents were old and vulnerable, and didn't want anyone getting the virus. He said I might have to self isolate in a motel for three days followed by a test. That means I've spent four days quarantined in India with 3 tests, 14 days here with 3 tests, and then 3 days in Victoria with a final test.

All this while I've been safe with eating Ivermectin. If everyone popped in a pill we'd all be fine.

Do you want an Ivermectin, it will keep you safe from tomorrow's test?

It's a great Prophylactic.

Raminder shakes his head, refuses.(mumbles/curses) chutiya...
(spits out) propalactic...
Lights fade.

ACT 1 SC 6

Lights on Dalip's room. His food pack is still lying on his porch. It's very quiet, late at night. Sound of a night jar. Dalip steps out of the room. Picks up the food packets, sits down and starts eating.
    Lights fade.

ACT 2 SC 1

Morning. Lights fade in. A canopy of bird sounds fill the air.
Light on all the dongas.
We hear "gargling" sounds. More than one person is gargling.
A cart with 4 nurses pulls up. It's the testing team. All with PPE suits.
They go one by one banging on doors.
Jack, Raminder, Chris, Larry come out of their rooms.

Nurse: Thanks for stepping up. Sorry we had to wake you up early. We start here and have the entire plane load to cover which is 200 people. Here goes. Please say your name, date of birth and room number. We will then take the test sample. We will then ask you if you have any of the following symptoms.
    Loss of taste and/or smell
    Nasal symptoms like a common cold
    Fever
    Cough or shortness of breath
    Sore throat
    Tiredness.
    Please answer truthfully.
    (Pointing to the two who haven't shown up) What about these two?

Bangs hard on the doors again.
Just then Peter shows up.

Peter: Sorry, I was saying my morning prayers. I am ready for it *Om Namo Shivah*

The testing ritual begins. After each test the nurse changes her gloves. She pokes in deep down the throat making the process very uncomfortable. The entire sequence is done very realistically, taking its natural time.

Chris: Chris Connery. Date of birth 03-10-1965. Room No C4 3D

Nurse: Chris Connery. Room No C4 3D

Performs the test.

Nurse: Any symptoms

Chris: No. Cold as a Salmon on ice, all good.

Peter: Peter Xu. Date of Birth 04-01-1955. Room C4 3C.

Nurse: Peter Xu. Room C4 3C.

Performs the test.

Nurse: Any symptoms

Peter: All well by the grace of Shiva.

Larry: Larry Johnson. Date of birth 29-07-1972. Room C4 2D.

Nurse: Larry Johnson. Room C4 2D.

Performs the test.

Nurse: Any symptoms

Larry: No cough, no fever, no other symptoms. All good.

Raminder: Raminder Singh. Date of birth 22-09-1985. Room C4 2C.

Nurse: Raminder Singh. Room C4 2C.

Performs the test.

Nurse: Any symptoms

Raminder: All *changa*, all fit and fine dear.

Jack: Jack Gold. Date of birth 04-11-1950. Room C4 1D.

Nurse: Jack Gold. Room C4 1D.

Performs the test.

Nurse: Any symptoms

Jack: Still as pure as gold, not a trace of dirt.

The nurse steps up to Dalip's door again. And bangs hard then steps back. A very sleepy Dalip steps out.

Dalip: Very sorry, once I sleep I just sleep, can't wake up.

Dalip: Dalip Singh. Date of birth 01-03-1988. Room C4 1C.

Nurse: Dalip Singh. Room C4 1C.

Performs the test.

Nurse: Any symptoms

Dalip: No no, just sleepy, all normal, thanks.

Much bonhomie and relief.

Nurse: We will have the results tomorrow. If anyone is positive we will land up and move them to the red zone. Any close contact will also be moved. So, If you don't see us again that's good news for you. Enjoy yourselves, just follow all the rules. Fever check from tomorrow morning, every day.

All six characters stand on the porch and watch the testing team walk away.

Jack: It's washing day. Let's go guys. One walk for washing clothes, another for drying them.

Chris: And if you split the load you can get four walks...beat the system, beat the system to its death.

Chris is happy, he plays an imaginary set of drums as he sings 'beat the system'

A very percussive Indian music plays from Ramindar's room.

Everyone takes a load for washing walking down the pathway up stage. It turns into a dance, a celebration. Those on the porch are dancing too.

Dalip is the only one missing.

As things quieten Peter takes over;

Peter: Hello friends I would like to introduce you to some yogic asanas. If you like you can join. I will put on some healing flute music to help with releasing the stress.

Raminder, John, Chris, Larry all follow Peter in a Yoga sequence.
A soothing flute plays over him.
Lights fade.

ACT 2 SC 2

Evening. Bulb light on porch.
Raminder is sitting on his porch. Jack sits on the opposite side.

Raminder: Mr. Jack I am sorry to say but vaccinations are our only hope. I should know, I had Covid. It's a terrible disease. I would cough so hard my head would start aching, alone in my room I had no choice but to bang my head against the wall to dull the pain. I thought I would die there. Would never get out. Never see my wife and child again, my parents, my father who has paralysis. Who I nursed back to some health, he can now at least sit up on his bed, eat his food himself, and get to the toilet with some help.

I am an Australian citizen, I was living in Sydney with my brother. I drove a taxi for many years in Melbourne, then my brother and I started a restaurant, The Grand Indian Chook House. I was the chief chef. Made all kinds of great Indian chicken curries, my butter chicken was so famous, people would drive 400 kilometres to have it. Great success. Then my father fell ill in India. Paralysis, his entire left side, was totally bedridden. My sister is married and lives in Italy. Mother was alone. I had to go back. My father had spent his entire life savings sending my brother and I to Australia. I owed him that. Couldn't bear thinking of him suffering. I went back and with my own hands nursed him back to health. I would give his entire body an oil massage everyday. The doctors had given up but I refused to. No one knows this but I also gave him some opium, every day for many months, slowly he started getting some movement, strength back. It's true, I started eating opium myself. Lots of friends in Punjab do that. It's easily available. I used to hide my ball of opium in the cupboard. One day my mother saw a trail of ants leading to my cupboard. She discovered the opium, and made me promise to give up. Then she decided it was because I was not married that all this was happening. She took it upon herself to find a girl for me. Don't get me wrong. In college I was known as Krishna, all I had to do was play the flute and many girls were falling in love with me. I had many relationships in Sydney and Melbourne. Indian girls, if they see you have an Australian passport, it's very easy to get them. I had many affairs. But I agreed to get married by my mother's choice. She was right. I have a nice wife. She asks for nothing, a very simple lady. Helped me take care of my father. After one year I had a son. Then the family started pressuring me to go back to Australia, 'think of your son's future,' they said. When I finally decided to go, Coronavirus began. All flights stopped. Then my brother found a travel agent who suggested I come by the Maldive route. In my guts I did not want to leave, but my brother, parents, even my wife said, go. I caught the flight to Maldives, landed at 12 noon, 2 pm we had a Covid test, that night they informed me I had Covid. The Police came in the middle of the night, isolated me in the hotel itself, and the next day they moved me to a hotel dedicated to Covid. I did not have a fever for the first two days, then the fever started in the evening and by night I had a very high fever, with cough and headache. They then moved me to a Covid Hospital 'The Indira Gandhi Covid Center for Healing.' There my symptoms became worse. I thought I will die here. Never be able to get out. I begged the doctors, I don't know what got into me how I could behave like that, but I was very alone and frightened, I went down on my knees and screamed I would pay any price, 5 lacs 10 lacs, I even held their feet shouting begging just put me on a plane back to India. I just wanted to die in India, not in Maldives. I was shaking crying god why are you doing this to me. The doctors were kind, they calmed me, assured me I would be ok. It was very difficult to believe them. I decided that I will not carry on to Australia even if I got better. Even though my ticket had cost 1.8 lacs. I would go back. I was so tense. My travel agent said wait for the result once you are negative the next day itself I will book you a ticket to India. That's what happened. I got my result on 14th day morning 9 am, by 2pm, I was on a flight. Since getting back I have slowly recovered strength. I still didn't want to leave India. Was very afraid. My family then gave me courage, said god has been on my side, I should not lose hope. So I registered with DFAT. My wife is having second baby any day now but I was lucky to get the 25th July flight so I decided to leave.

Don't mind me but I don't like your Ivermectin idea. It's a terrible illness. I have gone through it. I know. Vaccinations are our only hope.

Jack doesn't say anything.
Lights fade.

ACT 2 SC 3

Night. Moon, stars.
Some of the doors are open.
TV sounds from inside the rooms.
TV's are switched off.
Doors close.
Light on Dongas fades.

Act 3 Sc 1

Morning light. Bird sounds.
Loud banging on doors. One after the other the characters emerge. The nurse is holding a hand held 'gun' thermometer.
She is a joyous character. Like a little happy sunbird.

Nurse: Good morning it is fever testing time. Wake and shine.

Please say your name and date of birth and room number.

One by one all characters say their name and date of birth and room number.

Chris: Chris Connery. Date of birth 03-10-1965. Room No C4 3D

Peter: Peter Xu. Date of Birth 04-01-1955. Room C4 3C.

Larry: Larry Johnson. Date of birth 29-07-1972. Room C4 2D.

Raminder: Raminder Singh. Date of birth 22-09-1985. Room C4 2C.

Jack: Jack Gold. Date of birth 04-11-1950. Room C4 1D.

Dalip: Dalip Singh. Date of birth 01-03-1988. Room C4 1C.

Security: Dalip Singh. Room C4 1C.

She puts a gun to everyone's forehead, says the temp to her assistant who notes it down.
She asks for any symptoms.
Chris has the lowest temperature.

Jack: It was 36.5 on my thermometer and 36.4 on yours. So mine is pretty close.

Larry: What kind of range are you looking at?

Nurse: Anything between 36 and 37 we treat as normal.

Nurse leaves

Chris: My temp was 36.0. I woke up early and stood before the air con for ten minutes. Tomorrow I will stand for 5 minutes. Don't want it to go below 36 and get myself into trouble.

Peter asks: Yoga anyone.

> *Everyone mumbles no we are all right mate*
> *Raminder comes out of his room*

Raminder: Hey guys I've got some good news. I've had another baby, a girl this time. My family's complete. Spoke to my wife just now, she's in good health. I feel I am being blessed with a new life and hope for the future. All will be well guys.

> *Much celebration and joy around.*
> *On the upstage pathway 4 Cops come and stand. They watch the celebration looking very ominous.*

Cop One: Gentlemen. We have some news for you. Until further orders no one is to use the laundry.

Cope two: No more walking up and down this ramp till we tell you it's ok to. Just to let you know, there are five positive results from your flight. That means we are moving the 5 covid positives to the red zone.

Cop 3: Till they are resettled into the red zone no stepping off your porches. No going to the laundry. Please wear your masks at all times on the porch.

Cop 4: Just to remind you there is a $5000 fine for any infringement. We will apply the law rigorously regardless. Best of all, you comply.

The characters watch stunned from their porches.
The Cops leave.

Jack: Where were these guys seated in the plane?

Larry: No idea. What a disaster.

Chris: Fuck, we're doomed

Lights fade.

ACT 3 SC 2
Light on all the dongas. All except Dalip sit on their respective porches.
They are quite stressed, agitated. Jack is eating his lunch. Everyone else
is sipping tea or coffee. Their masks are lowered framing their chins.

Jack: I am not worried. I've been having Ivermectin every day since we quarantined. I am sure it's going to protect me. In the flight, with my bladder issues, I had to keep going to the toilet for a piss. I could've easily crossed the positive ones. If they told us where this group was seated we'd all be more relaxed. Hell the plane is the worst place to have to share space with Covid positives. That's even worse than hotel quarantine. There at least your room air gets to escape when the room door is opened. Though if the Covid is floating around the corridor you can get into trouble.

Larry: Yeah, the guards at the Leela Palace had no gloves when they accompanied the meals. What was the point of locking us up in the hotel for three days and then herding us in the aeroplane? I mean there were 150 passengers with no social distance. There was this family behind with a child coughing throughout. I was like, somebody stuff something down the child's throat. If it was them I may be in trouble, I was just a row away. But then it could be anyone in the flight. Why don't they tell us who it was and where they were seated?

Peter: I have this mantra my spiritual guru gave me. It is like a shield, it protects me from all dangers. I have to repeat it more than a thousand times. It's my practice. If anyone would like, I am happy to teach you. It will protect you. You don't have to worry. The mantra will take care of everything. That is why I have been in India for the past nine months but Covid is far away. Of course if you have no faith then it will not work. It's not like you are a parrot, just repeating.

Raminder: I will be happy to learn. It's now been four months since my COVID. My doctor said I am protected for six months, that is why I don't need to take vaccinations. I am protected but still will be happy to do the mantra. You know when I first saw you and you said you worked on the river Ganga, I thought you were the famous Japanese spy who had come to Banares to poison the water system. Did you hear of that story? It was many years ago.

Peter: Haha yes when I first came to Banares, people used to suspect me to be that Japanese man. He is very famous. Then I had to tell them I was not Japanese but Chinese. This time it was the opposite, initially when Covid struck people we were very afraid of me, I had to carry my passport everywhere, show them I was not Chinese but Australian. This Covid has made us all behave in strange ways. The real disease now is anxiety. Like the stress of these 5 positive cases.

Chris: (very angry) 5 Covid cases in the enclosed space of a flight. It's not good ole Alfa, it's bloody Delta Delta Delta….it's going to spread like wildfire. Something was telling me I was safer in India despite all the cases all around. I mean I stayed covid free for months and months. I was being forced to come to Delhi to quarantine in the hotel. From Hyderabad to Delhi is a two day train journey. The man sleeping opposite me in the 3 tier train had a terrible cough. I thought I was done for. When I arrived in Delhi, even before I got into the hotel I took a Covid test. Thank god it was negative. Then with the three negative tests in the hotel I thought finally I am now in Australia, I am safe. I will spend these 14 days and get back to see my Maya. Of course Scot Morrison screwed the vaccination program. Trusting Astrazeneca, not ordering enough, making a mess. So even when we get out it's months before we are vaccinated. Now that the U.K is celebrating freedom day they seem to have got into action. It's too bloody late and we are suffering. I don't recognize this country anymore, I want to get out even now, I want to go back to India, I love it there, it's just my parents and Maya. I am suffering, suffering great stress.

Jack: I don't trust these vaccines. The blood clots are just the surface of the problem. It's all too rushed. There has not been enough time to do all the trials in a proper scientific manner, its big money driving it all, its mega trials we are all being put through and I refuse to be a trial rat. On the other hand there is Ivermectin. It's safe and well tested, it's been in the market for years, doctors in India have been using it, it's a great Prophylactic. I am happy to share my medicine with you.

Chris: (*explodes*)...No ...please please stop this Ivermectin versus Vaccination debate. I am sick and tired of it all. You keep on banging on about Ivermectin, we have had enough arguments about Big Pharma and small Pharma and little Pharma. Please please please just shut down this Ivermectin business. I have had enough, I have had more than enough. Please...

Jack: (*very angry*) That's censorship. That's what you liberals do. Shut down conversations, stop people from thinking because you think you have all the ideas. Well I am not going to be shut down. I won't be bullied by you into accepting something that I feel strongly about, that does not work for me. You have no right to stop me from expressing my position. I believe this whole vaccination thing is a hoax. I have strong evidential experience that Ivermectin is working. I will not shut up talking about it. If you find it hard to listen, why don't you just go take a walk?!!!

Chris: (*exploding*) Go take a walk where to? The only walk I can take is to the garbage bin. You call that a walk!

Raminder:(*laughing*) Mr. Jack, that's the problem, Chris can't go take a walk, not even to the laundry now. He is also saying please...when a friend says please...we have to listen.(*aside to Peter*). They are behaving like my customers do on Friday and Saturday Nights. Fight like dogs in the backseat of my cars. Luckily we have no alcohol here. Otherwise we would see their inner demons coming out. Please do some mantra on them before we all get into trouble.

Peter:(*placating*) Friends, these are difficult times, we all need to destress, that's why there is Yoga, if you want I can hold a special session right now. Also, Mr. Chris, I have *ashwagandha* medicine perfect for mental balance. See I will play this healing flute, it will help the nerves settle down.

Peter plays the flute and everyone gets back to sipping their teas and coffees. Jack is eating his lunch. All their masks are off.
The four Cops return this time on the centre stage ramp.

Cop One: Gentlemen, your masks are off, that's breaking the rules! This is not amusing for us. You realise we get tested every day, every single day to protect you and the community. We need you to show the same commitment.

Cop Two: We will now demonstrate how the masks are to be worn. This is the first warning. We will be checking on you, if we find you breaking the rules we will issue you a second warning. The third time we will fine you $5000. Please let me repeat the fine will be $5000.

Cop Three: Please observe the mask wearing rule. While

you are drinking a coffee or tea, you can take a sip, but then immediately your mask must be back on. Mask off, take a sip, Mask back on. Mask off, take a sip, Mask back on. Of course if you are eating a meal (*pointing to Jack*) it's alright to take your mask off. We would appreciate it if you could all demonstrate the rule to us.

Cop Four: Mask off, sip, Mask back on.

> Mask off, sip, Mask back on.
> Mask off sip, Mask back on.
> *Everyone repeats under instruction*

Cops: G' day Gentlemen. We will be back.

> *Everyone sits back a little shell shocked.*

Chris: Its a fucking Police state. I hate it.

> *Lights fade.*

ACT 3 SC 3

Hey the Cops are coming! Is the theme of a game played out by the characters. The next set of scenes is like a collage.
Lights come on the Dongas. Everyone is sitting around with their masks on their chins. Then Chris on the extreme downstage porch whispers " The Cops are coming"
The Cops march past on the upper pathway, eyeing the characters suspiciously.

This transforms into a theatrical piece with music and marching, almost a kind of dance.
The Cops enter and exit in all kinds of creative ways.
The characters tense and mask up vigorously each time, then visually relax once the Cops have passed.

INTERVAL

ACT 4 SC 1

Lights on Jack sitting on the porch singing a song. Raminder sits listening.

Oh my darling, oh my darling
Oh my darling, Clementine
You were lost and gone forever
Dreadful sorrow, Clementine
In a cavern, in a canyon
Excavating for a mine
Dwelt a miner forty-niner
And his daughter, Clementine
Yes I loved her, how I loved her
Though her shoes were number nine
Herring boxes, without topses
Sandals were for Clementine
Oh my darling, oh my darling
Oh my darling, Clementine
You were lost and gone forever
Dreadful sorrow, Clementine
Drove the horses to the water

Jack: (*a little embarrassed*) It's a little old fashioned this, even for me, but reminds me of my first sweetheart, I was only sixteen then. Been married three times since. Last one lasted thirteen years. She was constantly trying some self improvement therapy on me, relentlessly, I finally told her I was fine, needed no improvement, healing nothing. Just peace. Man, women are difficult (*pause*). Maybe I was the problem each time my marriage failed...who knows...

Raminder: I like your singing. Very nice. You should try driving a taxi. Then you will have lots of time waiting for customers, you can really enjoy your own singing. I love singing, have you heard of Gurdas Mann...wonderful singer...

Sings a punjabi song.
Larry, Peter listen from their porches.
Everyone applauds.

Larry: I haven't seen the cops all day today. Maybe all our Day 7 tests have come out positive. We are safe.

Peter: (*angry*) If we are negative I can't understand why they cannot just send us a mail each time they test us. It is not rocket science. A simple software program and every time you test you get your result by email. Why are they holding back our results? Of course we will know if someone is positive because the entire medical team and the security staff will land up. Only you have to keep waiting for them to land up, and after all the tension when they don't, then you are safe.

Chris: It's how the Police state works mate, it's a system of surveillance and control. What is required for control is worked on in great detail, but individual liberty is repressed. Remember we were a Penal colony not too long ago. We are good at creating Prison systems. The camp is successful precisely because it builds off the prison model. Of course if the virus is kept out of the community the project is a success. It does not matter to them at what cost it was achieved. What it has done to our minds, to our beings, how broken so many of us are?

Larry: It's true mate. It's when you see the system working from the outside, like we have from India, waiting there desperately, day after day with no hope, that you realise how skewed the system is. This is our country, yours, mine, all us citizens, not these Politicians. We need to take our power back, our country back. I am not paying for this. They can't use these National Emergency Powers to impose anything on us. There is no legislation for all this. It's not going to hold up in court.

Chris: It's all because of Scot Morrison, he restarted the repatriation flights only when he felt his voter base was threatened. There is no humanity. He's a disaster especially for the Liberal party, they will lose the next election. He's going to be stabbed in the back very soon.

Jack: I prefer Peter Dutton. At least there you see what you get. Not all this glib stuff. He's a Cop at heart, at least we will know where he stands.

Chris: Christ Jack, we can't seem to see anything eye to eye. I promise you if Dutton becomes PM I will kill myself, I promise you I will kill myself.

Jack: There goes the wounded liberal not letting me speak again. I should just shut up, is what he wants. Well I am not going to.

Larry: (*sensing the tension is about to explode again*) Hey guys, on another note, today we are at the halfway mark. As children whenever we went for a holiday, at the halfway point my father would burst into a song...
     The bear went over the mountain
     The bear went over the mountain
     And guess what he saw
     And guess what he saw
     The other side of the mountain
     The other side of the mountain

Larry: We're past the halfway mark folks...just another 7 to go and we will be home.

     Everyone laughs, joins in the singing.
     The bear went over the mountain
     The bear went over the mountain
     And guess what he saw
     And guess what he saw
     The other side of the mountain
     The other side of the mountain

Larry: (*pointing to Dalip*) I really hope he is ok mate, he just never comes out.

Raminder: Nah, he's alright, I think he just sleeps, all the time.

Peter: He is *kumbhakarna*, from the Ramayana. Sleeps for six months and drives a truck for the other six.

Raminder: Haha you are a real *gyani* Mr. Peter. You know our *shastras* better than we do. Hey I got a message on my whats app group, we can use the laundry again. Time to go walking friends.

Chris (*does a little John Travolta dance*): You can tell by the way I walk I am a woman's man no time to talk...ah ah ah ah... stayin alive....

> *Everyone laughs.*
> *Lets go mates, time to do the Laundry walk*
> *Lights fade.*

ACT 4 SC 2

Laundry walk.
One by one the characters dance their way to the laundry. First taking loads to wash, then to dry and then to bring the clothes back.
A fun filled collage with music.

ACT 4 SC 3

Early morning.
Jack sits alone in the dark.
Very slowly, the light changes
Very slowly, one by one bird sounds fill the air.

Jack: I love waking up early, seeing the light change, hearing the birds come alive. It's my caravan habit. It's getting cold now. I needed a beanie this morning, and a sweater. I had a strange dream last night. In it all six of us were birds, I mean each a different bird. We were like sitting on branches, on trees, and we were singing, calling out to each other, but here's the complication, we were all stuck to the branch we were sitting on, we had forgotten how to fly, we were flapping our wings, desperately.

While he is talking the other characters walk onto the upstage pathway. Their silhouettes fill up the back screen. Jack joins them. Each is a specific bird making its own sound. The birds seem to be shaking, shivering, twisting and turning with an internal desperation to fly. It is both beautiful and agonising this creation of sound and body image.

ACT 4 SC 4

Early morning.
Jack sits alone in the dark.
Very slowly, the light changes
Very slowly, one by one bird sounds fill the air.
Raminder sits on the porch.

Jack: Tomorrow and tomorrow and tomorrow
  Creeps in this petty pace from day to day
  To the last syllable of recorded time
  And all our yesterdays have lighted fools the way to dusty death…

Raminder: It's a nice song, you are writing this, what's its meaning?

Jack: No, it's from a play, by a..er... famous playwright from Britain. Its saying life moves from one day to the next and then to the next, like our days are moving here, one day at a time, all the way to our final day, the day we die.

Raminder: That's great philosophy. You're a Pommie mate?

Jack: haha Yes I am British. I hold both British and Australian passports, get two pensions, British and Australian. Gives me enough to do my gallivanting. Though I am getting tired now. Want to buy a house. Will need to sell my gold. Am waiting for the price of gold shares to rise, which they will, then I will cash out. You should invest in gold. The dollar is going to crash and then the price of gold will shoot up.

Raminder: haha I have to earn and save money before I think of investing. I've never been on welfare, on Center link. Believe in hard work and earning my way. Didn't leave all my family, my country to be on welfare here. But for old age pensioners Australia is good, right?

Jack: yes, it's alright, helps you get by

Chris: (*barges in*) Hey guys great news India beat Australia 1-0. Women's hockey. Fantastic game. The Indian team played so intensely, right throughout the game. Three cheers for women's hockey hip hip hooray, hip hip hooray, hip hip hooray. Indian women, you are our hope for our future, for the future of the human race.

Raminder joins in with a hoorah
Peter and Larry have also come out on the porch and celebrated.
Chris goes back inside the room.

Jack: He is very excitable isn't he, quite unstable. We already have a Kamala destroying the White House, not sure if we need more of them around. Biden is such a weak President. Once he is dead Chris's prediction may just come true. We are doomed then.

Peter: I love Chris because like me he loves India so much. He is a good man at heart. Must also be excited now that we are all close to heading home. Tomorrow is the final test, the day after the results and then the next day we are free. By the way have you seen the mail from tele well being. We have to apply for an interstate travel permit. The numbers are rising in NSW. Has anyone applied for the permit?

Larry: I have applied for the permit for Victoria. It wasn't very complicated. Each state has a different permit. I can do it for you Jack, if you'd like me to.

Jack: Thanks Larry. You're a great help, wouldn't know what I would have done without your help. All these forms are just too complicated for me.

Raminder: Do we also have to do a Covid test once we return to our state? I got a message on whats app that we have to do a test on the 17th day.

Larry: Really? Why? We are going from a Green zone. Do they suspect we will catch it on the flight? There are no cases here in NT. I will check the legislation on this. This is all getting so arbitrary. Every state with its own rules and regulations is driving me crazy.

Just then a loud banging sound is heard coming in from Chris's room. He seems to be banging his head against the Donga wall. An anguished cry followed by more head banging follows.

Stunned, everyone waits, watches in silence. The banging continues, and is quite frightening.

Then Raminder breaks the rule, walks off his porch and approaches Chris's porch.

Raminder: (*calling out*) Mr. Chris. Mr. Chris are you all right? Mr. Chris I can come in and help you. What's happened? Are you ok Mr. Chris?

After a long silence Chris steps out of the room. His face looks anguished, desperate.

Chris:(*hysterical*) I can't cope with these digital forms any more (*screams*) I've fucking had enough. From the DRO forms in India to now this ...I am trying to fill the inter state travel form to WA, I have filled all the details, ticked all the boxes, but the fucking system rejects my application each time saying I will need to quarantine for 14 days in a hotel. I mean I am coming from a fucking camp in Darwin, I've quarantined for 14 days but the system wants me to quarantine in a hotel for another 14 days. There is no one to talk to about this, no human voice, it's all so mechanical, robotic. I've had it mate, I am done.

Everyone's a little relieved the issue is not more dramatic.

Raminder: (*empathetically*). Yes I know, these forms can make you crazy mate, but no worries there must be some confusion, I will call tele well being and ask them what the problem is. You just take it easy, we still have three more days to go. Maybe you are exhausted today, you could try filling in the form tomorrow. Sometimes if we just let the problem breathe, we can come back to it refreshed.

Chris: (*childlike*): But I so want to go home. I am so desperate to get to see my Maya, my sister called, said she was not doing well and that I should be prepared for the worst. I just panicked and decided to complete all forms and procedures. You're right though..maybe I should just let it be, I can wait to do this tomorrow. It's just I am so missing my Maya.

Chris goes back into his room. Raminder walks back to his porch.

Larry: Well done mate, sometimes you just have to break the law. Luckily there are no cameras here. And we promise not to dob you in.

Raminder does a namaste in thanks.
Jack has been watching the drama unfold, a little cynically.

Jack: Missing my Maya! What a drama queen.

Larry: It's been tough Jack. Tough for all of us. Sometimes you can deal with all the big stuff, but then the little things end up breaking you. It's not been easy for no one. Not for you, not for me, and especially not for Chris. He is a sensitive one.

Jack: (*muttering*) Well I am sensitive too but I know how to reign in my nerves. Bloody pretentious liberal.

Just then another head banging and anguished sound follows.
Chris walks out of the room. He looks like death.

Chris: My sister called again, said Maya had an infection, was dying, and was in terrible pain. The family were waiting for me to return but then had to make a decision. They called in a farmer who just shot her. It was a liberation for Maya, my sister says.

They couldn't wait another 3 days.

He is heartbroken. Breaks down crying.
Everyone stands watching, awkward in silence.
Lights fade.

ACT 5 SC 1

Morning. Lights fade in. A canopy of bird sounds fill the air.
Light on all the dongas.
We hear "gargling" sounds. More than one person is gargling.
A cart with 4 nurses pulls up. It's the testing team. All with PPE suits.

They go one by one banging on doors.
Jack, Raminder, Larry and Chris come out of their rooms.

Nurse: Thanks for stepping up. You all know the routine by now. This is your final test. Here goes. Please say your name, date of birth and room number. We will then take the test sample. We will then ask you if you have any of the following symptoms.

    Loss of taste and/or smell
    Nasal symptoms like a common cold
    Fever
    Cough or shortness of breath
    Sore throat
    Tiredness.
    Please answer truthfully.

(Pointing to the two who haven't shown up) What about these two?
Bangs hard on the doors again.
Just then Peter shows up.

Peter: Sorry was saying my morning prayers….I am ready for it….Om Shivah Namah

The entire ritual as described previously begins.

Chris: Chris Connery. Date of birth 03-10-1965. Room No C4 3D

Nurse: Chris Connery. Room No C4 3D

Performs the test.

Nurse: Any symptoms

Chris: No. Cold as a Salmon on ice, all good.

Peter: Peter Xu. Date of Birth 04-01-1955. Room C4 3C.

Nurse: Peter Xu. Room C4 3C.

Performs the test.

Nurse: Any symptoms

Peter: All well by the grace of guru ji.

Larry: Larry Johnson. Date of birth 29-07-1972. Room C4 2D.

Nurse: Larry Johnson. Room C4 2D.

Performs the test.

Nurse: Any symptoms

Larry: No cough, no fever, no other symptoms. All good.

Raminder: Raminder Singh. Date of birth 22-09-1985. Room C4 2C.

Nurse: Raminder Singh. Room C4 2C.

Performs the test.

Nurse: Any symptoms

Raminder: All *changa*, all fit and fine dear.

Jack: Jack Gold. Date of birth 04-11-1950. Room C4 1D.

Nurse: Jack Gold. Room C4 1D.

Performs the test.

Nurse: Any symptoms

Jack: Still as pure as gold, not a trace of dirt.

The nurse steps up to Dalip's door again. And bangs hard then steps back. A very sleepy Dalip steps out.

Dalip: Very sorry, once I sleep I just sleep, can't wake up.

Dalip: Dalip Singh. Date of birth 01-03-1988. Room C4 1C.

Nurse: Dalip Singh. Room C4 1C.

Performs the test.

Nurse: Any symptoms

Dalip shakes his head saying nothing.
Much bonhomie and relief.

Nurse: We will have the results tomorrow. Fingers crossed all of you are clear, else it's another 14 days quarantine I am afraid. Enjoy yourselves, just follow all the rules for your last days here.

All six characters stand on the porch and watch the testing team walk away.

ACT 5 SC 2

Raminder, Chris, Jack, Larry and Peter are sitting on the porch eating their lunch.
Loud Bollywood music plays from another block.

Raminder: Farewell party has begun in the next block. Everyone is feeling happy to finally go home. My two nieces have baked a cake for me. I am really excited to see them after four years. They were two and four when I left them. Now they are like two little ladies wanting to serve me tea and cakes. My brother told them why are you making this fancy cake, make butter chicken then Chacha will be happy. Haha it's true my brother knows what I like. Butter chicken with some beer. Staying dry in quarantine has not been easy.

Peter: My grandson and granddaughter are also so happy. We all stay together, my wife, my son and daughter in law, my grandchildren. Now with everyone working from home it will be interesting.

Larry: I plan to get my car and then head up the coast. I have family in Queensland, and will look them up before I plan my next phase. I am also joining a class action against this whole fucking quarantine business. I am not going to pay up. I will tear up the invoice when they send it. Just fucking delete it.

Jack: I called my friend John, he is an artist, very successful, his works sell for thousands of dollars, but he talks with this very working class accent (*imitates a working class accent*). He sounded very nervous about my coming back, poor bugger. I suppose I will have to stay locked up in the motel room. Not looking forward to that. In fact I am not looking forward to going back. I really have no friends there. This is all quite nice here actually, could happily carry on for another fourteen days. My caravan is parked in a paddock. Will have to see what condition it is in. I've asked the owner to tow it back to my spot. Will have to get the heating going. Gets quite cold there, in Victoria at this time. Weather here has been perfect. Will miss you guys.

(Starts singing)

Say good bye my own true lover
This will be our last goodbye
For the Carnival is over
We may never meet again

As he is finishing his song Dalip steps out onto his porch.

Dalip: Hey guys, anyone got medicine for a headache. My head is hurting so bad I want to bang it against the wall.

All watch, not saying a word. A sense of dread spreads amongst them.

ACT 5 SC 3

Light comes on all the porches. Everyone is in their rooms.
For a while nothing happens.
Then, as if on cue, the place is surrounded by PPE KITS.
The four Cops are on the upper ramp.
The medical team is on the lower rank.
Security too has joined this operation.
A cop walks up to Dalip's room and starts banging.
After a while Dalip comes out and looks at the Cop in horror.

Cop: Gentleman, I regret to inform you that your test has come positive. We will have to move you to the positive zone. You have 5 minutes to pack all your stuff. Then you will leave with us. Our staff will sanitise and move your luggage to the new location. We request this is done respectfully and with no resistance.

Dalip (*in shock*): How can this be? How can you do this to me? How can I be positive after 5 tests? Please I beg you, please take another test, I am sure there has been a mistake. Please I beg you I cannot do fourteen more days. I will die. I will go mad. (*He falls down on his knees*). Please God what crime have I committed that you are doing this to me. Please put me on a plane back to India. I will pay whatever money you want. I don't want to go to Australia. I will go back. You cannot do this to me. I have no one here. I am totally alone. I promise I will do whatever you say.

Please show some mercy.

He collapses onto the floor.
Raminder, Peter, Larry, Jack and Chris are all watching this scene
from the porch.
Lights out.

ACT 5 SC 4

Dalip is being carried in a stretcher, across the upper ramp. The entire
posse accompany him. It's like a funeral march. His luggage is brought
behind on a trolley.
All the characters watch standing on their porches with their trolleys.
Then one by one each character leaves, walking the pathway.
Lights slowly fade.

END

THE HOUSE OF A GREAT VICTORIAN PLAYWRIGHT

Characters

Hari Gunasekhra a 35 year old South Asian playwright and performer

Brandon Smith a 65 year old Australian male of Anglo Saxon origin

Arthur Hall a 54 year old male of Anglo Saxon origin

Margaret Smith an 85 year old mother of Mr. Smith

Set

The inside of a two storey Victorian Cottage

On the back wall is framed the sentence: The House of a Great Victorian Playwright

Below it is a large canvas painting of a statue of Queen Elizabeth seated on a park bench.

Through the centre of the house runs a wooden staircase

On the first floor is 'Mother's' room and the guest room, one on each side of the staircase.

On the ground floor live Mr. Brandon Smith and his married partner Mr. Arthur Hall

The ground floor is occupied by Mr. Smith's studio, a clutter with all things artistic. Musical instruments, costumes, props. A number of old/ used bathtubs litter the space. They are painted to look like ships.

Stage left is a writer's desk and 'library'

Stage right is the main entrance to the house

Upstage are doors that lead to the kitchen, bedroom, toilet/ bathroom.

ACT 1 SC 1

Stage is dark.
Music
Lights come on, we see the inside of a two story Victorian cottage
Brandon receives Hari at the entrance door. Hari Gunasekara enters with his travel bag. He is wearing a hoodie. You can barely see his face. He is hunched over like a gangsta.

Brandon:(*pompous and expansive*) Welcome to your Art residency Mr. Guna…sek…h..ara (*stumbling on the name*). It's such a pleasure to finally see you. I loved your production of er….

Hari: *Hanuman in Lanka*

Brandon: Exactly, and now I am really excited about our collaboration titled…

Hari: *Mahabharata* in *Gondwanaland.*

Brandon: Thank you, I always stumble on the Maha...bha... rata...It is indeed a long word. As a formal introduction I am Brandon Smith as you may have guessed, and this fine specimen of a human is my partner Arthur Hall. Your studio is ready for you, there on the first floor. Before we lock you away in your cell, and throw away the keys for the term of your sentence, turning you from a (*speaks with a broad accent*) 'mate into an inmate' (*laughs*), it would be nice to have a chat about the project. Please be seated.

Arthur, may I trouble you to please bring us two Coffees, if that's alright by you Mr. Gun..ase...khara or should I call you Harry?

Hari: (*mumbles*) Its Hari sounded with an ee as in Coffee, but written with an I and not a y as in Harry. Yes, Coffee's fine.

Brandon: He likes his Coffee... that's my friend Hari, don't worry, be happy. I could also use h..u...r...r...y, there's no hurry for Hari to drink his coffee...that should make it sink in for good. I always use a little ditty to remember things. Works wonders each time.

Now, I would like to tell you a little about myself, so you have some idea about the artist you will be collaborating with and this house you will be working in.

Hari's gaze has drifted towards the sign on the back wall that reads 'The House of a Great Victorian Playwright.'

Brandon: Please ignore that sign. Well, that self declaration is indeed a little embarrassing, very un Australian. I put that sign up to remind Arthur about my needs, you see Mr. Gunasekara, Arthur is a very practical man, and practical men can't appreciate the needs of men like us. I imagine you too like me, when you put your head down and write, forget this world, go into another world, more spacious, more cerebral, more beautiful and more kind. Arthur's world is full of chores. He is constantly cleaning something. The floors, the clothes, my Ute. (*whispers*) If he could, he would even clean my bank account haha. By the way the word Victorian here, is not suggesting a period of history as in Edwardian or Elizabethan …but instead…the state of Victoria…in which our little village of Star Dale lies. I may be getting old but I am not that old I assure you haha.

Hari (*mumbles*): …I..had gathered that…Victoria the education state.

Brandon (*on a roll*): Exactly, and now, I suspect your eyes have drifted to this beautiful painting of the statue of the seated monarch. The actual statue was sculpted by my grandfather and is there in our botanical garden. I busk there every evening playing the violin. This was painted recently by a local artist. By the way my father too was an artist, a musician, and played the saxophone.

Hari says very matter of factly

Hari: My father was a soldier, a warrior, a tiger…he was part of a….

Brandon doesn't seem to get it.

Brandon: Ah, the tiger is my favourite animal, Mr. Gunasekhara. The Bengal tiger. He is such a handsome fellow. Majestic.

Tiger Tiger burning bright

In the forest of the night

In what distant deep or skies

Burnt the fire of thine eyes

William Blake one of our civilization's greatest poets. I love his work. Don't get me wrong Mr. Gunasekhara, I do love Indian artists though it is really only in Tagore that I find the artist rising above religious compulsions. There are so many gods they seem to be everywhere. Too many Gods spoil the broth, is my twist to the well known saying? For me my one god is more than enough for my soul's salvation.

Hari: *(mumbling)* I am a Hindu. I love Shiva

Brandon: Ah Shiva, is he the one who plays the flute? I know Ganesha is the one with the elephant trunk. Right?

Even as Hari thinks of a response, Mother has stepped out on the first floor.

Mother: Arthur, Arthur....

Brandon quickly intervenes.

Brandon: Yes mother, I will tell Arthur to get you your hot water. In the meantime please meet Mr. Gun...a...sekhara he is a wonderful artist. He will be sleeping in the room next to you. Mr. Hari Gunasekhara, Mrs Margaret Smith.

Hari very awkwardly greets her.
Mother ignores him and shouts

Mother: Arthur, my hot water. (*returns to her room*)

Arthur comes out of the kitchen with a glass of hot water. There is an awkward pause

Arthur: She is a little theatrical. That's where Mr. Smith gets his talent from. I will go settle her down, it's her irritable bowel syndrome that gets her to be a little, well, irritable.

Brandon: (*after a slight pause and changing gear*) Thank you Arthur, Mother is indeed getting a little uncontrollable. (*clearing his throat*) So Mr. Guna...se...khara... Or may I call you Mr. G, once again welcome to your residency. I hope you will be able to put your head down and write one episode after another of the Maha...bha...ra...ta, set in dreamtime, in Gondwanaland, thousands of years ago when our civilizations crisscrossed quite ordinarily. I leave the rest to your imagination and talent.

Just remember to avoid the contemporary. Especially this contemporary obsession with black and white identity politics. You know what I mean, I hate it. (*he looks a little crazed*)

I trust I have made myself clear on that.

Hari doesn't react. He gets up, picks up his bag and moves towards the staircase.

As Hari moves up the staircase Arthur starts to come down. Brandon watches them cross. Then moves towards his desk. Arthur watches Hari exit.

Arthur: O you've got yourself a good looker haven't you Brandon. A dark and brooding Nicholas Brown he is. Oh this is exciting.

Brandon: (*laughs*) It is exciting isn't it. I better get down to applying for an Arts grant. I will have to pay him at some point I imagine, and not from my pocket. My takings these days are so low, with people reluctant to show up at the gardens. Hopefully with the lockdown lifting things will begin to cheer up. We may just be able to have our annual veteran cricketers party if all goes well. It's what you like, isn't it?

Arthur: Yes, that will be nice. We all do need some cheering up. We will have to get rid of some of this stuff Brandon, (*almost screaming*) this place is looking like a pig stye, there are things here you haven't touched for years, I am just going to have to decide myself and pile up the Ute and throw them into the TIP. And the garden outside is a mess. The bushes and the shrubs need to be trimmed, the lawn mowed, there is so much work to do? Do you think I could ask the young man to help me? He might be willing, it will give him a break. I felt instinctively he is not the grumpy beaverish writer you are. Who knows, I may help him come out and have some fun?

Brandon: He's straight Arthur. Lives with someone called Lakshmi in Melbourne. I checked on google Lakshmi is a Hindu Goddess. You think I would have let him near you if he wasn't! He is more good looking than his photographs I must admit.

Arthur: Doesn't look straight under that hoody of his. I can sense a crooked man Brandon, or maybe he is a violent one, yes, I sense some hidden violence in there. Maybe some explosions here will finally cheer things up. Oh this is so exciting.

Brandon: Stop fantasising Arthur. Just let him be and let me be too, I have to put my head down and make an application. So much paperwork. It's tiring for an artist.

Arthur: Well I am off to cook dinner, now for four people. It's just work and more work for me, when am I going to have some fun?

We hear a raucous Cockatoo calling

(speaks directly to the audience)

And here comes the fifth one demanding his feed. I love him for the noise he makes. He comes just as Brandon is deep into his work. And then he squawks and squawks till I feed him. The great Victorian playwright hates the sound.

The Cockatoo squawks again.

Better feed him quick, Brandon's threatened to shoot him with his rifle. I fear, he is such a monster he might just do it.

Brandon looks up at Arthur. Arthur mocks him imitating a Cockatoo squawking. Then quickly exits.

Lights fade

SC 2

Music

Lights come on the first floor, we hear Mother call out in a shrill, high pitched, affected voice

Bran...don, Bran....don, Bran....don.

She seems to sing out her son's name like a Magpie.

We see mother emerge at the top of the stairs. While Brandon is overweight and 'limp' as Arthur suggests, Mother for an eighty five year old is full of strength and stature.

Brandon is at his desk writing

Mother: Brandon, I need your attention this morning. I couldn't sleep last night. The wall between our two rooms is too thin, and that man, you have put in there, I could hear him snoring all night. At one point, I had finally fallen asleep, I woke up with the shocking feeling that I was sleeping next to your father. He was such a dreadful snorer, dear man, I was never really able to sleep well while he was alive. This man's snoring brought all those restless nights back. What a horror!

I really don't know why you have him here? We don't know him do we? He may just be a serial killer masquerading as a playwright. You may not think so but I am still an attractive woman. Who knows what's going around in that dark mind of his?

She starts walking down the steps.
Looks around at the studio.

Mother: This studio is such a continuing mess Brandon. If there has been one constant in your life, one talent really, it's your extraordinary ability to create a chaotic puddle around you, and then sort of slip into it, well like a Hippo into a swamp really. Ha, I really do like that metaphor, I should have been a writer if I didn't have to spend my life raising my two boys.

Of what use is Arthur if he can't put some order down here, how hard is it for him to use that Ute of his to dump this garbage in the Tip? You have spoiled him all along and you continue to spoil him and that worries me, that really worries me.

Can you at least get up and find me a proper chair to sit on? I feel exhausted like that Kiwi after his long climb down Mount Everest. That's where you have me placed. There, *(pointing to the first floor)* on the top of Everest. Next to that snoring Sherpa.

Brandon has placed a comfortable armchair for her. She settles down with all the appropriate sounds for her aches and pains, making sure she has his attention.

Brandon gives up his writing, grunts and settles down on another armchair with his pipe.

Mother: Brandon… *she points to the pipe*

Brandon 'gets' what his mother wants. Grunts, then hands over the pipe and prepares another one for himself. They both sit smoking for a while.

Mother: I've started smoking only now, in my ripe old age, I am sure it's too late for it to kill me. You're still young Brandon, you should be careful, take more care of your lungs. I miss that about your father. He always smelt of the finest cigars. This tobacco settles me down, I mean all my agitations, anxieties.

Richard called from Melbourne and asked me that one important question that has been on my mind. Once Brandon's gone Mum, he said, what will happen to the house? Do you know why that's a million dollar question Brandon, because it's a million dollar House, that's right, that's the price of this small little cottage your father bought for just a hundred thousand dollars, now it's worth a million. I was happy to put this house in your name, but I have concerns now.

Without anyone knowing Arthur has stepped outside his room and is quietly standing listening to the conversation. On the first floor we see the hooded figure of Hari also standing looking down at the mother and son who are not aware of being watched.

Brandon: Mother, I've always said I am happy with whatever makes you happy. Just let me know and I will consider it.

Mother: Brandon you are twenty years younger than me but the way you have let your body go to sin, I am not sure who will go first, you or I. You have no children, no heirs, no one after you. I have my fears, and you know I am not afraid to speak them out. There is no way that your brother or I can agree to let this house go to that housekeeper of yours. I know you have all kinds of silly sentimental attachments to him but I am afraid, after you are gone, it must return to the Smith family. Either to me or your brother.

Let your will make that clear.

You could begin showing your love for me, by replacing that painting with one of me sitting on a park bench. Who puts a huge painting of the queen right in the middle of the house?

Spits some tobacco out

This stuff you smoke is horrible. If you cared for your mother you would keep some fine cigars for my visit downstairs. But then I've always suspected you have never loved me the way your brother has.

Tries to get up from the chair

Anyway, help me out of this chair and put me on that Stairway to Heaven.

Starts singing

Nobody knows the trouble I've seen
Nobody knows but Jesus
Nobody knows the trouble I've seen
Glory hallelujah

She carries on singing as she climbs the stairs.
Hari withdraws into his room.
Arthur steps forward into the studio. Brandon realises he has been listening in and is horrified.

Mother keeps singing all the way to the top of the stairs. Then she turns around to see Arthur. She's forgotten everything that she has just said.

Mother: (*she yells*) Arthur, my hot water

She goes into her room
Arthur looks murderous
Brandon looks horrified, shamed and sheepish. Arthur is on the attack.

Arthur: How dare you, how dare you cut me out of your Will! After all I have done for you, you dog, you and that mother of yours are throwing me out on the street. You are just mean selfish nasty people. I will never leave this house, your mother will have to kill me to get me out of this house. I will squat till my last breath.

Brandon: Don't be ridiculous Arthur I am not dying, I am not dying anytime soon. And, I am not writing a Will, I was just amusing mother. We are married, you have natural rights to this house, no one can throw you out on the street.

I love you. I love you, just stop shouting at me.

He picks up his violin and slowly walks towards Arthur. He is on his way out to busk.
As he approaches Arthur mimes strangulating him with his hands. He seems to shake with rage but very soon the rage turns into uncontrollable laughter.
He hugs Brandon

"Poor little rich boy, off to busk at the statue of his dead queen, sometimes I hate her even more than I detest your mother. Am I not the real queen of your heart Brandon? It's my painting that should be up there, not your mother's nor that dead woman's. I feel so jealous I could cut her head off, I could! Haha don't look so horrified, I mean the statues, not your mother's!

Happy busking, hope you earn enough to at least pay for your supper"

Brandon relieved, mimes, "She's crazy"
They laugh
Lights fade.

SC 3

Lights come on, it is night time.
We see a torch light bring Hari down the staircase. He is exploring the studio.
Checking out the books in the library, picking up the costumes and props.
Hari finds a box full of masks. These are Indonesian masks. He wears the mask of a tiger. Then takes it off and holds it in his hand.

Hari (*speaking to the audience*): On my first night here I had a strange and frightening dream. In my dream I was working in a zoo looking after a tiger. I would enter the cage to feed the tiger. These huge chunks of bloody meat. The tiger was a very kind and friendly one, orange in colour with black stripes, a Bengal tiger. In the dream I was standing in the cage watching this huge beast feed itself. I can recall feeling happy and safe myself. I was his trusted friend. And then suddenly, the dream turned nasty, he roared and turned on me. Not only did he start snarling and growling, moving to attack, and maul me, but he had also been transformed from a gentle orange and black striped Bengal tiger, into a White Siberian tiger. Snow White in colour with these large curved ivory tusks for fangs. He looked like a strange beast. At the point that he was about to attack me I took out a pistol and shot the tiger right between the eyes. I woke up shaking with the horrible feeling of his slimy dead eyes staring back at me.

This mask reminded me of the dream.

I love reading plays from this library here. Mr. Smith even has a collection of plays by Indigenous playwrights. These plays are all about the pain of rape, murder, death in custody, the emotions are of anger and rage, the central character in one is a woman who has turned into a crow and, whose room has turned into in a nest, another has a long list of the dead.

I sometimes feel such a rage here, right in my chest, when I hear of what happened and continues to happen to the dark skinned people of this land. It burns me up, wakes this sleeping demon inside me. I feel like there is a demon in me that I have carried here to this land of plenty, from my childhood. The demon keeps threatening to tear open my chest and explode. Yet I know I have to stay civil to survive.

Put on my civil mask, not the mask of a tiger.

I have to thank Mr. Smith for this, the privilege of being able to read these plays and witnessing these rituals happening within this house. Mr. Hall has even persuaded him to invite me for dinner. I am looking forward to that.

Am I obliged to write only about the Mahabharata in Gondwanaland….(*a little viciously*) please for fuck's sake…

Lights fade

SC 4

Lights come on with Arthur and Brandon facing off each other. Through their fight Arthur is setting up a makeshift dining table.

Arthur: We have a guest coming to dinner tonight and look at this mess we are inviting him into. All these bathtubs need to be thrown out, Brandon, please. They are an embarrassment! You need to make a list of all the things here that you really really really want to keep, the rest I WILL THROW OUT. Give me one reason, one real reason why you want to hold onto this, this piece of trash. Why can't you just get rid of it, please explain. I need a reason Brandon or else I will scream.

Brandon looks grumpy refusing to give a reason

O for heaven's sake you're such a child. At least be of some use and get the bottle of wine and glasses. Our guest is here.

Brandon, relieved, disappears into the kitchen.
Hari walks down the staircase

Arthur: Welcome, Mr. Gunesekhara, we finally have your company for dinner. Please forgive this messy room, it's embarrassing to invite someone into this, but as you are an artist, I am sure you will understand, Brandon needs chaos to create as all artists do, so he informs me.

Hari: Please call me Hari, and no I disagree, I for one like a house in order, in fact, if you ever come to my home in Melbourne, you will see things neat, clean and organised. I believe it helps my writing be more organised and flow better.

Arthur: *(a little taken aback by Hari's articulation)* Well Hari, that is a surprise and here I've been fooled for all these years and have had to suffer this horror in the name of Art. Brandon is deeply attached to these bathtubs for example, if you notice he has painted them up to look like ships. They are part of one of his disastrous shows titled The First Fleet. You know the first set of prisoners to Australia arrived on The First Fleet. He had created this performance, with him sitting in a bathtub, singing songs about the prisoners and their hardships. It was a disaster, a huge embarrassment. Brandon will kill me if he finds out I have told you about it. He is a little more rational about his attachment to the statue of the seated monarch *(pointing to the painting)* that's a story he likes to tell himself, and I am sure he will, but if I had my way, I would go down to the botanical garden, tear out the statue and dump it into the tip. I just hate it.*(looks quite crazed)*

It's such an embarrassing nightmare all this mess here, I ask your forgiveness, please be seated.

Hari: Haha no embarrassment please, thank you for inviting me. By the way getting rid of statues is no more a radical idea, world over statues of the colonial past are being got rid off. You will be participating in a revolutionary moment of history were you to actually get rid of the statue of Queen Elizabeth.

Arthur: My word Hari, you are quite a surprise after

all. Brandon has said nothing about your revolutionary sensibilities, or maybe he just doesn't know, and if I were you it might be wise to just let them be with me, where they are safe of course.

Hari: I shall keep this mouth shut though I will have to open it intermittently to stuff in some of that delicious pork curry you have made. The spices smell divine!

Arthur: Haha thank you, I love a man with a sense of humour Hari. I would suggest you ask Brandon about the statue. Once he starts he can't stop talking about it.

They laugh together conspiratorially. Brandon enters at this point.

Hari: Good evening Mr. Smith, thank you for inviting me for dinner. Arthur has been telling me about your deep connection to the statue. I would love to know its story.

Brandon: Of course you would Mr. G. Please be seated.

They sit down at the table
Brandon launches into his story

Brandon: Mr. G, in 1954, when she was only 27 years old, Elizabeth visited Australia for the first time. My grandfather, then a young and aspiring sculptor of the little rural town of Star Dale, saw her when she visited the goldfield regions, and I imagine, on a hot summer afternoon, sat resting on a little park bench, under the shade of an Oak tree. He was inspired by that vision to create the statue of the seated monarch.

Every day when I busk and play my violin right next to it, I am so emotionally moved by it, both for it being the statue of my beloved monarch and because my own dear grandfather lovingly crafted it. I think sometimes, if something were to happen to it, my heart would be broken irreparably.

Arthur: (*Using the opportunity*)Brandon, I could take Hari there to see it, then he will be able to really appreciate what you mean. Hari, it is indeed an awe inspiring sight, though I do feel my husband's attachment to it is a little too intense, a little pathological even (*laughs a little hysterical*). Artists are strange beasts, as you would surely know. When my husband is in a creative mood, he looks possessed to me, he goes around the house, floating on air, in what I can only describe as the Waltz of a grand Walrus.

Brandon: (*has turned very cold, irritated*) Arthur will you stop chattering like a hysterical Otter. We need to feed Mr. G so that he stops wasting his time and goes back to doing what he has come here for. Write. Not gossip.

You may want to try the pork curry Mr. G. I have the right red wine for it. Arthur has always insisted this was an Indian curry. With you there, we will know if it is indeed an authentic curry or a fake one. (*laughs a little cruelly*)

The three of them settle down to eating. Hari gets up from the table and walks towards the audience

Hari: What kind of a play is this, this play that I've been invited to? A comedy, a satire, a farce, or a tragedy?

Am I to play the chorus to these characters? Stepping

out from time to time to let you know where their lives are going?

Is this the play that I am writing in my room upstairs? Crafting a story, set here in this village of Star Dale 75 kms from the city of Melbourne. Does Mr. Smith not remind you of Obelix from the comic series? I am inspired to cast these two, the Walrus and the Otter, as Obelix and Asterix the Gaul, now living together as a middle aged married couple. Through all their bickering and fighting they do seem to love each other.

The one line header would go something like this...'A decadent gay love in a little rural village where folks gather, play, have fun, fortifying themselves against the onslaught of the modern world.' Or something to that tune.

O I think I am going to have such fun with it all.

Looks back at them

They have just finished their dinner, I must get back.

(*Returning to the table*) Please allow me to clear up the table and let me do the dishes. This is the least I can do to express my gratitude.

Brandon: No, no, no, I insist Arthur does it, while we talk about the work. He is very efficient at these chores, far more than you can ever dream of being. Please be seated here.

It's a command Brandon can't refuse. Brandon lights up a pipe. Arthur clears up the table and goes into the kitchen.

Brandon: Mr. Gunasekhara, I may be growing old but I can assure you my hearing is as good as any hound's. I had gone into the kitchen to get a bottle of wine but got delayed in returning because in truth I was standing by the door listening. Now you may think this a devious act, but I do not. I am a playwright, and have always been keen to listen in on conversations. I am sure you will understand. Well, to cut a long story short, I heard what you said to Arthur. Every single word of it. To say I am appalled is an understatement. I am indeed horrified that I have living in my house someone who would support the destruction of a statue, indeed supports the wanton destruction of statues of some of the great men and women of the free world. It is this free world that has allowed you to find refuge here in this country, and has brought you here into my home. I didn't know you were a revolutionary but I am happy that at least you are now out of the closet, as it were. As Arthur seems quite fond of you, and as I am a rational man, not a hound, though my hearing may be of one, I will reign in the impulse to end this relationship. I am now more than keen to see your writing. I will need to see a synopsis of the play you are planning, so that I can add it to my grants application. You will appreciate that an Arts grant will bring in the necessary funds to make me pay you a professional fee for your contribution. Money, Money, Money makes us all do sensible things, not shoot off our guns like some wild Che Guevera.

I hope I make myself clear.

Hari doesn't say anything. He turns around and starts to walk back up the staircase. He is counting as he climbs the staircase. With each count he is opening a shirt button.

Hari: One, two, three…

Hari pauses at the top of the staircase to address Brandon. His shirt is open, we can see his tee shirt has an image of Lord Shiva.

Mr. Smith, you saw my play *Hanuman in Lanka* and thought it was an authentic representation of the Mahabharata. I had used traditional forms of theatre so it looked like a work of traditional Asian theatre to you. In fact the play had nothing to do with the Mahabharata. Hanuman is a character in the Ramayana. He goes to Lanka to save Sita and ends up setting the whole city on fire.

The play was a metaphor for the Indian armies presence on the island (*laughs*)

I just wanted to clarify that I am primarily a contemporary playwright! Also, I want to show you this *(he opens his shirt to show the image of Shiva the Hindu God of Destruction)*, this is Shiva, when he opens his third eye in anger, there is death and destruction everywhere.

Om Namoh Shivayah. (does a salutation then starts to button up his shirt)

Good night Mr. Smith

Turns and exits
As lights fade we see Arthur has been listening in to the entire conversation. He steps forward. Once again Brandon can see he is upset. He makes a gruff exit to the bedroom. Arthur follows him, on the attack, shouting 'how dare you, you bloody snoop'
We can hear them arguing violently in their bedroom.

Lights fade

SC 6

Music
*Lights on Hari. He is singing and dancing to…*Menage A Trois

Dreams and alcohol
I love this story when I'm all alone
I love my body
Dreams and alcohol
I love this story when I'm all alone
I love my body
Menage a trois
With me, myself and I
Menage a trois
Oh my god, ooh-la-la
Menage a trois
With me, myself and I
Menage a trois

Hari laughs and keeps on dancing and singing
Arthur enters to stand by the stairs. He is in a good mood. He calls out to Hari.

Arthur *(Calling out to Hari):* Hari, Hari, I hope I am not disturbing you but I have some good news for you, good news for us in fact. Brandon has asked that I take you out to the local Indian restaurant for dinner. The miser has even given me sixty dollars to spend. I am excited. I am not going to take no for an answer, in fact I am not going to let you say a word, just get ready and let's get the hell out of here before he changes his mind and returns to take back his money. Hurry Hari lets go get some Indian curry.

They laugh. Hari comes down.

Hari: I like you Arthur, you have a good heart. After all my creative tensions with Brandon, dinner out with a kind man may just be what I need. A hug may be the final persuasion.

Arthur:(*delighted*) This is so thrilling, I get to hug a Hindu god before I eat an Indian curry. Life's never been so good. Let's get out quick before the monster changes his mind.

They laugh, hug, sing 'Menage e trois' and exit
Lights fade.

SC 7

Lights come on Brandon, we see him agonisingly climb the staircase. He is counting each step while opening his shirt
One, two, three…
At the top of the staircase, he turns dramatically…He mocks and imitates Hari's accent

Mr. Smith I just wanted to clarify that I am primarily a contemporary playwright!

(he opens his shirt and imitates Hari) Om Namoh Shivayah.
Looking towards Hari's roon

A contemporary playwright ha! I smell a bloody Guna SKUNKera in here....Lets see what Shiva's third eye reveals to me Mr. SKUNKERA.

Exits into Hari's room
Lights fade

Sc 8

Lights come on Hari and Arthur as they enter the studio, laughing together, seemingly having had a good time at the restaurant.

Arthur: Your partner is not a Hindu goddess but A MAN! Lakshmi is also a Hindu man's name, who would have thought so! That is so funny, Hari. Brandon got it all wrong. He thought Lakshmi was your wife.

Hari: Indeed we are two men living happily together. You can always come visit and live with us Arthur. You're an amazing housekeeper. With you there I could indeed concentrate all my energies on writing. Who knows what the future holds for us? Che sera sera what will be will be. Just teasing you about the housekeeping bit, it is amazing the amount of work you do, and these two just lord it around here! *(whispers)* Dame Margaret and Lord Smith.

They both laugh. They hug each other

Arthur: I like you Hari

Hari: You're a good man Arthur, I like you too.

They laugh, dance together and sing, 'menage a trois' then become aware of a presence upstairs.

Lights come on Brandon standing on top of the staircase. He has the document he took from Hari's room.

Arthur and Hari are both taken aback to see Brandon on the first floor.

Arthur: You climbed the stairs Brandon. Why?

Brandon: Welcome home my dear bride. You are a little late for your wedding. The priest should be here any minute or is this man here going to dress up as a Hindoo priest and get us married singing Hare Krishna Hare Krishna. Oh, just in case you are wondering who I am, I am Obelix the Gaul and you, my dear, are Asterix the warrior. This celebration then, to quote from this document written by our wonderful friend here, the new Tagore, the modern genius of the east, who finds brilliant metaphors to create biting satirical stories of our contemporary world. Well, in his words, the party being thrown tonight in this little Village of the Gauls is to celebrate the marriage of Obelix and Asterix who lovingly refer to each other as 'The Walrus,' and 'The Otter.' Wonder where I have heard those fucking words before?

Hari (*very angry*): Did you steal that document from my room Mr. Smith? That's not very ethical of you to snoop into my private papers. I could never think you would stoop so low.

Brandon: (*in a rage*) Shut the fuck up and don't you dare throw your cheap morality at me. What you have done is abominable, unpardonable and criminal! Don't you dare raise another sound, keep that mouth of yours shut, or I will at this very instant ask my friend Constable Harris to arrest you on charges of lampooning an artist of my stature. Character assassination and defamation are serious criminal charges in this country, and I will not hesitate to use all my powers, which let me assure you are considerable, to even put you in prison if I need to.

Arthur (*still a little shocked*): Now, now, Brandon, putting Hari into prison may be overstretching it a bit. I think this is a private document, if he made it public it would of course be a very different matter, but as it is...I...

Brandon (*really wild*): Shut up Arthur, I have had enough of your self indulgences. I have made it a point to read out from this document, and I will continue to read some more relevant sections, primarily to show proof to you of why I am asking this awful man to leave this house. There is enough damning evidence here to put him into prison. Don't force me to. For once just listen to me.

(*reads*) The very Gay Marriage Of Obelix and Astreix the Gaul by Harry GunaSKUNKera

Story Synopsis

In this village of Gaul things have changed considerably since the 'good ole days.' The old druid Getafix has died and the Gauls have lost their magic potion. Without the magic potion, the Gauls are a weakened race and very concerned about their own survival. In large numbers they are exiting the big encampments, where other races jostle with them for equality. Instead they are finding refuge in little fortified villages like Star dale where at least some of their earlier magical powers, like their folk and country music, their literature and poetry, their drama and theatre are surviving. The village is in search of new druid, in the hope of once again finding the magic potion to give back to them their old powers.

And if that were not enough… here is another section by this genius

Asterix and Obelix have moved from being friends, to lovers and now, after the laws have changed, have decided to get married. The play opens with the party to celebrate their marriage. Their friends, the local cricket team, have come in, each carrying a part of a boar, a leg, a rump, a head. They dance by throwing around pieces of ham. In the midst sits the Gaul queen smoking a cigar and screaming…Give me more Ham, Asterix, Give me more Ham. Despite all her diamonds and pearls she looks bloated, and decadent.

Arthur, do you need more proof of this man's treachery?

Mr. Gunasekhara (*he says the name perfectly*), GET OUT, GET OUT OF MY HOUSE, before I call the Cops on you. You have no excuse, none for this bilge. This is a complete betrayal of trust. I will give you till tomorrow evening to organise yourself and get the hell out of here. I will keep myself out all day at the library and when I return from busking tomorrow evening, I want you gone. I promise you, I am in such a rage, if I find you here, I may just get my rifle out and shoot you. How dare you! How dare you! You are a SLIME BALL… that's really what you are, a bloody SLIME BALL. I can't bear seeing your face anymore. To protect myself from a terrible crime I will not enter this studio, till you are gone. Please I beg you, don't let me see you. Please, don't make me kill you. JUST GET OUT YOU FUCKING SLIME BALL.

He throws all of Hari's papers down into the studio.

He walks off in a rage. Arthur and Hari are left standing shell shocked. In a daze Hari moves to collect his papers.

Arthur: (*defensive*) I swear Hari, I had no idea this was his plan. He has made a complete fool of me. He lied to me about wanting us to have a good time. Now I understand why he parted with his precious dollars. I can't believe how devious he can be. I am not going to take this lying down. I have had enough of his rage and tantrum. I am tired of being used and abused. I can't be walked over as he did right now. He lied to me. I was so happy that he wanted us, that he trusted me to go out with you, and have a night of innocent fun. Now I feel betrayed, horribly betrayed. I hate him Hari, I hate him.

What are you thinking, Hari, speak to me?

Arthur moves to start putting all the clutter into the bathtubs etc.

Hari has moved himself down to the edge of the stage. He seems to sway, wanting to step off it.

Hari: I was thinking about the young aboriginal woman, who depressed by the hacking down of an eight hundred year old birthing tree in the Dja Dja Warrung Country, attempted suicide. An eight hundred year old tree in whose womb her ancestors were birthed, gone forever to build a road. In despair she drove herself to a cliff, from which she planned to jump, and kill herself. With a hardened and determined heart she forced her body right to the edge, now only a step away from ending all her pain. As she attempted to take that final step, which would have flung her down into the rocks, she heard a Kookaburra call. Precisely at the moment that she was attempting her last step. Hearing that call she took a step back, then after a little wait, she mustered courage again and tried once more to take that last step, and as she did, once again, she heard the Kookaburra call. Shocked, she waited, unsure of what this meant. Then determined to do what she had set out to do, she stepped out one more time, and this time again, as she lifted her foot, the Kookaburra called. It was when it happened the third time, that she realised this was a sign, calling her back, telling her, it was not her time yet. That she had to continue fighting.

Arthur: (*very moved*) Yes, what a beautiful story, you must write it out. It's very powerful.

Hari nods his head in agreement and is about to say something when mother screams out from her room.

Mother: Arthur, my hot water.

Hari:(*walking towards the staircase*) Fuck. That's it. That's the sign I've been waiting for. It's time to take off my mask.
   With an explosive rage he lets out a repressed scream.
SLIMEBALL, YOU FUCKING SLIMEBALL.

Arthur laughs then freezes sensing Hari's rage. Hari is shaking with a repressed rage.

Arthur (*trying to console*): Hari, that was so so so very nasty of Brandon. He's like that. He's torn me to shreds so many times, abused me, humiliated me. With his words. With his actions. And still I have stayed on here. I feel ashamed of myself. He has a power over me that I just can't escape from. I wish someone would just get rid of him for me, just kill him. He looked so mad I thought he was going to attack you, throttle you. You know Hari, I saw something in his eyes that I've never seen before. Your writing did get to him where it hurts. He looked shamed by the story of the decline of the Gauls, and being cast as Obelix. Maybe it was because it was coming from *you.* You know with this race thing there is so much history here. Don't forget, not so very long ago, we could legally shoot black fellas for trespassing on our property. He does have a rifle. With real bullets. I have seen it. On occasions he cleans his gun with real love. It's crazy. I wouldn't risk your returning here. I will leave you at the station. I will be so sad to leave you. I will miss you Hari.

He hugs Hari.

Talk to me Hari, tell me what's going through your heart. Speak to me. I am here for you, listening.

Tries to lighten the mood

Let me be a Parvati to your Shiva. Your eternal consort. I have been googling up on your culture, you know. I've even been reading the Maha…bha…rata…What an amazing story!

Hari seems to have moved into another space. He moves away from Arthur speaking directly to the audience.

Hari: I am the son of a tiger, the son of a warrior. The son of a broken, wounded, maimed warrior.

When I was twelve years old my father came back from war. He had lost both an eye and a leg. He had an artificial glass eye and a wooden leg. This was no surprise, there were many in the village who had returned from war, limbless, wounded and maimed.

As days passed we got used to his sullen, angry presence filling the home with a deep marauding silence.

One day, my mother showed my report card to my father. I had failed my exam. He asked her to get him a stick, then stood up on one leg, and without wearing his artificial leg, started to beat me. After a few blows I moved away from him, ran away, as my father tried to chase me forgetting perhaps that he had only one leg. The poor man fell on the floor, writhing in rage like an angry black python. As he fell, his artificial eye ball too fell out, rolling all the way across the floor, all the way under the bed. I crawled under the bed, to look for this slimy glass eye ball.

When I gave him his glass eye ball, my father quietly placed it back, then, after he had put on his wooden leg, picked up the stick again. This time I did not move. I let my father beat me, let him take his rage out on me. My father looked, felt like a demon, he seemed possessed by the devil.

This beating became a ritual, with him raging and me standing there taking a beating.

Over time however we grew close. My father started talking, sharing the ghastly stories of war. Slowly, the demon inside was exorcised by being passed onto me. All that war, violence, horror, death, rage, grief, came to sit inside of me. The devil was in me. I felt possessed.

My father saw what he had passed onto me, and fearing for my life worked to get me away, on a boat, to Australia. I came on a boat, carrying the demon with me. Years later when my father died, I asked for only one thing of his to be sent to me in Australia. It was his glass eye ball.

Alone in Australia, whenever I felt lost and depressed, I would go look at my father's glass eye, trying to see, to remind myself of what the old warrior had lived through.

A slimy glass eye ball. Like a slime ball.

(*mutters viciously*) Slime ball. You fucking slime ball.

Arthur:(*looking very distressed and seeking his attention*) That's such a sad story Hari, I can't imagine how tough things must have been for you. You've had such a hard life, my heart breaks hearing it. I wish I could just hug you, hold you and give you the love you deserve. I wish I could heal the thousand wounds of the demon inside of you. I want to see the demon Hari. Let him out. I am not afraid of him. Let the demon out and let him take revenge for what Brandon inflicted on you. Now I understand your rage, I understand how horrible it must have felt for you when Brandon abused you with that terrible word. I know Brandon deeply, I know what will destroy him. These bathtubs, that damn painting, these instruments and these books! Lets just get rid of all his dear possessions, and then you will see how it will kill him. He'll be like your father writhing on the floor, not with rage but with the agony of losing all his precious toys. A huge white python.... or whatever creature you can think of... writhing on the floor.... in the final throes of a myocardial infarction. How dramatic does that sound? How satisfying! How exciting! Let's go Hari, let's just do it before we cool off and start talking about sensible things. It's time to be wild. Let's get to work. This place will take us all night to clean out.

Hari: (*very quietly mad*) Yes Arthur. Let's go crush the serpent.

Arthur hugs him seductively and whispers

Arthur: You're amazing Hari. You're a Hindu god come to liberate me. O this is so exciting. You look like a hero from the Maha...bha..rata. You're my Arjuna the great warrior. I feel so safe with you, I want to come live with you. May I be your Draupadi?

Hari: Yes Arthur, but first we must kill the serpent. (*pause*)
You know Arthur, my father believed killing an enemy was like smashing a cockroach on the wall. That's all it was, he said. A cockroach smashed and gone forever.
It's time now for me to smash the cockroach. It is time for me to jump into the abyss.

Lights fade

INTERVAL

Stage hands clear all the house clutter

ACT 2 SC 1

Music
Lights come on Mother standing in an empty studio singing

Amazing grace, how sweet the sound
That saved a wretch like me
I once was lost, but now am found
Was blind but now I see

Mother: Oh I am so happy I could sing all day. (*calling out*) Brandon Brandon where are you my darling son you've made me so happy today. See I am crying tears of joy. Brandon.......Arthur.......Where are the both of you? The sun is finally shining on our house today, come and see for yourself. Oh I am so happy I could dance all day long.

(*sings*) I could have danced all night, I could have danced all night and still have begged for more...I could have spread my wings....

Just then Arthur walks in looking tired and dishevelled. He too is delighted to see Mother happy.

Arthur: O hallelujah mother, is this a miracle that I am seeing...you here and dancing and singing...this is wonderful.

Mother: Arthur...Where is my dear son? This must have taken him all night to get rid of all this stuff. And all those books. He had read all of them. They were just taking up so much space. Good he has got rid of them. Even that damn canvas made by a failed local artist. Gone. He is such a trooper, such a trooper. When he decides on something, however big a task, he just gets it done. I am so proud of him. I could even give him a hug at this moment. Where is he?

Arthur: Mother, I think he has gone to the library. If I am not mistaken he plans to work there all day, and then go and busk at the statue.

Mother: Well I will have to wait till dinner then, won't I? Doesn't this place look wonderful? I can finally fill it with the kind of furniture I like. Arthur, will you come up and help me? I am still so unsure of this online shopping business. I've seen some wonderful sofas, and a lovely dining table with chairs. I also think a carpet in the middle would just make this place look magical. Finally, finally, finally, there is a god in heaven...hallelujah...

Starts walking up the stairs

(*singing*) Nobody knows the trouble I've seen, nobody knows but Jesus
   Nobody knows the trouble I've seen glory Hallelujah
   Sometimes I am up sometimes I am down
   O yes lord

At the top of the staircase she turns around.

Mother: (*looking into Hari's room*) Arthur, I couldn't help but notice, this room is empty. That man is gone. I am so relieved. He looked so threatening in that hooded jacket of his. I kept a butter knife under my pillow, each night, just in case, you never know. I can finally sleep peacefully hallelujah

Exits into her room

Arthur: (*turning to the audience*) That's not the only thing that's gone today. I just lost my head and did what I had to do. Both for myself and for Hari. Especially for Hari. I feel so much relief, feel much lighter. Then again, there's the dread of Brandon's reaction after discovering all that has happened. I mean after all that I have said I do hope he doesn't have a heart attack or shoot me dead now that Hari is safe and away. I know I am over dramatising things but you never know how things shape up in life do you? O my god this is all so stressful. I think I will cook him his favourite Hungarian goulash to soften him up. If you know what your man likes to eat, then let the dark days descend, there is always a goulash to lighten things up.

Still, it is all so wearisome, I feel a strange dread. I hear no Kookaburras calling. Hell what a moving story that was. I've been crying since. It broke my heart. It really broke my heart.

And then Hari with his terrible story of his father and that slimy eyeball. That was creepy. He was so angry though, had such rage in his eyes. And that smashing the cockroach thing. That was creepy, frightening. O my God, I hope all this turns out ok, I feel such dread.

I think I will prepare Brandon a hot bath, this is all going to be a real shock for him. Now I am feeling bad for him. I didn't really have to bury the statue in the garbage heap at the tip. And his precious books! I just got carried away, with all those wild feelings.

Lights fade.

SC 2

Lights come on with Brandon entering the house in a rage. He is shocked to see everything gone. He curses violently, 'fuck you Arthur.' He throws his violin across an empty studio, then charges into his bedroom from where he emerges with a rifle in his hand. He goes up the stairs to Hari's room, then comes down to the studio, goes around the house, the kitchen, the bedrooms, bathrooms, rifle in hand making sure Hari is nowhere.

He steps outside the house. We hear a rifle shot. Outside he has shot a cockatoo.

He returns to the studio carrying a dead cockatoo.

He throws it down right centre stage, shouting ' Happy birthday Arthur.' He then exits into his bedroom.

Arthur creeps in from the kitchen

Arthur: Did you hear that? He fired the rifle shot just outside the kitchen window. It was so loud that I almost screamed. Thank god Hari is away. I am sure he would have shot him. I've never seen him so mad.

(*screams*) O my god, he shot a cockatoo. It's the one that always makes a noise demanding I feed him. I recognise him from this ring around his anklet. Brandon hated being disturbed by his raucous calling for me, had threatened to shoot him, and now he has. My poor baby is dead but I have no time to grieve. I must get rid of it quickly. If mother sees this she will turn hysterical and then all hell will be let loose. She will find out the truth. I will just hide this bird away and then bury it later.

Goes out with the cockatoo and then returns quickly

I am going to lock myself away in the kitchen for the next two hours and cook that Goulash. That's all I can do at this moment, right? Just put my head down and cook him something he loves. I need time, I need time. I can't bear to face him. O God please don't let this get darker. My blood is screaming, I am shaking with fear.

Just then mother comes out of her room

Mother: Arthur, did you hear that, I think it was a rifle shot. Someone must have shot a rabbit. Please go out and investigate. O I would love to have rabbit for dinner. Nothing tastes as good as a rabbit freshly shot. It's this meat from the market that has destroyed my guts. O how I miss my husband. He would hunt and bring home roos and rabbits, and all kinds of ducks, Mallards and Teals....I loved the salty bitter sweet fleshy taste of a Teal...It's all gone now...no one knows the pleasures of eating fresh game meat anymore.

Arthur:(*laughing*) 'the salty bitter sweet fleshy taste of a Teal'! You are such a scream mother. I never knew I would need you as I do today. I am cooking your son's favourite Hungarian goulash for dinner, I will serve up a bowl for you as soon as it is done.

Mother: Hungarian goulash for dinner, O that will be nice. It's not easy for me to say it, but there are some things about you that I am beginning to like, I mean maybe it's because you are finally growing old or something, at least you don't look young anymore...I don't know, I can't quite put my finger on it...but my feelings for you are changing...

Arthur: (*blows her a kiss*) O that's so sweet...that's just what I needed...now go into your room and soon I'll be up with your wonderful warm dinner.

I love you mother. You're the best

Sings away into the kitchen
Lights fade

SC 3

Lights come on in an empty studio. Things are eerily quiet. From somewhere in the house we can hear a clock ticking. For a while nothing happens. Then Arthur enters with the dinner tray. He is singing 'nobody knows the trouble I've seen…'He climbs the stairs, enters mother's room, then returns down the stairs. He stops in the middle of the studio. Decides to go to the bedroom. Stands there listening. Then returns.

Arthur: Not a sound from the bedroom. I suspect he has gone into the bathroom, got in the bathtub and fallen fast asleep. I will take his dinner to him there. He's always loved that. Being served goulash while lying naked in a hot bath tub. If I am gentle and quick about this his belly should be full of goulash even before he realises what I've done. He will be too 'goulashed' to think straight.

Now to get him his dinner. Fingers crossed all will be well soon.

Exits into the kitchen
A pause with nothing happening except the clock ticking
Arthur enters, tray in hand, crosses the studio to the bedroom, breathes in deep before exiting.
Long pause, nothing happens except the clock ticking.
Just then we hear Arthur scream. A real blood curdling scream. Then he comes rushing out.

Arthur: He's dead, he's dead, Brandon's dead, he's gone, I know he's gone. It's his neck. I am sure it's his neck. I could see it's been strangled. There are bruise marks on his neck. Mother, Mother, please come out mother....O help, someone help me please...

Mother steps out

Arthur: Mother, he's gone, Brandon's dead. He's there in his bathtub, with his eyes rolled up. I felt his pulse, there was none. His eyes are all rolled over. I thought he was just acting to frighten me or something. But when I touched him, he was cold, as cold as death. I mean, the bath water was still warm, but when I felt for his pulse there was none. That's when I screamed.

Mother: O don't be so melodramatic Arthur. Brandon is too young to die. He just hates having a bath and must be throwing a fit or something. I didn't think he was epileptic but who knows, with his eyes rolling up, it could just be that.

Arthur:(*breaking down crying*) No mother it's true, it's true... he's gone, my darling Brandon has gone, he's dead...I am sure he's been murdered, by whom mother? Why? Who would want to kill him?!!!

Mother: Don't go primitive on us Arthur, just try and reign in your emotions, it's so uncivilised to howl and weep as you are. Maybe he's had a heart attack. I had warned him to look after his health. These things happen quite unexpectedly. On the other hand if he has died an unnatural death a forensic report will confirm it. The Police will get it done. We just have to wait. You're not a detective, hysterical conclusions get us nowhere. Put yourself in order. Get yourself a glass of wine or swallow a calmpose. If what you are saying is true then I am going to call Richard to take charge, to call the Police, to verify what you are suggesting.

Arthur moves to pour himself some wine

Arthur: If you don't believe me mother, go in there and see for yourself…he's gone, my darling, the love of my life is gone….dead, murdered…

Mother: There is no way I am going in there to see for myself, no way that I will inflict the trauma of seeing my son naked and dead in a bathtub. What horror!

Turns to go back into her room, then stops.

And, if you are lying Mr. Hall, if this is some kind of melodrama you are playing out, know that I will have you arrested for causing me such trauma. You'll be in jail for this.

Exits back into her room

Arthur: (*to the audience*) O my God, this has all gone so horribly wrong. He's dead. I am sure of it. And murdered. Who could have done it? Who could have gone in to murder him? O my god! It has to be him. It has to be Hari. I had suggested he could come back home to take a video of Brandon throwing his tantrum, didn't I? O Jesus I can feel it in my heart that Hari has something to do with this. I left him at the train station after we did our work at the tip. He looked mad with anger. He kept muttering that awful word. I thought he would calm down after we got rid of the statue, but it seemed he didn't. He could easily have returned to the house, as I had so stupidly suggested, hid himself in the bathroom waiting for Brandon to return, then come out to surprise and strangulate him in the bathtub.

Is Hari the murderer then?

I can sense he is still there, hiding there behind that door, he hasn't left the house. How could he have? He has had no time to escape.

Should I go in there and confront him? Ask him why he did it?

He turns hysterically towards the door screaming.

Why? Why? Why?
Why did you have to murder Brandon, Hari?
Why?

Arthur collapses weeping wildly
As if on cue the bedroom door opens. Hari stands there looking menacing, then walks in. He speaks in the calm voice of a killer who has exorcised all his inner demons.

Hari: It's over Arthur. You're free. I killed the enemy. Stamped and smashed him as easily as a cockroach on the floor. My father would be so proud of me today.

You want to know why I did it? Would you believe me if I said it's just that one word that drove me crazy, that took me over the edge, into the abyss. It's as simple as that. Just that one word had all the power in it to turn me into a killer.

Slime ball. (pause)

You fucking slime ball. (pause)

When that one word was screamed at me, it felt like the slime ball had been shot into my head like a rifle bullet. Into my brain.

All day, that slime ball slowly spun itself around my head.

When we piled up all the house clutter into the Ute and drove it to the botanical garden the slime ball was turning in my head.

When we tore out the statue and buried it in the garbage heap at the tip the slimeball did not stop turning.

Even when I was dropped off at the railway station the slime ball continued to turn slowly transforming in my head into a slimy glass eyeball that could see, that was showing me things.

The death of an 800 year old birthing tree.

Brown and black people incarcerated in jails.

A helpless young black boy, hooded and tied to a chair in a prison being beaten by white prison guards

While the list was endless, beyond these images, was the relentless turning in my head of that slimy glass eyeball .

The eyeball turning in my head turned me into a demon

The demon wasn't satisfied with dumping the queen's statue in the garbage heap. The demon wanted more, wanted blood.

The demon returned to the house.

The demon got into the house and waited in Mr. Smith's room, hiding in a closet. Waited for the evening drama to unfold. The demon could hear Mr. Smith angrily stomping about the house, then coming into the room, into the bathroom, into this bathtub.

The demon waited for a while, then knew his time had come.

But it wasn't the demon who stepped out of the closet, it was another being, it was a being with a third eye, a third eye that had opened, a third eye that had opened to destroy. The slime ball in my head had turned from a glass eye ball into the third eye of Shiva, the god of destruction. It was Shiva who stepped forward, Shiva who held Mr. Smith by the neck, Shiva who strangled him.

After the murder, the third eye closed, the slimeball returned back into my head, where it continued to sit and turn...turning...

In a voice deep and possessed he keeps muttering....

Turning
Turning
Turning.....

He continues viciously

Slime ball
Slime ball
Slime ball

As lights fade we continue to hear Arthur weeping and wailing

SC 5

As lights come on, we hear mother laughing hysterically.
She stands on the balcony shouting for Arthur

Mother: Arthur, Arthur, where are you? I have news for you. If you listen to me and do what I tell you to, you won't get arrested.

Arthur, Arthur are you listening…

She starts walking down the steps

Mother: (*to the audience*) He's locked himself into his room for the last two days fearing that the police will come and get him. Well they haven't and if he behaves sensibly, they won't.

She moves to the bedroom and shouts

Arthur, come out and talk to me, it's good news for you, that is if you behave yourself. I know you are in there listening.

Knocks hard on the door. There is no response.

Damn, to hell with my trying to do this nicely, he is such a coward.

I know you are in there, so here goes. Constable Harris called Richard and informed him of the contents of the forensic report. Did you hear me? The forensic report. It seems Brandon died of a heart attack, a myocardial infarction. The heart attack seems to have happened at least ten minutes before your friend Hari got to him. Seems your friend was so possessed by the demon or some insane spirit that he didn't notice. As Richard explained, the case now is not of murder but of assault.

Talking to the audience

O Jesus, that is such a relief for me. To know my poor boy died a natural death. His time had come and the lord took him away. I won't have to be part of an Agatha Christie murder mystery for the rest of my life, that is such relief.

Continues to address the door

Arthur, your lover boy Hari is now going to be framed for battery, for assault, but not for murder. As a lesser crime it means a much shorter prison sentence. Richard asked me to tell you, now that it is not such a serious crime, that we are happy to let you off, to request the police not to pursue a case against you. Do you hear me? Richard can get you off the hook. There is only one thing that we ask of you in return. You pack your bags, and leave the house by tomorrow morning, and we will make sure that the Police hounds are off your heels. How does that sound? It's as simple as that. Leave the house and all the keys on the table, and move out. Tomorrow morning. Not afternoon. Not evening. Not the day after. That's all we are asking of you and you don't go to prison even for a day. Go by tomorrow morning and all will be well. I will let you digest that and I am sure you will make a sensible choice.

I will now go up to my room AND REST. This has been exhausting.

Walks towards the staircase. Stops to talk to the audience

Mother*:* Tomorrow I should have my house to myself. Fingers crossed (*winks*) wish me luck.

Lights fade.

SC 6

Lights come on Arthur. He is stepping out of his room into the studio carrying two suitcases. He stops centre stage looking up at mother's room.
On the back wall, instead of the painting of the 'statue of the seated monarch' now hangs a painting of Mother, sitting on a park bench in the exact pose of the Queen. Arthur stares at the painting.
After a while he turns his head to the audience.

Arthur: She won! The bitch!

He picks up his suitcases and exits
Lights fade.

Ingram Content Group UK Ltd.
Milton Keynes UK
UKHW011056310323
419467UK00001B/75